Eyes on the Prize

Tales from Grace Chapel Inn

Eyes on the Prize

SUNNI JEFFERS

Guideposts
New York, New York

Eyes on the Prize

ISBN-13: 978-0-8249-4787-3

Published by Guideposts
16 East 34th Street
New York, New York 10016
Guideposts.org

Library of Congress Cataloging-in-Publication Data

Jeffers, Sunni.
    Eyes on the prize / Sunni Jeffers.
        p. cm. — (Tales from Grace Chapel Inn)
    ISBN 978-0-8249-4787-3
        1. Sisters—Fiction.   2. Bed and breakfast accommodations-Fiction.
3. Friendship—Fiction.   4. Country life—Pennsylvania-Fiction.
5. Pennsylvania—Fiction.   I. Title.   II. Series.
    PS3610.E36E97 2009
    813'.6—dc22

                                                                        2008044039

Cover art by Deborah Chabrian
Design by Marisa Jackson
Typeset by Nancy Tardi

Printed and bound in the United States of America
10 9 8 7 6 5 4 3

GRACE CHAPEL INN

A place where one can be
refreshed and encouraged,
a place of hope and healing,
a place where God is at home.

Acknowledgments

For my wonderful children Laura and John. You grow more beautiful every day. You fill my heart with joy and make me so proud.

For my very special son-in-law Gary and daughter-in-law Ruth. I am so blessed to claim you.

For my very special granddaughters Madelaine, Kathryn, Mckenna and Shannon. My cup runneth over.

My dearest Jim. You made it all possible. I love running this race of life by your side.

—Sunni Jeffers

Chapter One

*J*ane Howard's feet hit the hard-packed dirt on Fairy Lane in rhythm with the country-western song on her Mp3 player. The headset cord swung in unison with her ponytail as she jogged.

At nine o'clock on Friday morning, Fairy Lane was deserted. She'd cooked an early breakfast for the guests at Grace Chapel Inn, the bed-and-breakfast she operated with her sisters, so she had the rest of her morning free to indulge her love of the outdoors. After a week of unseasonably cold, wet weather, the air was dry and clear. A slight breeze blew softly against her skin.

Jane loved the tree-lined lane and Fairy Pond at the end of it. She soaked up the surrounding scenery. This mid-September day, the hint of gold on the tips of the leaves foretold the brilliance that would burst forth in the coming weeks. Jane was happy that she'd moved back to her childhood home in Southeastern Pennsylvania, where each season brought dramatic changes to the landscape, but she particularly relished the fall. She couldn't wait to cart her paints and easel to the pond to capture the variety of maple, ash, elm and poplar leaves, with all their nuances of red and purple, yellow and gold. She could visit for weeks to come, and the scene would change constantly, from a place of soft, peaceful repose to one of a bold, wild riot of color.

Ahead, Jane fancied she saw fairies skipping and darting about upon the pond as shimmers of sunbeams danced across the wavy ripples scalloping the water. She snapped a mental photograph, filing it away in her mind in order to visualize it on some cold, stormy winter day for a painting. Jane could create pictures of Fairy Pond for the rest of her life and never run out of new scenes. In this one, fairies would inhabit the center of each sunbeam.

Something moved along the water's edge. Its reflection skimmed along the pond's surface, bobbing as it advanced steadily toward her around the edge of the pond. Curious, Jane focused on the moving reflection that grew larger as she drew nearer.

A figure emerged, jogging toward her from the deep shadows of the trees. She got an impression of long, powerful legs. She knew all the local joggers. She did not recognize this stride or the tall, slender female who displayed it.

As they drew closer, Jane was certain she didn't know the woman. Could it be a tourist or someone visiting from out of town? Jane smiled and raised her hand in a greeting, but she didn't slow her pace. There was room on the path to pass.

Suddenly, the woman stopped. She removed her head-phones and sunglasses and squinted.

"Jane? Jane Howard?" she called loudly enough to override the music from Jane's headset.

Jane stopped, slipping off the device. "Yes." She stared at the woman, but did not recognize her. "I'm sorry. Do I know you?"

The woman laughed. "A long, long time ago. I'm sure I've changed, but you haven't aged a bit. I'm Carrie Blankenship, er, Gleason, from Franklin High School. We used to run cross-country together."

In her lime green and pink spandex top and shorts, Carrie Gleason looked like a model for an energy drink ad. She looked young. She hadn't been a brunette when Jane knew her, so her hair must have been dyed. That might cover some gray, but she was a year older than Jane, not ten years younger, as she appeared to be. "I didn't recognize you. You look ter-rific," Jane said, smiling and holding out her hand in a friendly gesture. Carrie shook hands with her. Theirs had never been a close relationship. In fact, they'd been competitors. Jane had never beaten Carrie in a race, and Carrie had gloated over her victories, or at least it had seemed that way to Jane.

"So do you. Do you still live here?" Carrie asked.

"I moved back home a while ago, after my father passed away. My sisters and I run a bed-and-breakfast in our fam-ily home."

"Grace Chapel Inn. I ran past it on the way up here. It's lovely. So you're still running. Do you work out every day?"

"I try to. It keeps me in shape and gets me out of the house," Jane said. "I don't do the full course that we ran for cross-country training."

"Ahhh," Carrie said, drawing out her syllable, as if she understood something deeper than Jane's brief reply. "You must enter the Harvest 10K Run I'm setting up," she said. "That's why I'm here—to map it out. I'm part of a group that organizes charity races. We're working with the Children's Diabetes Foundation to raise money to increase awareness of the disease."

"Really? You're going to hold a 10K here in Acorn Hill?"

"Yes. We ordinarily plan these events well in advance, but our usual event fell through. I recommended our old course, from high school training days, but that wasn't long enough, so I've expanded it to include the north end of town. Then I thought I'd better make sure the roads and trails are still usable." She smiled. Even with a sweatband around her forehead and no makeup, Carrie was quite attractive, Jane thought. She was tanned and obviously in top shape. She must work out at a gym, Jane decided. Probably had a trainer.

"Not much has changed around here," Jane said.

"Which makes it perfect for our run. The course isn't difficult, but it has some hills, and it's out in the country, which is good. I imagine it'd be a piece of cake for you." She reached into the small zippered pack at her waist. "Here's my card. It has the race Web site address with all the details. You can sign up online. Maybe you could drum up some interest here in town. I'll have posters and flyers up here next week." She handed the card to Jane.

"Thanks. I'll look it up," Jane said.

"Great. Well, gotta run," Carrie said, flashing a grin at Jane that showed off her perfectly aligned white teeth. Carrie waved and took off down the path, passing Jane at the start of a flat-out run.

Jane glanced at the card. Carrie Blankenship, Events Planner, it announced in bold, raised blue letters. It listed the address, phone and a Web site for a consulting company. Jane slipped the card into her waist pack. She felt dowdy in her gray T-shirt and black running shorts.

"Show off," Jane muttered under her breath, after Carrie was out of earshot. "I could run like that if I wanted to." *But not for long and not very far*, Jane's unbidden thoughts added.

Louise Howard Smith glanced at her watch. Six-forty. Cynthia had said she would leave Boston at noon, so she should arrive at any minute. Her visit was a surprise, spur-of-the-moment trip, and Louise couldn't wait to see her only daughter.

"Traffic is always heavy on Friday afternoon, with everyone trying to get out of the city," Jane said from behind her at the butcher-block counter, where she was snipping chives to garnish the latkes.

"I'm not worried," Louise responded. Cynthia was a good driver and levelheaded. It had been three months since Cynthia had a break from her job as editor at a children's publishing house, and a weekend wasn't much time to catch up on their lives. They spoke on the phone frequently, but that couldn't replace talking face-to-face. "She said she'd be here for dinner. Especially when she heard you're cooking beef brisket and potato latkes."

"I know that's one of her favorite meals," Jane said. "And it won't be ready for at least a half hour. I figured she might get here by seven."

"I hear a car pulling into the driveway now, and all our guests have already checked in," Alice Howard, the middle sister, said. She was setting the kitchen table for the four of them. She came over to peer out the window. "That's her car. She's here," Alice said.

Jane rinsed her hands and wiped them on her apron.

Cynthia was Alice and Jane's only niece. Neither of them had children of their own and they doted on her. They loved her almost as much as her mother did, but they hung back, so that Louise could hug her first.

Louise opened the door and stepped out on the back porch. It was starting to get dark, but she could see Cynthia coming toward her in the light from the porch. She looked wonderful. Grinning broadly, Louise went down the steps and got caught up in Cynthia's enthusiastic hug.

"Hello, sweetheart, I'm so glad you decided to come," Louise said.

"Me too, Mother. I needed a break and where better to get one?" Cynthia picked up the bag she'd set down on the sidewalk. Louise reached for the smaller satchel.

"You'd better let me get that. It's heavy," Cynthia warned.

Louise started to lift it. It felt like it contained bricks. "Goodness. What's in here?"

"Work. What else?" Cynthia picked it up. "Now I'm balanced," she said. "I brought about a dozen submissions with me. I can't keep up with them unless I read on the weekends, but I promise I won't spend *all* the time reading."

"I should hope not. You came to get a break."

"Just being here, breathing the fresh country air and spending time with you is better than any other vacation. And I have an appointment in Philadelphia at noon Monday, so I can stay for church and Sunday dinner."

"That's wonderful, darling." Louise beamed.

Cynthia set down her bags inside the kitchen and stood tall. She smiled at her mother. They were eye to eye in height. Louise wondered if Cynthia had lost a little weight. She worked too hard.

"You look splendid, Mother." She cocked her head. "You look tan. I hope you haven't been out in the sun without sunblock. You have rather sensitive skin."

"I know better than that," Louise said, pleased that Cynthia noticed her tan and was concerned for her well-being.

"Of course you do." She inhaled deeply. "Smells like heaven in here."

"You're just in time," Jane said, stepping forward for a hug. "I'll let you wash up and we'll be ready to eat soon."

"I'll wash up down here and take my things upstairs later, after I've had some nourishment." She removed her jacket and hung it on a hook next to three other jackets.

"In that case, I'll start putting things on the table. You dish and I'll carry," Alice told Jane.

"I'll get our drinks. Milk or juice, Cynthia?"

"Do you have any buttermilk?"

"Oh no, not you too," Jane said, looking horrified. "It must be genetic."

"If that's the case, I'm glad it skipped me," Alice said.

"Me too," Jane added.

"You just don't know what's good," Louise told her sisters.

"It's an acquired taste. Not everyone has such a discriminating palate," Cynthia said, raising her eyebrows.

Jane nearly choked. Then she started laughing. "You look just like your mother when you do that."

Cynthia grinned. "I do a good impression, don't I?" She sashayed over to the table and sat down, picking up her knife and fork and holding them up. "I'm ready. I've been waiting for this all day."

Louise set a glass of buttermilk in front of her daughter. She wondered when Cynthia had started drinking the creamy, slightly sour drink. Louise loved a glass now and then, and sometimes drank it just to get a rise out of her sisters. That wasn't the only thing she used the rich milk for, but that was her secret. She smiled to herself as she took a seat next to Cynthia at the round oak table.

Chapter Two

Saturday morning, Alice came through the swinging door from the dining room to the kitchen, carrying a tray of dirty plates and bowls, which she set in the sink.

"The Burtons are almost finished. Mr. Burton would like another serving of the baked egg dish."

Jane opened the warming oven and set a pan of scones inside. "I just took a fresh casserole out of the oven," she told Alice. "It's in the chafing dish. Do they want more scones?"

"I'll ask when I refill their coffee," Louise said. She picked up the pot and headed toward the dining room.

"What can I do?" Cynthia asked. "Put me to work. I can't believe I slept in so late. Mother should have woken me when she got up." She had just come downstairs from Louise's third-floor room.

"Everything's under control," Jane said. "Have a cup of coffee and you can have some breakfast, if you'd like."

Cynthia took a cup out of the cupboard. "Have you all eaten?" she asked as she poured a cup.

"Not yet. We'll eat when the guests are finished. Remember, we have a full house this weekend."

"I'll wait for the rest of you. Again, I do hope I'm not putting you out."

"That'll never happen," Alice shot over her shoulder as she carried a plate of hot egg casserole to the dining room.

"You always have a place here, no matter how many guests we have. The only problem with a full house is that you have to share a room with your mother," Jane said. "I just wish you could stay longer than the weekend. You need a nice long break and we'd love your company."

"Thanks, Aunt Jane. I wish I could stay too. I'll be down for Thanksgiving, though, and I already put in for the whole week."

"That's wonderful! Does your mother know?"

"I told her last night. Let me start washing the dishes." Cynthia pushed up the sleeves of her rugby shirt and stepped up to the sink. She turned on the hot water and began rinsing off some of the guests' plates. "Did you go jogging this morning?"

"No, I'll go this afternoon."

"Mind if I come with you? I'm trying to stay in shape. I was doing really well, but we've had three book launches this month, and the hors d'oeuvres and canapés were fabulous. We had a chocolate fondue fountain at the last one. I nearly drowned myself in dark chocolate."

Jane rolled her eyes. Cynthia, like her mother, was slender. She'd never carried an ounce of excess weight.

"Something must be working. You should come down next month. They're doing a 10K race for charity."

"In Acorn Hill?"

"So I understand. I have a Web site address for the event, but I haven't looked it up."

"Are you going to run it?"

"I'm thinking about it. I need to do some training. My daily jogs are much shorter than that and a whole lot slower than I used to run."

"But you're so faithful with your exercise. You'll sail right through it."

"Maybe if I could wear my in-line skates, but I doubt they'd allow them."

Cynthia laughed. "I can see you now, gliding circles around the other runners. What fun! You'll have to get sponsors. Put me down. I'll be your first."

"So now you're caught up on all the exciting details of my life, my editing and never-ending proposal reading," said Cynthia, setting her napkin beside her fork. She leaned back. "That was delicious, Aunt Jane."

"I know your life is more than work," Louise said. "Last night you were telling me that your singles group at church attended the symphony."

"Well yes, I guess I do get out now and then. I even went bowling last weekend."

"Bowling and jogging—you have been busy," Jane said.

"Oh, and I discovered a new author. I'm very excited about his work." Cynthia gave them a dreamy smile. "Adrian and I have really hit it off," she said.

"Really?" Jane said, perking up.

"You'd love him, Mother. He plays the piano quite well. I first met him at a recital that I attended with his mother. She is in my Bible study." Cynthia laughed. "Adrian is nineteen and a child prodigy, although I suppose he's really an adult now. His fantasy stories are magical. He has quite a future ahead of him and he loves mint-chocolate-chip ice cream.

"He's fortunate to begin a career at such a young age," Alice said.

Jane was a little disappointed. Cynthia was such an attractive young woman; Jane didn't understand what was wrong with young men these days. Her niece's boyfriends became her best friends, more like brothers. But Cynthia seemed content.

"Enough about me. What about you? What's been happening around here?"

"Your mother's been busy," Alice said. "She's also been very secretive."

Cynthia looked at her mother. "Are you working on a new concerto?"

"We'd know if that were the case," Jane said. "We could hear her playing."

"True. So what is it that you're being secretive about?" she asked, giving her mother an inquisitive look.

"It's quite a phenomenon," Alice said. "Strangest thing I've ever seen your mother do. She'll have to show you."

"It's outside," Louise said.

"Now I *am* curious. May I see it now?"

"If you'd like." Louise rose ceremoniously and carried her dishes to the sink.

"The dishes can wait. I'm coming too," Jane said. "It's not a secret anymore," she told Cynthia. "It's not the kind of thing you can hide for long. But your mother managed to keep it a secret for almost two months."

The four of them trouped out the back door, and Louise led them across the lawn to the fenced-in vegetable garden. Even from the gate, Jane could see the huge, rounded leaves of the vine that dominated the far side of the garden. In the center of it, a large sheet was spread out, shading the vine. Normally, Louise and Alice spent very little time in the garden, other than to help pick the bountiful fruits of Jane's labors. It seemed Jane had inherited their mother's green thumb and her love of gardening. Neither Alice nor Louise had that interest, so they left the gardening to Jane, which suited her fine. She loved working outside, and the rewards brought her great joy.

The rest of the garden was a riot of color, with marigolds in dazzling red, orange and yellow; there were also nasturtiums in various pastel shades, surrounding full-headed broccoli, cauliflower, beet greens, carrot tops and cabbage as large as soccer balls. Jane watched Alice snap a bright red sweet pickle pepper off a loaded bush and rub it on her shirtsleeve. The pepper was clean. Jane didn't use chemical pesticides around her vegetables. Alice popped the pepper in her mouth. Jane wasn't surprised when her sister picked several more of the miniature specialty peppers that Jane grew. The crisp sweetness demanded another taste. She said a silent prayer, thanking the Lord for their bounty. She often talked to her plants and to the Lord while she worked. The verse about the plants and rocks praising the Lord was one of her favorites. Reciting it was like having a three-way conversation among her, the plants and God. And she believed the Lord heard, because she and her sisters had been feasting on the beans, carrots, assorted salad greens, radishes, cucumbers and tomatoes most of the summer.

They made their way through the rows of vegetables when suddenly, Louise stopped, held out her arms, hands extended, palms up, encompassing the back of the garden.

"Ta-dum!"

Cynthia looked dumbfounded. Jane could imagine

what was going through her mind. Long, thick twisted vines with huge, wilting, splotchy leaves ran all over across the back half of the garden like some kind of dying serpent. Jane laughed.

"You're reacting the same way we did, back when we first discovered your mother had invaded the garden with some sort of creatures that were attempting to take over the town," Alice said. "As you can see, they've nearly succeeded."

"It's time to get out the weed whacker—or a cannon— and drive this thing back again," Jane said, pointing to the pole beans. "Your monster has wrapped its tentacles around my beans." She'd already harvested the summer bean crop, but the vines remained.

Cynthia looked where Jane was pointing. "Unbelievable. It looks like a giant stalk climbing the beanpole. Are you going to climb it and look for a treasure of gold?"

Louise gave her daughter a look somewhere between insult and injury. "Don't talk that way in front of the plants. You're supposed to talk nicely to them, aren't you, Jane? You always talk to your plants and so did Mother."

"You're serious?" The incredulous look on Cynthia's face made Jane laugh out loud. "This looks like something out of a Grimm's fairy tale, Mother. It could be an illustration in one of my books. Only I thought it was supposed to be a beanstalk. Not a ..." Cynthia looked back at the monster plant and the sheet that covered three big bumps in the middle of the vines. One of the bumps was peeking out from under a corner. It was large and yellow. "What are they? Squash? And how did they get so big?"

"They're pumpkins. They've just started turning color. And they'll grow much larger. These are Atlantic Giant Pumpkins. Let me show you." Louise carefully pulled back the sheeting over one of them that protected them from pests and harsh weather.

"Me-ooow." The inn's black-and-gray striped tabby stole out from under the material, stretched and rolled over onto his back.

"Wendell, this is not here for your benefit," Louise said, lifting the cat and setting him on the pathway.

Wendell gave a little flip of the black tip of his tail and sauntered off.

Several large rounded leaves shaded the pumpkin. The gigantic yellow vegetable was the shape of a somewhat flattened and rather irregular beach ball.

"Wow! It's bigger than I thought. That's a pumpkin?" Cynthia exclaimed. "It must weigh a ton."

"Craig Tracy measured it not long ago. He estimated then that it weighed over seven hundred pounds. The others are smaller." She looked at her plants and beamed. "Aren't they amazing?"

"*Amazing* is certainly a fitting word," Cynthia agreed. "What are you going to do with them? Have a pie festival?

That's enough pumpkin to make pies for the entire town. I'll definitely expect pumpkin pie for Thanksgiving, Aunt Jane."

"Pie, cake, bread, cookies, soup, soufflé—I'll be searching my cookbooks and the Internet for new creative ways to cook pumpkin," Jane said. "At least there are only three pumpkins. We harvested a few smaller ones, and there were a lot of flowers. Your mother let me make fried squash blossoms out of them."

"They were good," Alice said. "I'd never had them before."

"So my pumpkins *are* good for something," Louise said, arching her eyebrows at her siblings. "You have to acknowledge, in front of my daughter, that I grew these by myself and that they've thrived under my care."

"*Thrived* is hardly the word I'd use. They're taking over the garden. We're out here every day, cutting back these vines," Jane explained to Cynthia. "If they weren't finally starting to die off, they might have taken over Acorn Hill," she teased.

Louise put her hands on her hips. "And you're the master of exaggeration, Jane Howard. You both said I couldn't grow anything. I've proved you wrong."

Cynthia began to laugh. "Remember when I was little and we grew an avocado from a seed? We had this tall, spindly stick coming out of the seed with two leaves on it. It lived a long time, but it never grew beyond those leaves."

"What about the sweet potato vine that grew up the sides of the kitchen window?" Alice said. "That was one of your science projects. It was very healthy, as I recall."

"Father called it the sweet potato monster. I was so sad when it died." Cynthia affected a downcast pout, her chin trembling as if she were about to cry.

"All right. Make fun of my gardening and my pumpkins if you must, but mark my words: I'm going to grow the largest pumpkin Acorn Hill has ever seen."

"You mean you're going to keep on nurturing it? When will it be ripe? I may have to make a special trip to see that." Cynthia linked her arm through her mother's arm. "You are *extraordinary*, Mother. In every way."

Louise patted her daughter's arm. "Thank you, sweetheart. It's nice to be appreciated," she said, giving her sisters a condescending look that only brought giggles from Jane and a chuckle from Alice. Louise sighed. "You see what I have to put up with?"

"How about if we help you trim back this monster?" Jane offered. "Will that make up for our teasing?"

"It might save the rest of the garden," Alice said.

"True. I do have an ulterior motive," Jane admitted. "Anyone want a pair of shears?"

Cynthia pushed up her sleeves. "I'll help."

"I'll get them," Alice offered, heading for the shed. She returned a moment later with three pairs of shears, four pairs of gardening gloves and two baskets. "I figure we should pick some vegetables while we're out here."

"The competition's been good for Jane's vegetables," Louise said. "They're not as large, but they're certainly plentiful."

"There's nothing like fresh garden produce," Cynthia said, slipping on a glove.

"We'll send some home with you," Jane said.

"Good. I was hoping you'd take the hint. I hate begging." Cynthia grabbed a long runner from the pumpkin vine and snipped it off. Lifting it gingerly, she followed it to a head of cabbage and carefully untangled it.

"I'll have to admit, I never really expected this much success," Louise said. "Next year, I'll need half of the garden, instead of just a corner."

"Half? Not likely. Those vines are running over half the garden now," Jane said, straightening up with a large stalk of broccoli in her hand. She wiggled it at Louise, then set it in a basket. "You'd get mighty sick of pumpkin, and our guests might never come back."

"*Hmm*. That could be a problem." She gave Jane a thoughtful frown, but the twinkle in her eyes gave away her mirth. The garden would be safe.

Chapter Three

"Yoo-hoo," a cheery voice called out. The garden gate squeaked and groaned as it opened.

Alice glanced up. She knew it was her Aunt Ethel, who lived in the carriage house behind them. There was no mistaking that greeting, but she had been expecting her friend Vera. During the school year, when Vera Humbert taught and the days were shorter, Saturday was their only regular walking date and was a highlight of Alice's week. Alice snipped a thick runner off the vine and tossed it into the pile growing next to Jane. Cynthia straightened up and removed her gardening gloves.

"I thought that looked like Cynthia's car." Ethel stepped gingerly along the hard-packed path between the rows of vegetables, taking care not to soil her pink paisley shoes. With her matching blouse and shiny, carefully coiffed Titian-red hair, she could have been a flower in Jane's garden. "Darling, it's so good to see you," she said, throwing her arms open dramatically. "Are you staying long? No one tells me anything around here," she complained, sending her nieces a chiding look as she hugged her grandniece and kissed her cheek.

"Hello, Aunt Ethel." Cynthia gave her a squeeze. "It's good to see you too. You look beautiful this morning. I came on the spur of the moment. I have an appointment with a new author in Philadelphia on Monday, so I took a long weekend to visit Mother. And all of you, of course," she added.

Ethel seemed mollified by the explanation. She made a point of knowing everything that happened in Acorn Hill, so not knowing about a visit from Cynthia could be an affront to her pride. She did look especially fine this morning. She always took special care with her appearance, but it was unusually early for her to be dressed to go out.

Ethel took a step forward and peered at the gigantic pumpkin leaves. The large yellow orb stuck out like a golden boulder through the leaves. "Those plants of yours have grown huge, Louise. I just saw them two days ago. I believe they're twice the size today. Whatever are you feeding them? With all those curly tentacles and runners, they remind me of a science-fiction movie. *The Invasion of the Whatevers.*"

"They have rather taken over, haven't they?" Louise gave her aunt a satisfied look. "Craig said I should shade the pumpkins, so they don't crack in the sun. They were growing twenty-five to thirty-five pounds a day, but they should be slowing down soon."

Astonished, Cynthia gaped at her mother. "How can they grow that fast? What are you feeding them?"

Louise raised one eyebrow but did not reply.

"You must have gotten a prescription for growth medicine," Alice said. Although she doubted that was the case, the pumpkin patch did look like a lab experiment in growth research. "I'll never forget the day I came home from work and found your mother kneeling in the garden."

"Mother never spent much time in the garden," Cynthia acknowledged, "but why did that surprise you so much?"

"She was so secretive. When I called out to her, she nearly fell over. Then she hurried out of the garden and came to meet me. I thought at the time she was hiding something. There was a row of plastic milk jugs with the bottoms cut out covering something in the garden. I didn't think too much about it. Jane often starts her plants that way. I might have forgotten the whole incident, but your mother specifically asked us at dinner to leave her corner of the garden alone. We asked her why and she wouldn't give an answer."

"Really? Mother?"

Louise just shrugged.

Jane shook her head. "She's found some magic pills or miracle plant food, but she won't tell us about it," she said. "Maybe she'll tell us later. I could use some help improving the size of my vegetables. Just think how much I could can for winter. We could give jars to shut-ins. Our mother used to do that."

"We'll see," Louise demurred. "These pumpkins might crack or rot before they're done. And I need to cover them with something better than a sheet."

"We could make shade with black plastic trash bags," Alice suggested.

"Good idea. We could put the patio umbrella over the big one," Jane said. "I just put it in storage." She headed for the shed, where they kept gardening supplies and tools, and stored extra patio chairs out of season.

Louise stepped carefully over to the one of the plants; she leaned down and uncovered a pumpkin.

Cynthia and Ethel followed her. They peered down at the large vegetable.

"It looks puny next to the other one," Ethel said.

"You call that puny?" Cynthia said, laughing. "It's not nearly as large as Attila the Pumpkin over there, but it's still big."

"Attila the Pumpkin? Is that one of your children's books?"

They all turned at the sound of a new voice. Vera Humbert walked into the backyard as Jane came back carrying a large umbrella and a handful of black bags.

"That's a great idea. I'll take pictures and we'll get someone to write a children's book about the giant pumpkins. Thanks, Vera," Cynthia said, smiling at her mother's friend.

"Help me with this," Jane said, twisting the umbrella pole into the ground beside the plant.

"Be careful! Don't step on the plant or break the roots," Louise said. She grabbed the upper part of the umbrella. "Will it stay standing?"

"It will if we get it deep enough. We'll prop it up with cement blocks."

Louise frowned. "I don't want to do anything that might hurt my plants."

"We'll be careful."

"Jane knows what she's doing in the garden, Mother. Where are the blocks? I'll go get one." Cynthia stepped across the plant, being careful to miss the leaves and stems. The leaves stood up off the vine, some reaching a foot or more above the ground, forming a canopy and partially shading the large pumpkins, but the leaves were turning dry and curling with age, and the pumpkins had grown too big for the leaves to cover the fruit.

"I want to bring Fred by later, if that's all right. He tried growing a giant pumpkin a few years ago, but he lost the whole patch to some kind of bug," Vera said. "He'll want to bring his camera. He likes to put up pictures on the bulletin board at the store, you know."

"I'm afraid I didn't buy my seeds or supplies at the hardware store," Louise said, giving Vera an apologetic look.

Vera waved her hand dismissively. "It doesn't matter. You've supported us for years. Besides, this is an Acorn Hill phenomenon. I doubt many people around here have grown a pumpkin nearly that large, Louise."

Lloyd Tynan's SUV pulled into the driveway and stopped. Lloyd stepped out of his car and turned toward the carriage house, then stopped and looked in the direction of the garden. He was dressed in smart gray slacks and a dark blue sport jacket, and his fringe of gray hair had been cut very short, giving him a clean-cut, rather dashing appearance. He strode into the garden.

"Good morning, ladies." He smiled at each of them, but saved his special smile for Ethel. They'd become close friends when Ethel moved into the carriage house to be near her brother, Rev. Daniel Howard, after her husband died.

"Heavens, is it time to go? I'm ready," Ethel said. "Lloyd is taking me to a political luncheon in Harrisburg, so we must be on our way."

Lloyd was Acorn Hill's mayor and liked to keep up on matters relating to regional government. Ethel loved attending functions with him. "We have a few minutes, Ethel," he said. "It's nice to see you, Cynthia. Jane, your garden looks wonderful. Your tomato plants are so loaded with fruit, it looks like they might break under the weight."

"I've had to prop them up. Would you like some tomatoes and broccoli?"

"I'd like some tomatoes. I'll pass on the broccoli, though."

"Have you seen Louise's pumpkins?" Ethel asked. "They're quite remarkable. Especially since Louise is raising them, not Jane. Show him, Louise."

"Is that your pumpkin beneath the umbrella?" Lloyd asked, stepping carefully over rows of carrots and beets.

"Yes. It's a giant pumpkin variety. Jane isn't the only one who can grow something around here," Louise said, sounding just a bit defensive. "Although," she added, "she's the one with the green thumb. I hadn't realized how much work is required to raise a garden."

Lloyd stepped closer, just missing an onion plant growing nearby. "But look at it!" he urged, as if they hadn't just been doing that very thing. "Don't they hold competitions for giant vegetables? You need to enter it in a contest."

"It's not that large yet," Louise said. "Craig told me about a giant pumpkin weigh-off in Baskenburg every year. I understand they hold contests all over the country. Mine isn't big enough for that, though. The record is 1,502 pounds. So far, this might be eight hundred pounds. That's a big difference."

"Is it finished growing?" Lloyd asked.

"Not quite," Louise said.

"Hello-o-o," another voice called. They turned toward the sound. Patsy Ley's arms were swinging as she strode down the slight hill on the path from Grace Chapel, the church Louise's father had pastored for sixty years just down the road from their home. Patsy's husband was the associate pastor, and they lived in the rectory on the other side of the church.

"I could hear you laughing all the way up at the church. It looks like you're having a party. What's the occasion?" she asked as she came through the garden gate.

"Be careful where you step," Ethel warned. Patsy looked down at her feet and picked her way between rows.

"We're admiring Louise's pumpkins," Vera said.

"Oh my," Patsy said, peering around the group at the large yellow orb. "Louise, that's fabulous! I thought you couldn't grow anything."

"Indeed, that was the common perception," Louise said, her tone dry. "As you can see, I have in fact grown something."

"Sorry. I didn't mean to offend you. It's just, I know I've heard you say..." Patsy stopped speaking and blushed.

Louise gave Patsy a kindly smile. "I've probably said that more than once. I haven't spent much time in the pursuit of gardening. On a whim, I decided to see if it was true. As you can see, I have a little talent. Not as much as my sister," she added. "It's just not... 'my thing.'"

Jane laughed. "I'm grateful for that. It is my thing, but I wouldn't have any room for my garden if I had to compete with Louise."

"Well, I love gardening," Patsy said, holding her hands up, framing the pumpkin with her fingers. "This is extraordinary. May I come take pictures of it for my scrapbook? With the bright umbrella, it looks like something out of a garden in Tuscany."

Jane stopped pruning and stood to stare at the pumpkin. She cocked her head to one side. "You're right. It does. I just may have to immortalize your pumpkin in a painting, Louie," she said, giving her older sister a smile.

"*Humph*," Louise uttered, but she didn't look displeased at all the attention her plants were getting.

"What's happening in there?" yet another voice called from the direction of the yard.

Clara Horn stood just outside the garden gate. She was pushing her baby carriage, and Daisy, her miniature Vietnamese potbellied pig, was sitting up, wearing a blue ruffled bonnet, eyeing the garden with rapt attention.

"Uh-oh," Vera said to Alice in a low tone. "Perhaps we should disperse this gathering and distract Daisy before she decides to join the party. She'd have a heyday in this garden."

Alice nodded as an image of a destroyed garden flashed in her mind. She removed her gloves and handed them to Jane. "We're going walking now. Aunt Ethel, you'd better get going too."

"Yes, it's time," Lloyd said, taking Ethel's elbow and

helping her around a row of carrots. "I'll be back with my camera later," he said over his shoulder to Louise.

Louise looked out toward the gate. "Yes. Good-bye," she said. Under her breath, she said, "I do hope Clara doesn't feel rejected. She's a sweet lady, but I don't want Daisy loose in here."

"Amen," Jane said.

"I'll help distract her," Cynthia said, heading for the gate behind Lloyd and Ethel.

"I'd better run along. I was doing a bit of dusting in the sanctuary. I get sidetracked so easily," Patsy muttered, falling into line behind Cynthia.

"Looks like you two have the garden to yourselves," Alice told her sisters, as she and Vera moved toward the gate.

"My helpers are all deserting me," Louise said, watching the exodus. The cat was watching lazily from the shade of a row of tall basil. "At least I still have Wendell. He comes out every day to help me."

Jane laughed. "I'm sure he's a big help, batting at your giant leaves," she said. "Guess you and I will have to pick the tomatoes and carrots and beets and…"

"Excellent idea," Alice said. "I can just see them trampled underfoot, or worse, rooted up by Daisy's snout."

"Heaven forbid," Louise said.

"I'll be back to help after Vera and I have our walk," Alice said.

"Don't be concerned. We'll be done by then. I don't want to take a chance on losing all this produce to an invader," Jane said, brandishing her hoe like a weapon.

"Let's go before she starts swinging, Vera."

"Right. See you later," Vera told Louise and Jane as she headed for the gate. Alice followed right behind her.

Chapter Four

*C*ute bonnet," Cynthia said, patting Daisy on the head, to which Daisy let out a little snort. "And how are you, Mrs. Horn?" she asked.

"We're as well as can be expected. It's been a long time, Cynthia. So nice to see you." Clara's brow wrinkled as she watched the departing crowd. "I didn't know your mother and your aunts were entertaining this morning. Were they having a garden party?"

"Oh no. We were checking on some plantings, and a few people stopped by to say hi."

"Good morning, Clara," Alice said. "Are you and Daisy out for a morning walk? Vera and I will join you if you like."

"Oh no. We're just finishing our walk. We're on our way home. Daisy tires so easily, you know."

Alice didn't know. She suspected Clara was tired from pushing Daisy in the baby carriage. She couldn't be sure, but Daisy looked like she'd put on some weight, as even miniature pigs were prone to do.

"Nice to see you again," Cynthia said, as she gave a brief wave.

Jane came hurrying up behind them and held out a sack. "Good morning, Clara. Would you and Daisy like some vegetables? Here's a head of cabbage, some carrots and beets, and I left the beet greens for Daisy."

Clara's eyes lit up. She took the sack and tucked it into the pouch behind the carriage. "Thank you. I'm sure Daisy will enjoy them. We'll have them for lunch."

"I'll be happy to save some of our peelings for Daisy," Jane said.

At Clara's affronted look, Alice said, "Vegetable peels contain the highest concentration of vitamins. Jane makes delicious broth out of them."

"Of course," Clara said, but she didn't look convinced. Daisy ate food prepared carefully by her owner. Clara wouldn't think of giving less than the best to her precious pet.

"I'll make sure to save the very best for Daisy," Jane added.

"Thank you, I'm sure," Clara said. She said good-bye and walked away, pushing the carriage.

"I didn't mean to insult her," Jane said.

"I wonder how Daisy would like pumpkin," Alice ventured.

"I heard that," Louise said, coming out to join them. "Don't get any ideas about my pumpkins. They're still weeks from maturity."

"And then we'll have enough pumpkin to give a pie to everyone in town," Alice said.

"Only if you help me do the cooking," Jane replied.

"I'll help," Cynthia said. "If I get one all to myself, that is."

"It's a deal." Jane headed back into the garden.

"Just the thought of pumpkin pie and whipped cream is making me hungry," Vera said.

"Me too. Let's stop at the bakery after our walk."

Alice fell into step next to Vera as they walked across the inn property and turned up Chapel Road. They walked in silence for a few moments, power-walking up the hill. When they reached the top they slowed their pace and breathed deeply.

"What a gorgeous day," Alice said, enjoying the sunshine and the cool breeze. "I love the approach of fall. I think it's my favorite time of year."

"Me too," Vera said, but then she fell back into silence.

Alice thought that was odd. They usually chatted away, catching up on the latest news. They hadn't walked since the previous Saturday. Finally, Alice asked, "Is everything all right?"

"Yes. I think so. Fred and I are fine. I do have a dilemma, though. What do you know about assisted living centers?"

"We often have patients at the hospital from the ones in Potterston. I've been to them to visit some of my former patients. From what I've seen, most are wonderful facilities. Why?"

"I got a call from my cousin Reggie in Shelton Cove. Remember I told you that my Aunt Agatha fell and broke her hip several weeks ago. She had surgery and then she developed pneumonia. Well, she's recuperating in a rehabilitation center. They have her using a walker to get around."

"That sounds encouraging. So what's the dilemma?"

"The doctor, the physical therapist and the occupational therapist all want her to move into an assisted living center, where she will have professional staff and help in case she falls again. Reggie said that she has gotten fragile since her accident and she's supposed to use a walker from now on."

"That often happens. An assisted living center would be a good choice for her. I suppose she's against the idea."

"Adamantly. I doubt she'll keep using the walker either, if she can help it. Personally, I think the move makes sense. She's eighty-six and she's showing her age. But she's used to being independent."

"What is her house like? Can she get around easily?"

"No. It's a monstrosity, at least for someone who has trouble navigating. It's a big, three-story house with a long sloping yard that goes down to the Delaware River. It's a lovely old home with a beautiful view, but she shouldn't be climbing stairs anymore."

"That's a problem. What are you going to do?"

"I told Reggie I'd go to see her and help him find a place for her. She can afford a nice apartment. Convincing her to move is the problem. She trusts me, but she won't like it."

"I see that kind of reaction all the time. Patients can't take care of themselves, but they don't want to leave the security of their homes and all that's familiar. No one wants to give up his or her independence, and that's what it amounts to."

"That's it exactly. She ran the family business after my Uncle George died. It's only been the last few years that she stepped aside for Reggie to take over, but he complains that she won't completely relinquish the reins. Now we're asking her to give up some control of her own life." Vera stopped walking and turned to Alice. Frowning, she put her hands on her hips.

Alice stopped too. She could see that this problem weighed heavily on Vera's mind. Vera was one of the most capable, levelheaded people Alice knew. "How can I help you?"

"I'm taking a week off to go see the situation for myself and talk to Aunt Agatha. I hate to ask you, but would you consider going with me? I remember that you were only scheduled at the hospital for two days next week, and you would be able to tell better than I can whether she's healthy enough and strong enough to go home." Vera's eyes widened hopefully.

"Of course I'll go with you," Alice said, giving her friend a reassuring smile. "I don't know how much help I can be, but I can put on my sternest Nurse Ratched face and sound very official with your aunt. When do you want to go?"

"Next week. I thought we could drive down Saturday morning, then come back the following Sunday, if that's all right with you. You'll miss one week of your ANGELs group."

"No problem. I'll ask Jane to cover for me. The girls love her. I'll make arrangements to take off the time from work. It's been slow at the hospital, so they won't miss me."

Vera gave Alice a big hug. "Thank you, dear friend. I know that I'm asking a lot, but I feel that I can always count on you."

⁓

"It's warmer than I thought," Jane said, bending over, resting her hands against her knees and breathing deeply, waiting for her heartbeat to slow down.

Cynthia came up behind her, plopped down on the grassy side of the path and let out a sigh. "It's all the expended energy. I know we're supposed to keep jogging in place, but I'm too tired." She laughed breathlessly. "And I thought I was in good shape."

"Me too. I'm not used to that many hills. I can feel this

in my shins," she paused for another breath, "not to mention my burning lungs." Jane dropped down next to Cynthia. "I'll never be ready for that race if I keep stopping like this."

"How long have you been training?"

"This is day one," Jane said, wiping her forehead on the sleeve of her T-shirt.

"Oh well, no wonder. But you walk and jog regularly, don't you?"

"Most days. I do just about a mile or two. So far, we're getting well beyond that."

"This is way more than my typical walk. I usually wear my walking shoes to work and speed walk to the T or the bus or to lunch."

"I did something like that when I lived in San Francisco," Jane said. "It keeps you in shape."

"Yes, but doesn't train you for distance runs. How much time do you have to get ready?"

"I have a month."

"You can do it." Cynthia pushed to her feet. "How much farther do we have to go?"

"Ten kilometers is 6.21 miles, but we don't have any more steep hills."

"So is there a reward at the end of the trail?" Cynthia asked.

"Carrot cake. I plan to make it this afternoon and use

up some of those carrots I pulled this morning." Jane took
off jogging slowly. Cynthia caught up and paced herself in
stride and rhythm to keep even with Jane.

"I'll peel the carrots," she offered. "That is, if I can do it
sitting down."

Jane laughed. "It's a deal."

They'd reached a level stretch of farmland. The landscape shone with the evidence of summer's end. Across a
field of hay stubble and acres and acres of corn, the stalks,
beginning to dry and turn golden, rustled in the sunshine.
Off to the west, branches in an apple orchard hung heavy
with red fruit.

"I need to get out here and pick apples. By next weekend, these orchards will be crawling with people," Jane said.
"I canned peaches a few weeks ago. I'll send a couple of jars
home with you."

"I'd love that. I wish I could stay and help you do up the
apples. I'd like to learn how to can fruit and make jam.
Mother and I made apple butter one year. It was fun and so
good, but we made so much that we got tired of it."

Jane laughed. "Too much of a good thing isn't so good.
I usually go easy on the apple butter. I make apple chutney
and mix the apples with rhubarb or raspberries for jam."

"Yum. I remember your chutney. You served it at Easter
with the ham, didn't you?"

"Good memory. Yes. It goes really well with pork and chicken. And there's something very satisfying about putting up food. You should take off a week and come help me with the canning. Then you can take home some of the results."

"Maybe next year."

The road curved around a field, and they jogged along a stretch of evergreen forest for a while. The trees gave way to a cultivated field, bright green with alfalfa. Set back from the road, a long, white, two-story Victorian farmhouse came into view.

"That's Bellwood Farm, isn't it?" Cynthia asked, pointing at the house. "I remember years ago coming to Grandpa Howard's for Christmas. He brought us out here to see the living nativity they had set up in their barn. They used their own cows and sheep. It was so cool."

"It was probably *cold*, but I know what you mean. They've hosted a lot of activities for the townspeople. There's Rose now. Hey, Rose!" Jane shouted, waving her arm.

A petite woman was walking down the driveway toward the mailbox. She was looking down, and the sun glinted off her shiny brown hair. She looked up and waved back. She had an envelope in her hand. The three women reached the end of the driveway at the same time.

"Hi, Jane. Cynthia, it's nice to see you. Are you just down for the weekend?"

"Yes. I have to leave Monday."

"That's too bad, but how nice for your mother to see you. I live for the weekends when Samantha can get home from college. Why don't you two take a break and come up to the house for a glass of iced tea. You look parched."

"That's probably because we are," Jane said. Cynthia's face was flushed and her hair clung to her forehead in damp tendrils. "We'd love a glass of iced tea. Thanks, Rose."

"Let me put this in the mailbox so the mailman will pick it up." She walked over to the weathered white wooden box that surrounded the mailbox. The name Bellwood Farm was painted on the side of the box, framed by cheery red and yellow tulips and hearts around the edge. She set the envelope inside and raised the metal flag. "I suppose you have all the zucchini you need," she said to Jane.

"I do. The pantry is full from the garden. I've made zucchini relish and piccalilli and I'll freeze some for cooking this winter. I'll still have half a bushel leftover."

"Any you don't use, I can feed the hogs, so don't throw them away. Don't you wonder why zucchini and cucumbers are so prolific? I wish I could do so well with some of my other plantings."

They walked to the front porch, where Jane and Cynthia sat on rocking chairs while Rose went inside for refreshments. A silvery wind chime tinkled in the light breeze.

Hummingbirds vied for a spot at the feeder hanging from the porch beam next to an overflowing basket of pink and purple petunias. A round, red and green hex sign with tulips, hearts, birds and a star bid *Wilkum* over the front door.

The door swung open, and Rose came out carrying a tray with three tall glasses and a plate of homemade rolls.

"These are apple crescents," she said, offering them to Jane and Cynthia. She set the tray on the small table between them and pulled up a chair.

Cynthia took a bite of one. "*Mmm.* Delicious. Not too sweet."

"I just wrap apple slices in crescent rolls, roll them in cinnamon sugar and bake. Makes an easy breakfast treat, but I always have too many for just Sam and me. With school, the grandsons don't come over as often. You don't usually jog this far from town, do you, Jane?"

"No. I heard about the Harvest charity run next month, so I thought I'd check out the route. It's supposed to go right past the farm."

"Yes. Carrie, the organizer of the race, stopped by and talked to us about it. We're going to provide a water station for the runners. We'll set it up at the end of the driveway. She said she expects over one hundred runners and walkers. So you're going to represent Acorn Hill?"

"I'm sure there will be plenty of local participants. I'm thinking about running it. Would you like to sponsor me?"

Jane asked, taking a swallow of iced tea. It tasted good. She hadn't realized just how thirsty she'd become. She didn't usually go far enough to need a drink until she got back home. Perhaps she should look up distance training and see what else she hadn't considered.

"Yes, we'll sponsor you. We'll probably have to support our grandsons too, so we'll divide our contribution between you. How're Louise's pumpkins coming along? Craig told Sam they had prize potential," Rose said. "They must be getting large."

"*Large* isn't the word for them," Cynthia said. "They're huge. One is over eight hundred pounds."

"Really? That's good for mid-September. She still has a couple of weeks of growing season."

"You always plant a big garden. Have you ever tried the giant pumpkins?" Jane asked.

"One year I grew several that weighed in around two or three hundred pounds. That's not large enough to compete, so I gave up."

"That's pretty big. Why didn't you try again?" Cynthia asked.

"Well, it seemed like a waste of time to me. I can't compete at that rate, and pumpkins that big aren't good eating. The boys had fun carving them up for Halloween, though, I'll have to admit."

Jane leaned forward. "So you couldn't use them for baking?"

"No. When they get that large, they're usually water-logged. They don't have much flavor and they turn mushy. I like the baby pumpkins. That's what I grow. They make wonderful pies and soups and anything that calls for pumpkin."

"Aha! So I don't need to look for ways to cook Louise's pumpkins."

"I wouldn't bother. Just take lots of pictures. Unless she grows a contender and catches the bug, this may be her only crop."

"Catches the bug?" Cynthia asked.

"Yes. Growing giant pumpkins is addictive. There are organizations of pumpkin growers all over the world. They hold contests and haul their huge pumpkins to designated weigh-in stations. Around here, people tow their pumpkins all the way to Baskenburg."

"That must be almost two hundred miles from here," Jane said. "Louise won't want to go there."

"Oh no? Just wait and see. I'd have gone there if I'd grown one large enough."

"What is large enough?" Cynthia asked.

"It'd be worth going if you have a pumpkin that weighs somewhere around eight hundred to a thousand pounds," Rose said.

"Mom's just might get that big."

"It'll keep growing through September if it gets enough nourishment and water," Rose said. "What is she using for fertilizer?"

"I have no idea," Jane said. "It's a big secret.

"If Craig's advising her, she's using a good fertilizer. Obviously, she had a good early mix with a boost of phosphorous, then increased nitrogen to set the fruit. Now she's probably feeding it a higher concentration of potassium."

"I haven't seen any fertilizer containers. Louise's pumpkin patch is a complete mystery to me. She's out there every day fussing over her personal patch, but she waits until I'm finished doing my gardening."

Cynthia laughed. "Now that's a side of my mother I haven't seen before. When I was growing up, if I ever acted mysteriously she would demand to know what I was up to. She never cared for surprises, even if one was for Christmas or her birthday. Now she's the mysterious one. Very interesting. I think there's a story in this. You'll have to keep me informed, Aunt Jane."

"I could sneak around with my camera and see if I can catch her doing whatever it is she's doing. I can see the book now—*Louie and the Giant Pumpkin.*"

"Very catchy title," Rose said. "I need to get over and see these marvels."

"Why don't you and Sam come to dinner after church tomorrow. I'm sure Louise will be happy to show you her pumpkin patch."

"We'd love to. Do you have others coming?"

"I imagine Aunt Ethel and Lloyd will join us."

"I just picked apples. I'll bring a couple of caramel apple pies for dessert, just in case."

"Oh, I'm glad I don't have to rush off right after church." Cynthia winked.

Chapter Five

Louise was setting the dining-room table for dinner after church when she heard a knock at the front door. At the same time Ethel and Lloyd came through from the kitchen.

"I'll get that," Ethel said. She sailed into the entryway, while Lloyd stayed in the dining room.

"Afternoon, Louise. Can I be of assistance?" Lloyd asked.

"Thank you, but I think everything's under control. I imagine that's the Bellwoods at the door. Perhaps you and Ethel could visit with them until Jane serves dinner."

"Delighted. I brought my camera to photograph the pumpkins. I'll just set it on the buffet if that's all right."

"That's fine, Lloyd," Louise said.

Sam Bellwood's rich voice could be heard in the hallway, as Sam talked with Ethel. Lloyd went out to join them.

"Need any help?" Rose asked from the hallway door. She was carrying a pie basket.

"Thanks, but we're finished here," Louise said.

"Dinner will be ready as soon as everyone is seated," Alice said, poking her head through the doorway from the kitchen. "Hi, Rose. Those must be the pies Jane told me about. I'll put them in the kitchen," she said, relieving Rose of her burden.

"I'll help serve while you call people to the table, Mother." Cynthia disappeared into the kitchen behind Alice.

Fifteen minutes later, Lloyd asked a blessing on their meal and their time together. When he said "Amen," Sam Bellwood followed with, "Amen, and please pass the biscuits."

The platter of baked chicken was nearly empty by the time it got back around to Louise. She put a piece on her plate, then went into the kitchen for a refill. She pushed open the swinging door, returning to the dining room, and almost ran into Alice, who was holding an empty coleslaw bowl.

"Excuse me," she said. "I put some salad on your plate. I hope there's more in the refrigerator."

Jane came up behind Alice. "The sweet potato fries are almost gone too. Have you tasted them? I like them better than French fries."

"Looks like everyone else likes them too," Louise commented, scooting through the doorway. She set the platter on the table and returned to her seat.

As talk and laughter filled the room, Cynthia leaned

over to her mother and said, "I'm so glad I could stay today. It's easy to see why you love it here so much. I have friends in Boston who get together and go out after church, but everyone is so busy, we rush through a meal and off to other obligations."

Louise looked around at the friends and family gathered in their dining room. In a few short years, they'd shared many joys and shed a few tears together. She'd lived away from Acorn Hill most of her adult life, until her dear Eliot passed away. When her father died four years later, she was ready to move back to the small town and join her sisters in starting a bed-and-breakfast in the old Howard home. She'd never regretted it. "We're particularly blessed here," Louise said. "We'd be happy to make room for you."

Cynthia gave her a quick hug. "I know. And I'd love it for a while, but I'd miss Boston and all the energy and activity in the city. Maybe someday, when I'm ready to settle down."

Louise patted Cynthia's hand and gave her a knowing smile. She'd felt the same way thirty years before. "Yes. When I'm old and grayer and shuffling around with a walker. Then you can move home and take care of your ancient mother."

Cynthia laughed. "That picture does not compute. You won't ever be an old lady. You're too independent for that."

I wish, Louise thought. But she hoped she would never become a burden to her daughter.

"When are we going to visit your pumpkin, Louise?" Lloyd asked.

His plate was clean. Looking around, she realized everyone was finished except for Jane and her. "I don't know why you're all so eager to see a pumpkin patch when there's still a couple of pieces of chicken left, but give me a minute to finish, then I'll take you out. We'll save dessert for later. The Leys, the Humberts and Craig Tracy are coming over in a few minutes to take pictures and measure the pumpkin."

Most unusual. For the life of her, Louise couldn't understand their fascination with her pumpkin.

"Stand there to the left and hold the hoe as if you're weeding," Patsy instructed Louise. She'd set up her camera on a tripod in the garden, while the covering over the pumpkin was removed.

"I don't want to be in the picture," Louise objected. "Jane, you come hold the hoe."

"No way. I'm not the gardener here. That's your plant. You need to be in the picture."

"Go on, Mother. I want a picture of you with your remarkable pumpkin, for posterity's sake."

"Oh, all right." Louise picked up the hoe and went to the side of the big pumpkin.

"Careful," Craig said. "You don't want to break it off or stress the plant." He stepped forward to help. The large leaf was drying out, turning brown in big splotches. It crinkled when they moved it. Together, they tucked a leaf out of the way to fully expose the pumpkin. Then Craig moved out of the way and Louise posed for Patsy.

The gathering reminded Jane of an old-fashioned garden party. The guests meandered around the garden. Rose and Sam stood in back with Ethel and Henry Ley, watching. Alice and Cynthia stood to one side with Vera, talking softly. The umbrella shading the pumpkin completed the festive scene.

Trying to envision Patsy's finished photograph of Louise and the pumpkin, Jane held her hands out in front of her, forming the bottom of a square with her fingers. Patsy took flora and fauna pictures as a hobby. Her framed photographs had won several blue ribbons and rosettes and best of show in the county fair.

The scene didn't work for Jane. Louise's navy blue skirt and royal blue sweater set didn't fit with the hoe. It would be fun to do her own picture for Louise, though. She'd use pastels to sketch Louise on her knees, pruning or perhaps watering.

Craig and Fred stood off to the side, watching the photo shoot. Craig had a tape measure in hand, ready to check the current size. Jane thought that the pumpkin looked larger, but big was big and it was huge. She'd heard about giant pumpkins and squash, but she'd never watched one grow before. She'd even stood and talked to the amazing plant when no one was around to hear her. This was Louise's project. Although she had teased her sisters for their brown thumbs, she was thrilled with Louise's success and didn't want to interfere in any way.

While Patsy gave Louise directions, Lloyd was up close, taking shots of the giant pumpkin. Jane had to admit it was impressive. The patio umbrella was very large and it shaded the entire pumpkin, but they would need more coverage if the pumpkin continued to grow at the rate it had been.

"Smile."

Louise tilted her head just slightly and gave Patsy a forced smile.

"Say 'whistle,'" Jane told her sister.

"Whistle," Louise repeated. One camera clicked.

"My camera didn't take. Do it again," Lloyd said.

Louise glowered at him. Jane knew how much Louise hated having her picture taken.

"Just one more, please," Patsy said.

"All right, but this is it. Are you ready, Lloyd?"

Lloyd held his camera up and looked through the viewer. "Ready."

Louise smiled and said, "Whistle."

This time, two cameras clicked.

"Okay, that's it." Louise walked to the shed and put the hoe away.

Craig bent over the pumpkin and took out his tape measure.

"Let me help you with that." Sam started to step over a leafy runner.

"Be careful," Rose said.

"I will." He practically tiptoed across the vines to the center, where the giant pumpkin lay.

"Sam can do anything around the farm except help in my garden," Rose said. "He's so big, he has trouble in tight areas."

Watching him, Jane was amazed that he managed to miss the vines. He'd been described as a gentle giant and he fit the nickname well. His feet were like small boats.

Sam took the end of the tape from Craig and they stretched it around the girth of the pumpkin.

Craig bent lower to read the tape. "I've got almost one hundred sixty-three inches." He looked up at Louise. "Growth has slowed down, but it's nearly three inches larger than last week. That's still good." He took a folded piece of paper out of his pocket. "According to the weight table, it weighs approximately nine hundred and fifty-three pounds."

"Wow!" Cynthia said. "Mother, that's unbelievable."

"But it's true," Craig said. "In two weeks, it's gained a hundred and twenty-four pounds." He checked the stem and the vine where the pumpkin connected to the main plant. "There's some stress, but it looks good. Whatever you're doing, keep it up."

"You mean you don't know what she's feeding the pumpkins?" Jane asked. She'd been certain Louise was following Craig's advice. Plants were his business and his passion. His greenhouse business had grown so quickly, he kept very busy managing both the nursery and his florist shop.

"I've advised Louise on compost and garden pests and recommended which pumpkins to nurture, but she's been mum on her fertilizer supplement. I extracted a promise from her that she'll share her secret if it's successful. I can't wait to hear what she's using."

"Me too," Fred said. "Whatever it is, I'll be sure to stock it at the hardware store next spring."

Louise stood watching them all, a sly smile on her lips and a twinkle in her eyes. Jane was baffled. What miracle product was her sister using that she wouldn't share—not even with her advisor, their resident plant expert? Whatever it was, it didn't come from Jane's ready supply of plant and garden products. Nothing was missing.

Chapter Six

After a leisurely breakfast with Cynthia, then a warm farewell for their dear daughter and niece, the sisters tackled their Monday routine, cleaning the guest rooms.

Louise bent low and peered under the bed in the Sunset Room. She'd learned from experience to look before she vacuumed beneath furniture. Sure enough, a tan sock stuck out from behind a bedpost, where it was caught. She went around and retrieved it. The sock was fine wool and looked new. She dropped it in the laundry basket with the used towels and linens. She would wash it, then tuck it into an envelope and mail it to the guests who'd stayed in the room.

The sisters couldn't always match items with guests, but this was obvious and cost very little in time or postage. Most hotels kept left-behind articles in a lost-and-found bin for a short while, in case the guest called looking for the item. The sisters went the extra mile as often as they could.

Turning on the vacuum, Louise bent down and cleaned beneath the bed, then stood and turned to get around the bedside table. A movement caught her attention. She shut off the vacuum. Alice stood framed in the doorway.

"You had a phone call from Carlene Moss," Alice said. "She saw Lloyd's picture of the pumpkin, and she wants to come take a picture and interview you for the *Nutshell*."

"Oh dear. I had no idea my pumpkin patch would gain so much attention." Louise unconsciously reached up and smoothed her short, silver hair. "What did you tell her?"

"I said we're cleaning today, but we should be finished by this afternoon. She said she'll come by at one o'clock, unless we call to make other arrangements. She wants to get it in this week's edition of the paper."

"Carlene isn't pushy, but she won't give up if she's after a story. I might as well talk to her and get it over with." Louise looked down. Her cleaning clothes consisted of a pair of slightly worn slacks and a knit shirt. She'd want to change before Carlene came over. "I'm almost finished here. I still need to vacuum the Garden Room and the hall."

"I'll take the laundry," Alice said, picking up the basket. "I'll bring clean linens in a moment. Jane's finishing up in the Garden Room. Then she plans to go running."

"It's supposed to warm up today. She'd better get going before it gets too hot."

Alice left with the laundry. Louise turned on the vacuum and resumed her task.

Jane topped the long grade coming down Hill Street to town. It was the last leg of the 10K Harvest Run course that started and ended in the parking lot behind City Hall. The air felt cool against the damp sweatband around her forehead, but her feet and her lungs felt as if they were on fire.

Ahead of her, two women were walking down the hill. One was tall and thin, with short blonde hair. The other was a little shorter and large. Although her momentum was good, Jane slowed as she came upon them. They turned as she approached.

"Hey, Jane," Betsy Long said.

"Hi, Betsy. Briana." Jane dropped her pace to a walk, falling into step with the two women, who were in their early thirties. "Nice day for a walk."

"Hope told me you're training for the Harvest Run," Betsy said.

"I thought I'd give it a try," Jane said, her words coming out between short breaths.

"We're going to enter too," Briana said. "Only we're just going to walk the course."

"I picked up a brochure at the Coffee Shop," Betsy said. "They want runners, walkers, and they even have a section for wheelchair participants."

"Sounds like it's going to be quite an event," Jane said.

"We walked half of the course today," Briana said. "I told Betsy I needed to start walking. I need the exercise, and it's for a good cause. My cousin's daughter has diabetes and my mother has it too, so I'm a prime candidate to get it. We're going to walk a little farther every day to get ready."

"You're smart to do it that way. I just did the full course and I'm exhausted. I think I'll slow it up a bit and work on part of the course every day for a week. I saw Eleanor Renda, the high school track coach. She was checking out the course for her students. She's encouraging them to participate."

"That's terrific," Briana said. "They'll be hard to beat, though."

"Oh, I don't expect to win the race," Jane said. "I just want to do my personal best." She almost winced after she said it. She *did* want to beat Carrie Gleason or whatever her name was now. Just as in her school days, she wanted that very badly. "I'll see you later," Jane said, and she resumed jogging with a burst of speed to put as much distance as possible between her and Betsy and Briana. She hadn't lied. She didn't care about coming in first in the race. Only about coming in ahead of one particular runner.

"If you could sit on the stool and put your hand on top of the pumpkin..."

With a sigh, Louise complied. She wasn't sure how it had happened, but here she was, posing for another picture with her pumpkin. This picture would appear, Carlene had informed her, on the front page of the weekly Acorn Hill newspaper. Louise grimaced. Some people were photogenic. She didn't feel that she was one of them.

"Smile, Louise. This is a happy occasion. I get enough bad news." Carlene knelt down on a straw-strewn path in the garden. She squinted into the camera viewfinder, then looked up at Louise. "Lean forward a couple of inches. Your face is in the shade."

That could only be a good thing, Louise thought, but she obeyed.

"Much better. I didn't know you were a talented gardener. Jane is the one who always enters her flowers and vegetables in the fair. Have you done a lot of gardening in the past? There, say 'geese.'"

Louise sighed. "Geese," she said without much enthusiasm. She hoped the pumpkin story would overshadow her picture. After all, that's why Carlene wanted an interview.

Carlene snapped off three pictures in succession, then looked into the back of her camera. Finally she stood.

"Great. I got three good shots. Shall we get out of the sun?"

"Let's sit on the front porch," Louise suggested, picking

up the stool she'd been sitting on and carrying it back to the house.

The covered porch still had shade in the early afternoon. Louise and Carlene sat on the padded wicker chairs from which they could look out toward the downtown area. Jane brought out fresh coffee and crumbly dessert bars.

"Those look delicious," Carlene said, taking one. "Maybe I should include some pumpkin recipes along with Louise's article."

"I've been collecting pumpkin recipes since Louise planted her giant pumpkins. I've found recipes for desserts, soups, salads, stuffed potatoes, ravioli sauce, cookies, waffles and pancakes. I haven't tried many of them yet. I usually come up with ideas as I cook."

Carlene took a small bite of the bar. "*Mmm.*" She looked up at Jane. "What's in this? I taste pecans and cheesecake."

"All of that plus apple and pumpkin."

"Very good. Is this an original?"

"I suppose so. I combined and adapted several recipes."

"Would you be willing to share it?"

"I don't know. I'd have to think about that." Jane giggled.

"Perhaps I could run some recipes closer to Halloween."

"That would give me time to create something. Now

I'll leave you alone to talk." Jane left the goodies on the wicker table between them and went inside.

Carlene turned to Louise. "You're all so talented. You amaze me." She took out a small notepad and pen, and put on her reading glasses. "Tell me about your pumpkin patch. What made you decide to grow a giant pumpkin?"

Louise steepled her hands together. "I saw one when I visited Connecticut several years ago. It was so fascinating that I bought a small package of the Atlantic Giant seeds. Then I put them in a drawer and forgot about them. This year, I found them and decided to plant them to see what might happen." She smiled. "I admit I never expected to succeed so dramatically."

"So what did you do to make them grow so large? I imagine you did more than just put them in the ground and water them."

"Oh yes. Much more. I kept a diary." Louise pulled a small bound book out of her pocket. She opened it. "I found a book at the library on growing vegetables. Pumpkins are actually a fruit, by the way, but they are treated like a vegetable. Where do you want me to start? You don't want all this detail."

"Give me some highlights. What special things did you have to do and what problems have you faced?" Carlene was already writing in her notebook. At Louise's pause, she stopped and looked over at her. "Go ahead. I can jot notes as you talk."

"All right. I picked May 19th to start my seeds. I followed the instructions and filed the edges, using an emery board. I soaked them several hours, then laid them between damp paper towels inside a plastic bag. I kept them under a light bulb, so they'd stay warm and germinate. It took about three days. Out of eight seeds, seven of them sprouted, but two were sickly." Louise turned the page. "I planted them in peat pots on May 25th and kept them under the light bulb. It took about a week to get the first leaf."

"That sounds pretty standard for starting seeds. Did they all keep growing? I only saw three plants in the garden. What happened to the others?"

"Well, all kinds of things. At first, I covered the plants with milk jugs with the bottoms removed. I'd seen Jane do that. It worked quite well, until the leaves started growing out of the tops. I removed the jugs, and the first night something ate the top off one of the plants. Every leaf was gone. We never did figure out what it was, but Craig gave me chicken-wire baskets to cover them.

"Then it turned cold unexpectedly. I went out first thing in the morning with a blanket, but one of the sickly plants died. It was kind of sad. I'd been nursing it along." Louise stopped and shook her head. "I suppose that sounds silly, treating a pumpkin plant like a child or something."

"No, not at all. Well, maybe a little. I think all serious

gardeners treat their plants with TLC. That's why their plants grow so well." Carlene laughed, showing her dimples. "Mine have to survive severe drought, since I keep forgetting to water them, poor things. They've got to be tough."

"To be honest, that's always been a problem for me as well."

"I find that hard to believe. You're a meticulous and caring person, Louise. I can't imagine your neglecting anything."

Louise smiled. "Thank you. That's a fine compliment, Carlene. I suppose it comes down to priorities. I love my family and my music, foremost, so my attention goes to my students and to my sisters and our family business. That's why I've kept a diary and a calendar for my pumpkin venture. They help me to stay on track." She flipped forward several pages. "I've battled heat, cold, too much humidity, not enough humidity, root rot, powdery mildew and aphids. Craig Tracy showed me how to hand-pollinate the plants and he's been invaluable, advising me at every step how to deal with the weather. I'm a novice when it comes to gardening."

"That's what makes your pumpkins so remarkable. You have at least one contender for a champion pumpkin. Are you aware of the competitive nature of giant pumpkin growers?"

"I've heard about that. I guess I still don't know about the sport of giant pumpkins."

"Well, your pumpkin is news. You might put Acorn Hill on the map."

Louise raised one eyebrow. "I doubt that."

"We'll see. Just remember, I said it first." Carlene put away her notebook and stood. "Thank you for the interview and picture. And thank Jane for the pumpkin bar. Remind her I'd like a recipe for the paper. I'll be sure to mention the inn."

Louise watched Carlene stride purposefully down the sidewalk. She operated and published the *Acorn Nutshell* by herself since the death of her father, serving as editor, reporter and photographer and every other position a weekly publication required. Louise had to admire her hard work and tenacity. Acorn Hill was fortunate to have her.

Louise enjoyed the celebrating of her gardening success, but she'd had enough picture-taking to last a year. She'd set out to prove a point to her sisters and the entire project had gotten out of hand. She hoped Carlene's article would be the end of it.

When Jane opened the front door, Louise was standing on the other side. She was carrying cups and the leftover pumpkin bars. Jane stepped aside to let her enter.

"How did your interview go?"

"I'm sure I bored Carlene with all the details of my

agricultural achievement. She's determined to do an article on the pumpkin, so I suppose she'll pull together something to make it interesting."

"She's good at that. I'm going downtown to see if I can drum up some support for the race. Do you need anything?" Jane said.

"Are you stopping by the General Store?"

"Yes. I'll make it my last stop so I can pick up some bananas."

"In that case, would you bring me a quart of buttermilk?"

"I'd be happy to."

"Thanks." Louise went down the hall.

Jane stopped at the Coffee Shop first. Hope Collins was ringing up a customer's tab. She finished and turned to Jane. "Hi. Have a seat, Jane. I'll be with you in a moment."

"I'm not here to eat this time, Hope. I'm looking for sponsors for the 10K Harvest Run for diabetes. I was wondering if you and June would be willing to help out?"

Hope's shoulders slumped. "I'd really like to, Jane, but I've already committed to supporting Betsy and several of the kids on the track team. They come in here a lot, you know. Besides, I'm walking it, so I'm sponsoring myself. I'm sorry." She turned to the kitchen. "Hey, June. Jane's here to talk to you."

Hope hurried off to wait on a customer. June Carter

poked her head out of the kitchen. "Hi, Jane. What can I do for you?"

Jane walked over to the kitchen entrance. "I'm looking for supporters for the Harvest 10K Run. Sounds like you're already committed though."

"I can pledge fifty cents per kilometer. I'm doing that for any customer who asks. So far, you're the sixth person."

"Thanks, June. I appreciate it. Louise and I will be down sometime this week for lunch."

"All right." She waved her spatula in the air and disappeared back into the kitchen.

Jane went next door to the antique shop. Joseph Holzmann was behind the counter.

"Good afternoon, Jane. Lovely weather, isn't it?"

"Beautiful. Have you heard about the Harvest 10K Run for diabetes here next month? I'm looking for sponsors."

"I'll need to confer with Rachel. She isn't here right now, but I'm sure we can give you something. We bought an ad for their brochure. The lady said we should have lots of out-of-town visitors for the race. We put in a coupon for ten percent off that day. We're always busy during the fall color season, but a little extra business doesn't hurt."

"Yes, it sounds like quite an event. I'll check back when Rachel's here. Thanks."

Jane stopped at the Good Apple Bakery, where Clarissa

promised her a five-dollar donation, and she left with two loaves of fresh focaccia bread that smelled divine. She stopped at Sylvia's Buttons, Nellie's dress shop and Time for Tea. Each of them pledged support, but Jane began to feel guilty asking them to give on top of the pledges they'd already made. She didn't want people supporting her just because they were friends, although it was a worthwhile cause and she wanted to support the effort.

By the time she got to the General Store, she realized that she might have to look outside Acorn Hill for pledges if she wanted to do a good job for the Diabetes Foundation. She bought bananas and Louise's buttermilk, and trudged home.

Chapter Seven

*C*oming off her run Wednesday afternoon, Jane stopped at the mailbox and leaned against it, breathing hard. Her shins hurt, but she shouldn't have stopped abruptly. She needed to wind down. Straightening, she looked at her watch as she started walking down Chapel Road toward town. Forty-five minutes. She'd gone four miles, but that included hills. Still, she needed to do better than that.

As she walked, her heartbeat returned to normal. She reached the corner of Hill Street, turned around and walked back to the mailbox. Leaning over, she touched the ground, then stood and stretched her legs back, first one, then the other.

She collected the mail and the weekly newspaper, and started up the walk to the house. The headlines and picture beneath it caught her attention. Louise looked small seated next to her pumpkin. Jane smiled. It was a nice picture, but she could detect a slightly irritated look on her sister's face. The average person would see a composed half-smile. But Jane knew better.

Jane saw that the parlor door was closed, an indication that Louise was conducting a lesson. She placed the newspaper on the kitchen table for her sister to see, knowing that Louise would make a cup of tea after her student left. Then Jane hurried upstairs to shower before she started dinner.

When she came downstairs, the parlor door was open and the piano was silent. She headed for the kitchen.

Louise was standing at the counter, waiting for her tea to steep, reading the paper. She looked up and frowned.

"Well, it's not too bad, but the picture would be better without me in it."

"I think it's a good picture of you, Louie. Besides, it gives perspective to the size of your pumpkin."

Louise put down the paper and picked up her tea. "I suppose people will come by now wanting to see it."

"I'm sure they will."

"Can I help with dinner?" Louise offered.

"I'm experimenting tonight. Sit down and drink your tea."

Louise took a seat. "What are you concocting?"

"Carlene wants a pumpkin recipe, so I thought I'd make a pumpkin sauce to serve over penne pasta. Is that all right with you?"

"Pumpkin sauce? I can't even begin to imagine how

that will taste, but I'm game." The telephone rang just as she took a sip of tea. "I'll get it," she said.

"Grace Chapel Inn, Louise speaking."

Jane couldn't hear the other end of the call, but Louise looked flustered.

"I suppose that would be all right. Tomorrow at three o'clock." Louise said good-bye and hung up.

"Who was that?"

"A reporter from the Potterston newspaper. He wants to come see the pumpkin and do an interview with me."

"So you'll get even more publicity."

"If it appears in the Potterston paper, more people will see it. I suppose that means visitors." Louise looked dazed, as if the implications were just beginning to sink in.

A knock at the back door interrupted them. The door opened and Ethel walked in, holding a copy of the paper. "Did you see this? You're famous, Louise."

"Yes, I saw it. Would you like a cup of tea, Auntie?"

"Certainly, thank you." Ethel sat down at the kitchen table. "Lloyd and I ate lunch at the Coffee Shop. Everyone stopped to ask me about your pumpkin, Louise. Of course, I was happy to tell them what I know, which is very little. I'd appreciate it if you'd keep me informed. Fortunately, I was there Sunday when Craig and Sam measured and weighed it."

"They didn't weigh it," Louise objected. "They estimated its weight. They could be off by quite a bit."

"True, and I stressed the fact that it may weigh much more than nine hundred fifty pounds. I hope you don't mind that I told everyone they can come by and see for themselves."

"I hope they'll have the courtesy to call first and make sure we're home."

"I wouldn't worry about that. One of you is always home. If you're not, I'll be happy to show them your pumpkin."

Louise raised her eyebrow. A knock at the back door turned her attention. *Probably a good thing*, Jane thought. Louise might have been tempted to reprimand their aunt. Ethel had a tendency to take matters into her own hands, which wasn't always convenient or welcome.

"Come in," Louise said, opening the door to Vera. "Would you like a cup of tea?"

Jane filled the teakettle as Vera entered the kitchen.

"Thanks. I'd love one. Do you have chamomile?"

"Yes. Busy day at school?" Jane asked.

"Very. It's always a little chaotic the first month. Things are settling down. Speaking of school . . ." she turned to Louise. "I . . . uh . . . promised our principal that I'd ask you if we could bring the kindergarten and first grade classes on a field trip here to see your pumpkin. I'd like to bring my class too, perhaps on a different day. We could work out dates later on."

Jane pictured a hoard of children running around in the garden, stepping on vegetables and bouncing on Louise's pumpkins. She almost laughed at the image. It would make a great illustration for the book Cynthia had talked about producing. Although her first thought was an emphatic "No," Jane quickly reconsidered. They could occupy the children with games on the back lawn, while they escorted small groups to see the pumpkins. She looked at Louise, to see her reaction.

"How many children are we talking about?" she asked.

"I'd guess about thirty children combined in the kindergarten and first grade classes. I have sixteen students this year. We wouldn't stay for long. I suggested making a stop here, then taking the children to Fairy Pond for a picnic."

Jane avoided Louise's gaze and nodded.

"Yes, that'll be all right."

"Oh, thank you. The kids will be delighted!"

The teakettle whistled. The back door opened, and Alice came in from working at the hospital. "Hello," she said. "What's the occasion? Are we having a party?"

"No, but we're having tea. Would you like to join us?" Jane asked.

"I'd love to, as soon as I change out of this uniform. I'll be right back," she said and went through to the hallway.

Jane carried the teapot and a plate of apple and cheese slices and homemade gingersnaps to the table. Louise set out cups and napkins.

"How's the race-training going?" Vera asked Jane.

"Not as well as it should. I doubt I'll be passing anyone. Hey, want to sponsor me?"

"Sure. I can give you a dollar per kilometer. I've pledged to support several of the teachers from school too. Most of them are planning to walk the course. Don't people usually train for months for a race?" Vera asked.

"Probably. More time would sure help me. I can't seem to pace myself for very long. I need someone riding a bicycle or driving along beside me, so I can run at a steady rate."

"Maybe you need a running partner, so you can encourage each other and set a steady pace. You could try running with the cross-country team from the high school."

"Those young people could run circles around me. No thanks. I'm not into training by humiliation."

"If you think the team would be too much of a challenge," Alice said as she entered the kitchen, "several of the young people from church are training for the race. I bet they'd be happy to have you join them."

"I don't know. I'll think about it," Jane said. She didn't

have to think very hard to know she didn't want a bunch of teenage athletes seeing how out of shape she was. Besides, she reminded herself, it wasn't about winning, at least not against the young runners. It was about performing at her personal best. She'd keep working out, jogging daily, training on hills. She'd be as ready as she possibly could be.

⤳

"Did you walk here?" Alice asked, as Vera got up to leave.

"Yes. Care to walk back with me?"

"I'd like to." Alice turned to Jane. "Do you need anything in town?"

"A loaf of fresh French bread would be good with dinner if you would drop by the bakery," Jane said.

"While you're there, you could pick up some cinnamon bread for breakfast," Louise suggested.

"Happy to."

"Pick up a loaf of sprouted wheat bread for me, please," Ethel chimed in. "Maybe a couple of Clarissa's bagels too. The ones with sesame seeds."

Alice got her wallet while Vera said her good-byes. They went out the front door and down the steps.

"How's your aunt doing?" Alice asked when they reached the sidewalk.

"Not so well. My cousin Reggie says she's failing fast."

"That's too bad. It happens, though. For some reason, the trauma of a broken hip can mark a turning point for the elderly. She's getting physical therapy. Is that helping?"

"She suffered a setback with the pneumonia. She's on antibiotics and oxygen, and they're giving her breathing treatments."

"That usually takes care of it, but she might be weak for a while."

"Reggie's hoping that'll help convince her to move into an assisted living facility."

"And you're not?" Alice asked.

Vera shook her head. "I'm having a hard time believing it's necessary. Aunt Agatha's always been so independent, I hate to see this happening to her. I can't imagine she's gone downhill so fast. I just saw her over Easter break."

"That's almost five months ago. A lot can happen in that amount of time to someone who's elderly. On the other hand, I've seen some remarkable recoveries. She might bounce back and be fine."

Vera stopped walking and turned to Alice. "That's why I'm glad you're going with me."

"I hope I can be of some help. What kind of clothes should I take along?"

"Mostly casual, but we'll go to church, and my aunt's church is very traditional, so something churchy as well."

"Do I need to take a skirt?"

"Oh no. I think one of your pantsuits will be fine. We might go out to dinner at the club too, but one nice outfit should be enough. I don't plan on doing a lot of socializing while we're there."

They arrived at Vera's house and said good-bye. Vera went inside and Alice walked on. She got to wondering what kind of club Vera was referring to, but it was too late to ask. She'd pack her two Sunday pantsuits. Both were knit. One was black, the other blue. They were conservative but flattering.

"I'd like to make a reservation for Friday night," the woman on the telephone said.

"I'm terribly sorry. We're full all weekend," Alice said, looking at the reservation book. "I have rooms available during the week."

"What about tomorrow night?"

"Thursday? For one night? I do have a room, but only for the one night," she repeated, wanting to be clear.

"What time is check out?"

"We ask our guests to check out by noon," she said. She started to mention their policy of sometimes allowing late checkouts, but stopped herself. The room had to be ready for Friday night and that meant one of them would have to clean it. Since she was working until midafternoon, she didn't want to burden her sisters. "Did you want me to reserve a room for you for the one night?" she asked.

She heard a sigh. "Yes. We'll have to drive down after work, so it will be late."

"How late?" she asked.

"We're coming from the Wilkes-Barre area. I estimate we'll arrive around eight o'clock."

"That's fine. We'll have the room ready. Could I have your name, address and telephone number please?"

Alice took the information and filled in the reservation form. Jane came out of the kitchen as she hung up. "We have guests coming tomorrow night," Alice said.

"Just for one night?"

"Yes. It sounds like they're making a special trip. They'll be arriving late."

"Interesting. I took another reservation for tomorrow night."

"That's odd. The fall colors won't be full for a while yet."

"Well, whatever the case, it's nice to have the business. Shall I make pumpkin waffles with maple pecan topping for breakfast Friday?"

"Sounds wonderful. I'm sure they'd love them." Alice

picked up the book she'd checked out of the library and started up the stairs. She looked back at Jane. "I'm glad I'm going out of town with Vera next week."

"Why's that?" Jane asked.

"I think I'd start to hate pumpkin if I weren't."

Jane's laughter followed Alice up the stairs.

Chapter Eight

I'm sorry we're so late," Reba Gladstone told Alice as they stood in the entry hall, registering. She was a petite woman with white hair arranged in a neat bun on top of her head. Freckles liberally sprinkled her upturned nose, and her eyes seemed to smile up at Alice. "We tried to leave earlier, but Harry couldn't get away."

Harry, her husband, was of average height, but towered over his wife. Alice took the key to their room off a hook. "It's no problem. Our other guests for tonight haven't arrived yet, so you're not the last ones. If you'd like to follow me, I'll show you to the Garden Room."

Alice led the way up the stairs. She opened the door for them and stood aside so they could enter. A bedside lamp gave the room a welcoming glow.

"What a lovely room," Reba declared, turning around in a circle, taking in the soft shades of green and the floral border along the wainscoting and the ceiling. "I'm an avid gardener, so this couldn't be more perfect. We must come back when we can stay more than one night, Harry."

"Yes, dear," he said, carrying their suitcases to the end of the bed and setting them down. He gave his wife an indulgent smile.

Alice loved this room. They had decorated the room that had belonged to their parents in honor of their mother, who'd loved gardening. The rich rosewood bedroom suite added elegance to the space. It always gave Alice special satisfaction when they picked the perfect room for their guests.

"Breakfast is served from seven to nine, so come down whenever you're ready. I hope that you'll be quite comfortable here."

"Thank you. I think we'll turn in early. We keep farmers' hours," Reba explained.

"Good night then. If you need anything, let me know."

Alice went downstairs in time to see Jane registering another couple. They looked about the same ages as the Gladstones. The man was stocky and also of average height. His gray-streaked brown hair curled around the edges of his ball cap. He removed the hat and ran his hand over his smooth, shiny scalp.

"I hope you don't have railroad tracks running right through the backyard," he said. "Can't stand the noise of the city."

Alice couldn't help wondering where this couple lived, if he considered the tiny metropolis of Acorn Hill a city.

"We don't have trains running anywhere near the inn," Jane said. "I've given you the Sunset Room, which has a private bathroom, but I can put you in the back of the house if you'd prefer. It might be quieter."

"The Sunset Room will be fine," the wife said. She gave her husband a challenging look. He didn't respond.

"Let me show you to your room then," Jane said. She turned to lead the way, but the woman marched to the stairs in front of her. Alice stepped out of the way. Jane rolled her eyes at Alice as she passed. The man followed, dragging a large suitcase.

The woman marched like an army sergeant, hands fisted and swinging purposefully at her sides as she climbed the stairs. At the top, she stood aside, waiting for Jane to take the lead. Then she fell into step after Jane, but in front of her husband.

Alice went to the kitchen, shaking her head. What a difference from the sweet couple she had just registered. She brewed a cup of tea and was removing the tea bag when Jane came into the kitchen.

"Whew. Delmer Wesley is not a happy camper. Makes you wonder why they would travel all this distance for one night." Jane shook her head.

Alice had wondered the same thing about both of their

guest couples. Both had wanted to come for the weekend, but settled for this one night.

"I don't know. Whatever the case, they'll only be here until noon tomorrow."

"I'm going up to my room. Can I help you before I retire for the night?" Alice asked.

"No, you go ahead. I'm going to try a batch of pumpkin popovers before I go to bed. Sleep well," Jane said.

"Thanks, I will." Alice took her cup of tea and headed for the stairs. She opened the door of the parlor, where Louise was working on an arrangement for a duet for her piano students.

"Goodnight," Alice called out. Louise looked up over the top of her reading glasses.

"Is it that late already?" Louise looked at her watch.

"Nine thirty and I have to work tomorrow. I'll see you at breakfast."

Alice could hear voices on the second floor as she reached the landing. There was usually something satisfying about the sounds of guests occupying their home, but not this time.

"I will not be a party to your shenanigans," a harsh voice said, coming from the direction of the Sunset Room. The voice was shrill, causing the words to carry. It was the wife. Alice was not inclined toward eavesdropping on the argument, but she couldn't help hearing. She hurried across the landing and up the stairs to the third floor.

Whatever did she mean, his shenanigans? What was the man planning to do? And where? Probably nothing important, Alice decided. Maybe the man was a practical joker.

Jane rolled out of bed and shut off her alarm clock on the third ring. She flipped on her bedside lamp to the lowest setting and squinted against the glare. Rubbing the sleep out of her eyes, she slowly opened them and let them adjust to the light.

Four thirty. She hoped her alarm hadn't awakened her sisters. The three of them occupied the only rooms on the third floor, leaving the second floor for their guests. Louise and Alice rose early, but not two hours before dawn. Jane dressed in canary yellow sweatpants, a white T-shirt and a soft yellow sweatshirt. She wasn't likely to encounter vehicles at this hour of the morning, but if she did, they'd be sure to see her.

Jane tiptoed to the back stairs, carrying her running shoes, and descended to the kitchen as noiselessly as possible. She had to suppress a giggle. If anyone saw her, they'd think she was a thief sneaking around. But the guests wouldn't use the back stairway, which was marked *For Emergencies Only*.

I must be crazy, she thought, looking out the kitchen window as she put on her shoes. *It's pitch-black outside.* Only a sliver of moon was visible. There'd be little illumination while she ran.

Grabbing a small flashlight, Jane went out the back door. Skirting the driveway, walking on the grass close to the house so she wouldn't make any noise, Jane reached the street. The cold penetrated her cotton pants. At least the grass didn't have the telltale white sheen of frost yet, but weather could change quickly this time of year, so Jane kept an eye on the forecast for the first dip below freezing so she could cover her plants. She didn't want to lose anything in her garden. Her breath puffed little clouds in front of her as she headed down Chapel Road to town, where streetlamps would light her way.

She'd forgotten her Mp3 player, so her only music was the sound of her feet hitting the sidewalk, pounding a beat as she ran. Fred's Hardware was dark inside except for a dim light over the front window display of rakes and leaf blowers. The light was just enough for Jane to see her reflection whizzing by in the front window.

The pharmacy and the General Store were dark and deserted. The streets were empty of cars. She'd never before ventured downtown at such an early hour. She shivered at the lonely, unnatural feeling.

A bright overhead light illuminated the front of the fire department, raising her spirits, although the building looked deserted too.

As she ran past the Cat Rescue Center, she triggered an alarm of meowing and caterwauling that set off a dog somewhere nearby. She smiled, glad for the sound of company on her solitary run.

She circled around to Village Road and ran past the lovely old stone Presbyterian Church with its backlit stained glass windows sending soft colors into the dark night. Its modern sign was lit inviting all to enter and find fellowship and rest for their souls. Jane felt suddenly warmed and comforted.

As she ran up the hill, leaving the streetlights behind, she flicked on her flashlight and shined it out in front of her. It bobbed as she jogged. She grunted out a laugh. What a sight she must be.

Past the houses, the world seemed suddenly vast and empty. Dry corn stalks rustled in the slight breeze on her left. She startled some animal and it scurried away. She shined her flashlight in the direction of the sound, but the creature had moved out of sight.

Jane alternated walking and jogging past farmland and forest until she finally circled back and came down the hill on Chapel Road toward the house. Still an hour before sunrise, the sky had lightened to the color of brushed steel as she walked the last quarter mile, letting her breathing slow and her muscles relax. She'd turned off the flashlight and was enjoying the muted landscape as she neared the driveway.

A movement on the far side of the house caught her attention. A deer, perhaps, headed for the garden. So far, the fence had kept critters out. She hurried her steps, intent on scaring the animal away, when she realized the early morning visitor moved on two legs.

Not wanting to disturb a guest, Jane slowed her pace and hung back. Having early risers for guests happened frequently. Jane usually started her day by 6:00 AM and had the coffeepot going soon after. She'd hoped for time to shower before she started breakfast, so she'd decided to start the coffee before she went up to change.

The early morning guest wasn't wandering leisurely along the path to the garden. He or she was skulking, slightly hunched over, moving slowly, as if sneaking through the yard. Perhaps it wasn't a guest. But who else would be moving through their yard at such an odd hour?

At the garden gate, the figure turned and looked to the left, then to the right, then lifted the latch and pushed open the gate.

Jane couldn't imagine what the intruder could be after. A carrot? A fresh tomato picked and eaten right off the vine? If the guest would come to the kitchen, Jane would be happy to give him whatever he desired and it would be washed. There was a bench in the garden. Maybe the man just wanted to sit in the garden and pray.

Jane moved along the grass, so she wouldn't disturb anyone. Before she reached the back porch, another figure stepped out from the side of the house and moved toward the garden.

At first she thought it might be the man's wife, but the form plodded along, a man with heavy steps, making no attempt to keep his presence a secret. Curious, Jane kept close to the house so she wouldn't be detected. When she reached the back door, she heard a deep cough.

"Who's there?" the man in the garden called out in a hushed but audible voice.

"What are *you* doing here?" the other man asked. He kept his tone low. Nevertheless, Jane had no trouble making out his words. By his inflection, she got the impression that he knew the other man.

"I might ask you the same thing."

"I'm here for the same reason you are, but I'm not the one sneaking out here like I was up to no good. Couldn't wait until daylight, could you?"

"You're here, aren't you? I guess your motives aren't so pure."

Jane listened to the men banter back and forth, accusing each other of something nefarious, though she couldn't imagine what.

"I just want to get a look."

"What can you see in the dark?"

A light suddenly shot across the yard, aimed at the man still standing outside the garden gate, just missing Jane where she hid against a tall bush. She instinctively pressed back, moving closer to the bush. A thorn pricked her arm. Too late, she realized she was cuddling up to a pyracantha bush full of berries and thorns. She didn't dare move.

"I can see plenty. You might as well come over and see for yourself as long as you're here."

The garden gate creaked open. Jane peered out from behind the bush. The man made his way across the garden to the other man. Jane could just make out their silhouettes as they stood in front of the umbrella. Hunched over, so she couldn't see any difference between them, they faced the pumpkin patch.

Jane's jaw dropped. She closed her mouth as understanding dawned. *The pumpkins. The couples who'd made special trips to the inn are here to see Louise's pumpkins. But why in the middle of the night? Why couldn't they wait until morning, when Louise would be proud to show off her giant pumpkin? Because they are up to no good. That's why.*

She stood there wondering what to do. Should she make a racket and scare them away and wake up the neighborhood in the process?

"Yup. It's a beauty for sure. Now you've seen it, I suggest you go back inside and wait for the lady to show us her prize."

"I'm not leaving until you do."

"We'll go together."

"Yeah, all right." The man's tone sounded begrudging, but the light shined out toward the gate again. Jane hoped they would go around the side of the house to the sunroom door. Since they'd come from that direction, she assumed that was how they'd left the house.

The flashlight beam danced around the backyard, sweeping across the grass as the men came out and the garden gate swung closed. Jane held her breath, not daring to move. She didn't want to be caught observing, even though it was her house.

The footsteps moved away. She waited. Finally she heard the sunroom door shut. Exhaling, she stepped away from the prickly bush and crept back to the kitchen door, feeling like an intruder herself. Before she entered the house, she looked back toward the garden. It was safe. The conversation she'd overheard sounded like one between adversaries. The men would watch each other, so she probably didn't need to worry.

She didn't know why she felt concerned about the two guests. Visiting the garden wasn't a crime, but people didn't travel halfway across the state to look at a pumpkin unless it had some value. Jane suddenly had the urge to post a guard at the garden gate.

She hurried up the back stairs to her room. There was no time to relax in the shower, letting the hot spray work the strain out of her sore muscles. Instead, she took a quick shower and slicked her hair back into a ponytail. She had work to do and a giant pumpkin to protect.

Chapter Nine

I hope you like these," Jane said. She placed a steaming hot Belgian pumpkin waffle, topped with pecan-fried apples and whipped cream drizzled with maple syrup, in front of each of the men.

Harry Gladstone said, "Thank you."

Delmer Wesley, the one she'd registered, gave her a sharp glance, then quickly looked down. "Not my favorite. You got something else?" he muttered.

"We have ham and egg frittata, cheese biscuits, bacon and sausage and fresh fruit."

"I'll have that," Delmer said.

"This looks delicious," Harry said. Delmer glared at him. He glared back.

"It all looks wonderful," Reba Gladstone said, injecting a cheerful tone into the icy looks between the men. "I'd love a pumpkin waffle, please. And it's nice to see you again, Genevieve," she added, smiling at the other wife.

"You too," Genevieve said, giving Reba an apologetic look.

So they do know each other, Jane thought as she returned to the kitchen and took the frittata out of the oven. She wouldn't tell him it was made with pumpkin. Perhaps he wouldn't notice. At least the women were cordial. She'd guessed the men were competitors. She'd been puzzling over the garden confrontation while she prepared breakfast, and she'd concluded that the men were giant-pumpkin growers. That was the only thing that made sense. They'd come to check out the competition. Louise would be floored to learn *she* was considered the competition. Jane couldn't wait to tell her.

$\backsim$

"I have to confess, we came here because we saw the article in your newspaper about your pumpkin, Mrs. Smith."

Louise finished refilling Reba Gladstone's coffee cup and set down the cup before she responded. The woman's statement stunned her.

"How did you get a copy of our newspaper?"

"It's on the Internet," Genevieve Wesley responded.

"You read about my pumpkin too? Why? You drove all this way because of my pumpkin?"

"Yes, we did. Would you mind showing it to us?" Harry asked.

Louise couldn't miss the challenging look he shot Delmer Wesley. "I'd be happy to show it to you," she said.

"Can we go now?" Genevieve asked.

"I need to help my sister in the kitchen." Louise looked at her watch. "It's eight-thirty now. I'll show you the garden at nine o'clock, if that's all right."

"Certainly. Take your time," Reba said. "Meanwhile, I'll enjoy my coffee. It's so rich. I'd love to know the brand."

"You can talk to Jane. She's in charge of all the food. The tea is available at a local shop, Time for Tea. It also carries our Madeleine and Daughters truffles, which are made from our mother's recipe."

"Are they the ones in our room?" Genevieve asked. "They're to die for. I ate all of ours." She blushed.

Louise smiled. "They are. Would you like more coffee?"

Genevieve said that she would.

Louise offered coffee to the men, but they declined, so she returned to the kitchen where Jane was washing a pot. "I could do that for you," she offered.

"I've got it." Jane turned and looked at her. "What's wrong?"

"Nothing. Why?"

"You're frowning."

"It's our guests. Do you know why they came here?"

"I have a pretty good idea. Are they finished?"

"Yes, I think so."

"Good. Take your coffee and sit down. We have time to chat." Jane poured a cup for herself and carried it to the table.

"Where's Alice?" Louise asked.

"She already left for work. She'll be getting off early, so she'll have plenty of time to pack. Vera wants to leave first thing in the morning. I'm going to help her after our guests leave."

Louise stirred her coffee, then set the spoon on a napkin and looked at Jane. "They read about my pumpkins. Evidently, Carlene puts the *Acorn Nutshell* on the Internet."

"She told me she wanted to post it online. I didn't know she'd already started. They must have done a search for giant pumpkins." Jane shook her head. "Louise, they've already been out to the garden. The men, at least. I saw them sneak out there in the dark when I came back from my run. They were talking and I overheard them."

"That's really odd." She leaned forward, hardly believing her pumpkin patch was causing such a stir. "What did they say?"

"They were arguing, sort of. I gathered neither one knew the other was staying at the inn. They both came in late last night, so they might not have seen each other. Kind of funny, when you think about it."

"Indeed. So what were they arguing about?"

"Your pumpkin. One of them was suspicious of the other's motives, but I couldn't tell which was which. One talked the other one into going back inside. Honestly, Louise, I think one meant to harm your pumpkin."

"No. Why would he want to do that?"

Jane crossed her arms. "Competition."

"From me? But I'm not planning to do anything with it. I missed the county fair. Besides, I'm just an amateur gardener. Very amateur."

"Most gardeners are amateurs. They must think you plan to enter it in some weigh-off, like the one Craig told you about in Baskenburg."

"Well, I'll just tell them I'm not going to enter my pumpkin in any competition. Then they'll go away and that'll be the end of it."

"I think you should reconsider. They read the article and they immediately came to Acorn Hill. You must be a contender. And it hasn't done growing yet."

"How would I get that huge hulk to Baskenburg? No, that's just silly. I can't go running off to the other end of the state. I have better things to do with my time," Louise said.

Jane leaned back and crossed her legs. "Suit yourself. I'm just saying, don't make any rash statements. Let them sweat for a while."

Louise raised her eyebrows. "I don't know what to say."

"That's the point." Jane stood and took their cups to the sink. "Don't say anything. Let them come to their own conclusions. I'd really like to know why it's so important to them. Other than for winning a weight contest."

"But the winning pumpkin last year was over fifteen hundred pounds. Mine won't get nearly that heavy."

"That was last year. It doesn't mean anyone will grow such a large one this year. Just leave your options open. You never know what's going to happen."

"All right." Louise stood. "I'd better escort our guests to the garden. Would you come with me?"

Jane removed her apron. "You bet. I wouldn't miss it for the world."

At nine o'clock, Louise and Jane met the Gladstones and the Wesleys in the parlor. All four of the guests had chosen to dress for the garden in long-sleeved shirts and jeans. They'd come prepared, which didn't surprise Jane at all. It just confirmed their reason for being at Grace Chapel Inn.

Jane led the way out through the sunroom to the garden. She knew the men had already taken that route earlier, but she didn't say anything to them. Louise was right behind her and the guests were in the rear.

"Lovely garden. You're a talented gardener," Reba said to Louise.

"The gardens are Jane's domain," Louise said. "I've only grown the pumpkins."

"Then a gift for growing things must run in your family," Harry said.

Jane was about to thank him for the compliment, but she caught herself just in time. She did not want to become friendly with garden vandals, assuming that her suspicions were correct. She wondered if the wives knew about their husbands' early morning escapade.

She opened the gate and stood aside for them to follow Louise inside. She watched the men's feet as they stepped across her paths. They were careful to avoid disturbing any plant life. So far, so good. Jane shut the gate and stepped over to where the four people surrounded the giant pumpkin beneath the umbrella.

The men feigned surprise at seeing it.

"That's a beauty, all right," Harry said.

Reba nodded, but didn't say anything. Genevieve pursed her lips and looked at her husband.

"Not bad," Delmer said.

"What do you mean, not bad," Harry said. "I'd wager it weighs more than yours."

Delmer shot Harry a look toxic enough to wilt the

cabbage growing two rows over. "You don't know what you're talking about."

Harry shrugged.

"Are you both growing giant pumpkins?" Louise asked.

"Sure are," Harry said. "I don't have a contender this year. I might have a winning squash, though." He grinned and tilted his head toward Delmer. "We've been competing against each other for years. Neither one of us has come up with the champion yet. Maybe this year, Delmer?"

"You'll just have to wait and see," Delmer said.

"Mind if we measure this beauty?" Harry asked Louise.

"I don't know. Really, I haven't thought about entering it in any contest, but I don't want anything to happen to it."

"Harry won't let anything harm your pumpkin," Reba assured Louise.

"Our local nurseryman measured it Sunday. He estimated it at 953 pounds," Jane said.

"That's almost a week ago. It should be quite a bit heavier now. Did he use the three-way method?" Harry asked.

"I don't know what that is, but he measured it around its middle," Jane said.

"That's the circumference method. It's not the most accurate way to estimate weight. I use the over-the-top method, which requires three measurements." He took out a large tape measure. "May I?"

Jane stared at Louise, who gave her a questioning look. Jane didn't know what to say. She wanted to protect her sister's patch, but it was up to Louise to decide. She shrugged.

Louise sighed. "All right," she said. "Please be careful."

Harry turned to his wife. "Honey, will you help me?"

"Of course." Reba stepped over a runner and moved to the other side of the pumpkin. She ran her hand over its smooth skin. "Amazing, aren't they?"

Harry handed her the end of the tape measure, and she held it against the pumpkin. He carefully took measurements, then removed a small pad from his pocket, wrote a number on it and put it back.

"Let's get the stem-to-blossom end measurement," he said, stretching the tape across the pumpkin once again. Reba held one end to the ground next to the stem. He lowered it to the ground by the end where the flower had broken off. "Got it." He recorded that number on his pad.

"One more." He stood to move and nearly lost his balance. With a leap, he jumped away.

Louise gasped. Jane held her breath.

He landed well off to the side, out of harm's way. "Whew! That was close," he said.

"You could have been hurt," Louise said.

"But I'm not. Fine as a fiddle," he said, waving his arms to show he was in one piece.

"Maybe you should forget about measuring the pumpkin," Louise said.

"If you don't want me to finish, I understand. I could have damaged it with my clumsiness," Harry said.

"I'm not concerned about that pumpkin," Louise said. "I'm concerned about you. I don't want anyone getting hurt trying to preserve my plant. It's not worth it."

"I promise I'll be careful—of your plant and my clumsy body too," he said.

"All right." Louise allowed him to go back.

They took a measurement of the circumference, just as Craig had done on Sunday. Harry wrote the number on his pad, then did some calculations. He looked up and smiled at Louise.

"Three hundred sixty-seven inches total." He gave Delmer a triumphant smile, as if it were his own pumpkin. "That makes it about 988 pounds, give or take a few. Pretty good, I'd say."

"Harry, there's a split on the main vine," Reba said.

He immediately redirected his attention. "Where." He moved carefully to the other side of the vine and hunkered down. He examined the vine, then looked up at Louise.

"It's a hairline split. That's not uncommon. It could be a cross split, which would be worse. This could affect the pumpkin's growth, though, if it doesn't heal. I don't see any squash vine borers, so that's good. We'll just cover this split with soil and it should be all right," he said, carefully mounding the dirt over the stem. "Keep it covered," he instructed, standing.

Delmer stood off to the side, arms crossed, watching the proceedings. He didn't say anything, but Jane thought that he looked highly agitated. He was not a happy man. She believed he had been the man inside the garden with the flashlight in the morning darkness. Harry had been the one to stop him from doing any harm.

Genevieve watched her husband warily. Poor woman. She took several pictures of the pumpkin. When they moved away from the patch, she was the first one out of the gate. Harry hung back, talking to Louise, waiting, Jane suspected, for his rival to leave. Delmer finally shuffled off after his wife.

"I think you should consider entering this in the weigh-off at Baskenburg," Harry told Louise. "You have a very good chance if this keeps growing at a decent rate. What are you feeding it?"

Louise glanced over and caught Jane's eye. She smiled. "Oh, just a little something I thought up. An experiment, you might say."

Harry laughed. "I'm impressed. I'd sure like to see if your secret formula produces a winner."

"I'm not planning on moving this behemoth out of our garden," Louise said.

"You'll have to move it eventually," Jane said. "Otherwise, it's going to stink to high heaven."

"I hadn't thought of that," Louise said. "I just wanted to see if I could make it grow."

"I'd say you've been more than successful," Harry said. He opened the gate and let the ladies walk through. "Much more than successful."

Chapter Ten

I hope I'm taking the right clothes," Alice said, carrying her suitcase down the stairs Saturday morning. "Vera told me to take casual outfits."

"What you packed should be fine. Take along your light jacket for evening, when it cools off," Jane said behind her.

Vera stood at the foot of the stairs. "Do you need some help?"

"We have everything," Alice said.

Alice set down her suitcase in the entry hall. "I'll take my bag, just in case." She retrieved her black nurse's bag from the hall closet. "I never know when I'll need this."

"I hope you won't need it at all, but it's good insurance," Vera said, taking it from Alice.

Jane and Louise followed them to Vera's car, and stood waving as they drove off. Alice adjusted the seat belt and settled back for the long ride. "I haven't been on a trip for ages."

"Neither have I. With both of us working, Fred and I don't get a chance to get away very often."

"Oh dear. Maybe he'd have liked to go with you on this trip," Alice said.

Vera glanced over at her. "Are you kidding? He said he'd rather go to the dentist than spend a week trying to talk Aunt Agatha into moving to an assisted living center. He's very grateful you agreed to come with me."

"That's good. I mean, I wouldn't want to take his place if he wanted to go. Of course, it's not a vacation. I know this will be difficult for you and your aunt. I hope I can be of some help."

"Just knowing you're with me will help, believe me. I'll need an ally." Vera turned onto the state highway and headed southeast toward Delaware.

"I remember how I enjoyed meeting your aunt when she spent Christmas with you and Fred years ago. She reminded me of an older Aunt Ethel, very spunky and capable."

"That's Aunt Agatha. Or at least it was. She must be at least ten years older than Ethel. How old is Ethel, anyway?"

"I don't know. She won't tell anyone. Probably around seventy-five."

Vera chuckled. "They're a lot alike. Aunt Agatha won't tell either. I'd guess she's at least eighty-seven. She was still driving until this accident."

"If they're recommending an assisted living facility, her driving may come to an end," Alice said.

"I dread her reaction to that the most. She loves her old black Lincoln town car. It's as big as a boat and she barely sees over the top of the steering wheel, but she loves it."

"Sounds like Louise and her old white Cadillac." Alice chuckled. "I can just picture Louise in twenty years, still driving her old Caddy. But at least she's tall, so the steering wheel won't present a problem."

Alice was disappointed when the drive only took an hour. She loved the seasonal changes, but she'd been too busy back at home to get out and enjoy the subtle signs of autumn's approach. She soaked in the scenery of wild asters and goldenrod blooming in purple and golden profusion along the roadside. Dogwoods and shrubs showed patches of reds, and poplar and ash trees displayed early touches of yellow. Hints of red foliage shimmered from the red maples and black gum trees in the brilliant sunshine and light breeze. They passed rolling farmland with picturesque old barns, grazing cattle, horses and sheep behind weathered split-rail fences. Rows of graceful old maple trees overhung the country road, creating a dappled, multicolored canopy as the sunshine poked through their branches.

Descending from the farmland, the road wound down into the Delaware River Valley. From the hill, the river shimmered like a silver ribbon weaving through the landscape. Large, old stone and brick homes with long expanses of green lawns overlooked the river.

"That's Shelton Cove right below us," Vera said.

"It's lovely. It must have been hard to leave."

Vera smiled. "Not when I was young and in love. I couldn't wait to settle in my own home with Fred, no matter where we lived. Fortunately, he'd already chosen Acorn Hill. It has a similar small-town atmosphere, although Shelton Cove is a river town, so boating and fishing are mainstays here."

The road took them through the middle of town. Bright flower baskets hung from every streetlamp, and barrels of yellow, white and orange mums sat along the sidewalks next to the curbs.

They came to a stoplight. Ahead, the road crossed a steel bridge over the river to the New Jersey side. Vera turned left onto the main street.

"Goodness, it's busy. Are these all townspeople or tourists?"

"These are mainly tourists. Most of the locals stay home on Saturdays, except for the merchants, of course."

Alice looked around as Vera navigated the crowded street. The buildings were all stone or brick, with brightly painted shutters beside the windows. They looked very old, Alice thought. She remembered from her history classes that whalers had settled the area in the late 1600s. She doubted that any of the buildings dated back that far, but some looked like the historic buildings she'd seen in Boston and Philadelphia.

The road curved inland around a cove, with stores on one side of the street and a river walk along the other. She spotted an ice cream parlor with a large painted wooden ice cream cone hanging out front, and decided she must remember its location and treat Vera, if they had time, after a visit with her aunt.

"We'll have time to tour the town during the week, when the tourists have gone home. We'll need to get some exercise after sitting with Aunt Agatha most of the day."

"Good. I'd love to explore."

"We'll have to make up our beds at Aunt Agatha's house, I imagine. Reggie wouldn't think about it, and I doubt Aunt Agatha keeps rooms ready for company."

"That will keep us from getting lazy," Alice said.

A mile out of town, as they rounded the far side of the cove, the road climbed to run along a ridge. Large homes overlooked the cove. Alice saw signs for a yacht club and a boatworks. Through the trees she caught a glimpse of a busy marina filled with sailboats and motor yachts. Just past the marina, Vera turned down a driveway. They passed a hedge of bayberry bushes laden with clusters of silver berries, and the landscape opened up. A stately brick mansion dominated the gently sloping hill.

A wide, manicured lawn swept down from the house to the river. A copse of evergreen trees sheltered each side of the large property, but the view of the cove and river was unobstructed. A small, flat structure, surrounded by railing, perched on top of the three-story home. It reminded Alice of a gazebo or an oversized cupola. She'd seen homes with similar features, called widow's walks, when she'd visited Cape Cod.

"Here we are." Vera parked on the side of the house under a columned, covered *porte cochere*. Alice could imagine horse-drawn carriages pulling up to the entrance and uniformed servants helping ladies in hoop skirts to alight from the carriages. A porch light was on in the middle of the day. The house was perhaps twice the size of Grace Chapel Inn.

As they got out, Alice said, "You didn't tell me your aunt lives in a mansion."

Vera looked up at the massive structure that rose three stories. "It's quite a monstrosity, isn't it?"

"Hardly that. It's beautiful."

"If you like austere and imposing," Vera said, opening the trunk and lifting out their suitcases. "There should be a key under the doormat."

Alice walked over and lifted the mat. Sure enough, a large key lay beneath the mat. She picked it up and tried it in the solid oak door. It opened with a click.

"We're in." Alice opened the door, then picked up her suitcase and bag and let Vera precede her.

They stepped into a large entry hall that curved around to another entrance at the front, facing the cove with massive double doors. The dining room was on the left. Across from them, a set of glass French doors led to a parlor, furnished in pale green and white, with a formal upholstered sofa and Queen Anne style chairs clustered around an ornate marble and carved-wood fireplace. An elegant curved stairway rose from the center of the entry hall. The banisters and steps were polished mahogany. Alice envisioned regal ladies in long, full gowns sweeping down the stairway.

"There's a music room and a study and library around past the stairs," Vera said. "I'll give you a tour of the main floor later. Right now, let's go find our bedrooms." She started up the stairway.

Following her, Alice looked around. "Are all the bedrooms upstairs?"

"Yes. I suppose the study could be made into a bedroom. They converted the coatroom into a bathroom when I was a child, but it doesn't have a tub or shower. Aunt Agatha insisted on being modern. She loves to remodel, so the house should be in good shape."

"Is there another way to get to the bedrooms?"

"There's a servants' stairway at the back of the house. Aunt Agatha employed a live-in housekeeper and a cook for years, and Reggie and I used to sneak up and down it when we were children. We could get to the attic and the basement without anyone seeing us. I doubt it's been used in years."

"There's no elevator, though, so your aunt couldn't get to her bedroom?"

"I'm afraid not. If she came back, we'd have to close off the upstairs."

"This banister looks like it's been polished recently. Does your aunt have a staff to maintain the house?"

"Not full time. I'm sure she uses a cleaning service. One person couldn't keep it up." Vera reached the second-floor landing. They stepped out onto an open sitting area that surrounded the stairs. There were rooms on all sides. The stairway continued up to the third floor. Vera set her suitcase on the plush champagne-colored carpet. "Leave your bags here while we explore," she said.

She looked inside the first room. "Everything in here's under covers. Let's check the others." She closed the door and went to the next room, toward the front of the house. Its furnishings also were covered in sheeting.

"Here's Aunt Agatha's room," she said, cautiously opening another door, as if she expected her aunt to catch her going into a forbidden area. She peered inside, then stepped into the room and stood aside for Alice.

"I've only been in this room a few times in my life," Vera said, flipping on the light switch.

The room blazed to life. Alice blinked twice. Even with

the curtains drawn, the room seemed on fire in bright, vivid red, coral and yellow.

"Amazing, isn't it?" Vera said in an awed voice. "Last time I was here, everything was green and electric blue. I know to expect something wild, but it still surprises me."

The corner room had tall windows on two sides. The sun backlit the satin drapes, making the shades of yellow, orange and red glow. In contrast, the subdued shade of coral carpet matched the walls, making the drapes and bed all the more dramatic. A white marble fireplace took up one corner, with a low red-velvet chair and matching daybed nearby. A crystal chandelier hung from the high center of the room, surrounded by cherubs liberally decorated with gold. The polished red wood of the ornate dressers and bedstead shone from the glow of the lights overhead.

"Has she always used such vibrant colors?"

"As long as I can remember. My Uncle George said her colors were so loud he had trouble sleeping. Aunt Agatha's personality matches her bedroom. Flamboyant and bright."

"I see." Alice wondered how Vera would convince her aunt to give up her house and wild decorating for a small, bland apartment in an assisted living center. It promised to be a daunting task.

"Let's pick our rooms." Vera waited for Alice to step into the hall, then shut off the light and closed the door. She went to the next room and the next. All the rooms were closed up and cold, even though the day outside was warm. They checked six bedrooms in all. Only Agatha's room was made up.

Vera opened a door to a walk-in linen closet. She took out sheets and towels for both of them, and carried them to the front room next to Agatha's room. "You take this room, and I'll take the one next door. They have views of the cove and the town. It's beautiful at night with the lights reflecting on the water."

Alice pulled back the draperies. A small, private balcony extended from each room. She opened the glass-paneled door and let the light and warmth of the sun into the room. The house faced south, with a view of the town directly across the cove. Off to the right, where the lawn met the water, she could see beautiful boats docked at the marina. A cluster of tall pines hid the boatyard and most of the buildings, but she could hear hammering and some kind of power tool. How disappointing it must have been to live in such a beautiful home, then have a boat repair business move in close by.

Vera had begun removing sheets from the furniture. Alice helped her. Within minutes, they had uncovered a lovely dark walnut bedroom set and a green and peach, damask upholstered daybed. Alice liked the quiet, calming colors after seeing Agatha's room.

Together they made up the bed. Vera found a light

down blanket and down pillows packed in zippered plastic cases in the closet. Alice took the blanket out on the balcony and shook it to fluff it and air it out.

"The bathroom is here," Vera called, carrying a set of towels through a doorway.

Alice followed her. The large bathroom had an old-fashioned claw-foot tub. Vera placed towels about and then they left to make up Vera's room. It looked identical to Alice's room, except the colors were rose and blue.

After they deposited their luggage in the rooms, Vera suggested getting some lunch. "I'd prefer to face Aunt Agatha on a full stomach," she said. "Who knows what the afternoon holds. Besides, I'm dying to go to the Blue Claw Diner. They make the best lobster rolls and hot fudge sundaes."

Alice's stomach rumbled. She laughed. "Sounds good to me. I didn't realize I was hungry." They opened windows to air out the house before they left and headed for town.

Chapter Eleven

ey, Jane. Jane Howard. Wait up."

Jane barely heard the words behind her, carried away on the breeze. She stopped in her tracks and turned. About fifty yards back, Eleanor Renda was jogging toward her, waving. The high school track coach had been Vera Humbert's college roommate, but her petite size and freckles made her look more like the teenagers she coached.

"Whew!" She took a deep breath. "You'd think I'd stay in shape with my job, but I don't always run with my students." She took a couple of breaths. "I doubt I could keep up with them, but don't tell them that. I can take most of them in a short stretch."

"I know I couldn't keep up with them. Besides, you're the coach. You can take it easy. The football and basketball coaches don't work out with their teams."

"You have a point." Eleanor laughed. "And they're a lot younger than I am."

"Would you like to join me?" Jane asked, wondering if Eleanor wanted a partner.

"That would be a nice change. Thanks. I usually run alone. Gives me time to think and plan. You probably do the same."

As a matter of fact, Jane was used to jogging alone, and she did a lot of thinking and praying on her runs.

They began slowly, jogging side by side at a comfortable pace.

"You're entering the 10K race, aren't you?" Eleanor asked.

"I sent in my entry form and I've gathered a few sponsors, so I guess I'll run. You?"

"Thinking about it. I can't train alone. No one to pace myself by. Most members of the cross-country team are running. Gets them in shape and helps a good cause. I have an aunt with diabetes."

They ran in silence for a mile, their feet pounding out a rhythm in unison, their breathing huffing in and out in time.

"I thought . . . I was in shape," Jane said. "I run at least . . . four times a . . . week."

"Me too. Different when you . . . push yourself. Got to pace ourselves."

Jane's ponytail plastered against her neck. She felt a trickle of perspiration run down her forehead. She wiped it with the back of her hand.

"Let's slow down gradually," Eleanor said, decreasing her pace.

Jane matched her, stride for stride, until they were walking at a steady rate.

Eleanor took a water bottle from her waist pack. She took a swig. "Do you have water?" she asked Jane.

"Yes." Jane took a small plastic bottle out of the pocket of her windbreaker, which was tied around her waist. She took a big swallow.

"You should get a bigger bottle," Eleanor said. "You must stay hydrated. They'll have water stations along the race, but get used to drinking when you work out."

"You're right. I normally don't run this far."

"No one does around here. I ran marathons in college and the first few years I taught, but that was a long time ago."

Jane gave her companion a smile. It was nice to run with someone. The time went faster and the distance didn't seem so long. They came around the back side of Fairy Pond and connected with Chapel Road about a mile north of Grace Chapel Inn.

"Did you come up from town?"

Eleanor nodded. "I parked near the General Store, so I can do my shopping before I head home."

They jogged slowly down the hill toward the inn.

"I'm glad you caught up with me. I enjoyed running with you," Jane said.

"Let's do it again midweek ... say, Wednesday after school. Could you run then?" Eleanor asked.

"Sure." Jane liked running early in the morning, but she could adjust her schedule. It would be worth it to run with a professional coach. Like having her own personal trainer. "Where shall we meet?"

"I'll come to the inn. Four-thirty all right?"

"Great." They'd reached the inn. "I'll see you then."

"So long." Eleanor waved as she ran on.

The Kramdens stood on the path in the garden, next to Louise's pumpkin patch. The husband's arms waved about as he demonstrated his knowledge of garden pests.

"My daddy's an amotogist," their four-year-old daughter announced, squinting up at her father with a toothy smile. "He plays with bugs."

"That's entomologist, dear," the mother corrected. "Geoffrey just received his doctorate," she explained.

"Congratulations," Louise said. He barely nodded. She stood in front of them, trying not to look inhospitable while still blocking their way to the pumpkins. She didn't relish having their guests digging through her vines looking for bugs. Perhaps she'd feel different if he'd left the children outside the garden, but he hadn't and they made her nervous.

"Plants of the squash family, which includes your pump-kins, are susceptible to a variety of insects. I did my doctoral thesis on biointensive integrated pest management. From here, your plants appear to be relatively clean, but those lit-tle buggers can be elusive," he said, wagging his finger.

His wife giggled. He looked pleased that she appreci-ated his humor, or at least that's what Louise surmised. Janine Kramden held their squirming two-year-old son in her arms, rocking back and forth with jerky motions, whis-pering in his ear and kissing his cheek, but holding on firmly. The girl sat at her mother's feet, fascinated by a caterpillar, which Louise was certain Jane would pick up and evict from the garden.

Louise kept eyeing the children. Normally, she would take the little girl by the hand and let the child experience the wonder of pulling a large carrot out of the ground or unearthing a potato, but not today. She just wanted them out of the garden.

She'd come out to give her plants their daily feeding and discovered the little family entering the garden. She'd hurried after them to run interference between the helpless plants and the children.

Louise spotted Wendell sleeping beneath the foliage of Jane's potato plants, just beyond her tomatoes. The toddler let out an ear-splitting screech. Wendell jerked awake and jumped up, then darted away. The little boy saw him, stopped screaming and reached out his arm, his hand grabbing toward the cat, his little body wiggling. "Cat, cat, cat," he repeated in a rising crescendo.

Absorbed in her own world, the girl stood and worked her way around her mother to her father. She tugged on his pants pocket.

"Daddy," she said in a quiet, conspiratorial voice.

"Do you use chemical insecticides in your garden?" he asked, ignoring his daughter and son.

"My sister is in charge of the garden, except for my pumpkin patch," Louise said. "She uses an insecticidal soap. Purely organic."

"Daddy, Daddy, Daddy," the girl said louder than before.

He glared down at her, then looked at his wife. She reached for her daughter. In the process, her son wiggled out of her grasp and took off running across the garden as fast as his chubby little legs would allow.

"Timmy," she yelled. "Stop this instant!" She took off after him.

Timmy didn't stop. He didn't even slow down. He scrambled up Jane's tomato trellis and tumbled over the other side.

"Daddy, look!" the girl demanded, stamping her foot.

He looked down with an exasperated frown. "What? Can't you see your brother..."

She held up a tiny bug and beamed at her father. "I found a yellow ladybug, Daddy. See?"

"*Hmm.* That could be a serious problem." As he reached down for her hand, he turned, stepping on the end of a vine in the process.

Louise didn't know which way to turn. Chase the boy or guard her pumpkins. This scientist was so single-minded, he was as likely to damage the garden as his son.

"Yellow ladybugs are herbivores," he said. "Whereas most ladybugs eat other harmful insects, such as aphids, the *Epilachna borealis* eat cucurbits or plants of the gourd family, such as pumpkins."

He opened the girl's clenched little hand and removed a small, yellow bug with black spots. "Well, well," he said.

Louise clamped her lips together and resisted the urge to scold the man for ignoring his wife's mad pursuit of their son. She glanced from the man, whose attention was focused on a tiny ladybug, to the little boy, who was entangled in one of Jane's trellises. She was glad to see his mother scoop him up, but her relief was short-lived. Screaming and squealing, he wiggled and broke loose again.

Just then, Jane came through the gate, and Wendell escaped, tearing out of the garden. Louise breathed an inaudible "thank you." The cavalry had arrived. Jane jumped the rutabagas and caught the child as he fled from his mother. He closed his mouth and stared at his captor. Jane smiled and wiggled her eyebrows.

"Hello," she said in a jolly voice. Louise wanted to hug her. The little boy's mouth turned into a pout. His lower lip jutted out and began to quiver.

"I have something to show you," Jane said, and carried him toward the shed.

"Is she going to spank him?" his sister asked.

"Oh no. She wouldn't do that," Louise said. Janine hurried after Jane and her whimpering son. Disaster averted, Louise turned her attention to Geoffrey. He put the little creature in his palm and held it in place with the tip of his finger.

He leaned down to show his daughter. "This is *Diabrotica undecimpunctata howardi*—otherwise known as a spotted cucumber beetle. You'll notice it has twelve spots on its wings and it's elongated. This little beetle will go after roots and leaves of corn and cucurbits, like cucumber, squash, pumpkin and melons." He stared at the pumpkin patch for a few seconds.

Jane had the little boy under control. He sat by a patch of beets that he was pulling up by the leaves and stems. Jane knelt down beside him, helping him lift the dark purple root vegetable out of the ground. He tugged so hard that he nearly fell backward, but his mother, hovering behind her child, caught him. He lifted the bulbous vegetable, flinging dirt over their heads, squealing with joy. Louise caught Jane's eye and smiled. Jane gave her a thumbs-up signal.

"I don't see leaf damage to your crop, although it's hard to tell this late in the season. Your leaves have turned skeletal, but that's normal, I believe," he said. He stood straight and looked around. "Did you plant trap crops?"

Louise wasn't sure she'd heard him correctly. "Trap crops? You mean like a Venus flytrap?"

"No." He chuckled. "Perhaps I should speak with your sister."

With his daughter in tow, he turned and walked toward Jane and his wife and son. Louise glanced at her pumpkin patch, still intact, and followed him.

"You have a fine garden, Ms. Howard," he told Jane.

She looked up, then stood. "Thank you. I noticed that you've been admiring my sister's pumpkin plot."

"Yes. I was wondering—she doesn't seem to know—if you have purposely planted trap crops."

Jane frowned. "I've planted repellent crops, like the marigolds, and many of my herbs repel certain insects."

"Interesting." He rubbed his chin with one finger. "This little pest could have wiped out your sister's pumpkins, your squash and any melons and cucumbers you might have planted. You may have saved them by accident. The idea is to concentrate the insects on certain plants to prevent them from spreading to your other crops. Commercial producers of organic cucurbits often plant a small plot of a desirable species of squash nearby, and the offending beetles will feed on the trap crops and leave the other crop alone. It can be quite effective."

Contemplating the little bug in his hand, he stepped over the row of cabbage and followed a pathway to the gate. His wife watched him wander off, leaving her to deal with the two children.

"Go with your father, sweetheart," she told her daughter. "And be careful. Don't step on any plants."

"But I want to look for bugs," she whined.

"We'll take a walk later. Go on now."

The girl let out an exaggerated sigh. "All right." She scuffled her feet, raising little puffs of dust as she went.

"I'm sorry," Janine said. "I hope Timmy didn't harm any of the tomatoes."

Jane glanced in the direction of one of her tomato plants, now fallen on the ground. "We're near the end of the season, so we've harvested most of the tomatoes. The plants will be fine." Jane smiled at Timmy. "Thank you for helping me pick these vegetables."

Timmy picked up a beet and put it to his mouth, leaving little teeth marks and turning his mouth purple. He made a face, showing his surprise and distaste.

Jane pulled a carrot, wiped it off thoroughly and handed it to him. "Try this instead," she said.

He stared at it with a dubious expression, then reached out and took it from her.

"Thank you. We'll leave you alone now, before he gets his second wind," Janine said. She took his grubby hand. He dropped the rest of his carrot and reached toward Jane.

"I'll see you later, Timmy," Jane said.

As Janine led him away, he looked back and waved his free hand. Jane and Louise waved back at him.

"Phew," Louise said when they were out of range. "I wasn't sure the garden was going to survive the Kramdens. Poor Mrs. Kramden. Her husband seems oblivious of anything around him except insects."

"I noticed that." Jane chuckled. "I imagine the garden looks like a great playground to a little boy. How did you keep him from climbing on your pumpkins?"

"I stood guard between the pumpkin patch and the family. I was prepared to fight for my pumpkins if necessary."

"I wish I'd seen that." Jane laughed, then went over and looked down at the flattened tomato trellis. "These vines are so heavy, it's a wonder it didn't fall over on its own. Could you help me lift it?"

"Sure." Louise got on the other side and they tried to

lift the trellis. It was so tangled with vines, they couldn't make it budge.

"Guess I'll have to prune it first."

"I'll get the pruning shears," Louise said, already heading for the shed, feeling guilty for the damage to Jane's garden, although how she might have stopped the lightning quick child, she didn't know.

"Bring another basket too. We'll pick what we can salvage."

Louise came back, set the basket on the ground and handed Jane the pruning shears, then pulled on a pair of gardening gloves and held the heavy trellis so Jane could get down to the bottom vines.

Jane snipped off a long runner and held it up. Louise counted seven large tomatoes. Three were pale, but the rest were bright red. "Looks like we'll have fresh tomatoes to eat," Jane said. She handed the vine to Louise, who plucked the tomatoes and put them in the basket.

"I won't argue with that. Add some eggplant and Parmesan cheese and we'll have a meal," Louise said. She loved the summertime when Jane's garden produced an abundance of wonderful fresh vegetables for their table.

They worked together until they reduced the tomato vine to a manageable bush and the basket overflowed with tomatoes. Then they propped up the trellis.

Jane stood back. "That should hold it. What a year. There are still plenty of tomatoes to ripen on the vine."

"And a bushel's worth of work for you in this basket. I'll help you."

"I can't do them until tomorrow afternoon, but I'd appreciate your help now if you can spare the time."

"I can."

Jane gathered several large onions from the row where they were toughening in the sun. She picked a few green, orange and red peppers, and added them to a basket of kohlrabi. "We have enough unripe tomatoes to make chutney and salsa. If you'll take this basket, I'll get the tomatoes."

Louise didn't argue. The tomatoes were the heavier basket, but Jane was fifteen years her junior and Louise's back was already feeling the strain of garden work.

As she lugged the basket of vegetables to the kitchen, she wondered what misguided impulse had prompted her to plant giant pumpkins in the first place. Her special crop was attracting all sorts of unwanted attention. For a moment, she was tempted to cut them loose and end the project. She'd merely wanted to prove to her sisters that she *could* grow something. She'd accomplished her goal with amazing success.

Chapter Twelve

*V*era sucked in a sudden, deep breath and looked visibly shaken by her aunt's appearance. Fortunately, the lady was snoring softly and didn't witness her niece's reaction.

When she had visited Acorn Hill years before, Agatha had been spry and energetic. Alice had expected her to look frail now from the pneumonia she'd suffered in addition to a broken hip and surgery, but the tiny, pale wraith lying in the hospital bed reminded Alice of a dried apple doll that she'd seen at the county fair.

Vera quietly moved a chair to the side of the bed and sat facing her aunt. She reached over and touched her arm. "Aunt Agatha," she said in a low voice.

Agatha's eyes opened. She stared blankly for a few seconds, then recognition dawned and she smiled. "Hello, dear. I knew you'd come. I'm glad." She looked over toward Alice. "Who's that? A nurse? I don't want another one of those horrible shots. They hurt like the dickens."

"That's Alice, my friend from Acorn Hill," Vera said. "She's a nurse, but she doesn't work here."

Alice stepped closer to the bed. "Hello, Mrs. Jamison. It's nice to see you again."

"Have we met before? Oh no. I can't see a thing without my glasses. Be a dear and get them for me, Grace." She reached toward the bedside table.

Vera shot a distressed look at Alice. "I'm Vera, Aunt Agatha, not Grace. That was my mother. She's not here."

"Of course she's not here. Don't you think I know that? She died years ago."

"Yes. I'm her daughter, your niece, Vera."

"Alvera Lorinda Jamison, I know very well who you are. If you'd get those glasses for me, I could see you as well."

Vera found the glasses and handed them to her aunt, who fumbled to put them on. She managed, then peered up at her visitors as if examining something strange. "So you're a nurse, are you?"

"Yes, ma'am."

"Come here. I don't want to have to shout. Those buzzards out there spy on me all the time." She beckoned Alice with a bony hand.

Alice moved close, next to Vera, and they both leaned over the bedrail to hear better.

"They're drugging me," Agatha announced in a loud whisper. "They think I don't know it, but I do and I can't stop them. I don't take their pills. I spit them out when they aren't looking. But they inject stuff in this tube. I pulled the needle out of my arm twice. They punished me with a big shot in my poor hip that stung like a hornet."

"That's probably a vitamin shot to build you up. You've been very sick, Mrs. Jamison. You need your strength to get well."

"Oh, that's what they've been telling me, but they want to put me away. My nephew's in cahoots with the doctor and those nurses and the lady that makes me get around with that silly walker thing. Ridiculous."

"That's for your protection, Aunt Agatha. They don't want you to fall again."

She turned a sharp eye on her niece. "Have you been talking to Reginald? Don't you listen to him. He wants to put me away so he can run the business by himself. I don't trust him."

Vera gave Alice a helpless look. She turned to her aunt and patted her hand. "I came to help you figure out what to do when they release you from here. The doctor told me that could be in a couple of weeks if you keep improving. You have to get stronger first, though."

"I know. That's why I need to get out of here. The food is terrible and there's a bunch of sick people in here. I don't belong here. Bring me my clothes and take me home, Alvera."

"I can't do that. You don't have anyone at home to take care of you."

Agatha wiggled, trying to scoot up in the bed. Her hand shook as she reached for the bed controller. Vera found it and handed it to her aunt. Alice went to the other side of the bed and helped Agatha to sit up.

"That's better. Now you listen to me, missy," she said, shaking her bony finger at Vera. "I don't need someone taking care of me. I've managed on my own for years and I don't intend to stop now, so don't go listening to that rapscallion nephew of mine or that charlatan who calls himself a doctor. I know what's best for me."

Vera sat and took her aunt's hand. "I came to help you, Aunt Agatha. I'm on your side. Sometimes circumstances in our lives change and we have to make the most of them. You've been through that before. I've always admired your flexibility and your strength, no matter what happens."

Agatha's eyes became watery and her hands shook. "This time is different. This time I don't have control. Help me, Alvera. Don't let them put me away. Promise me."

Vera took a deep breath. "I won't lie to you, Aunt Agatha. You don't have a lot of options. You can't go up and down your stairs like you used to. I won't let them make any decisions for you without your consent. That's all I can promise."

Agatha stared into her niece's eyes for several seconds. Then she nodded. "I know I can count on you." She patted Vera's hand, then looked up at Alice. "I hope you aren't here to convince Alvera that the doctor is right."

"I'm here to support Vera and that means I'm here to support you, Mrs. Jamison."

She nodded. "I hope you're staying at the house and not at some expensive hotel."

"We already went to the house and we're airing it out. We'll be in the bedrooms in front next to your room," Vera said.

"Good. That house needs to be lived in."

"You have a beautiful home, Mrs. Jamison."

"Quit calling me that. It makes me sound old. Call me Agatha. Now where's my Bible. My eyesight isn't so good anymore. I want you to read to me. Reginald's too busy to spend time with an old lady."

Vera found the worn, black Bible on the bedside table. She opened it to a lacy bookmark in the middle of Psalms and read, "Have mercy on me, O God, have mercy on me, for in you my soul takes refuge. I will take refuge in the shadow of your wings until the disaster has passed. I cry out to God Most High, to God who fulfills his purpose for me. He sends from heaven and saves me, rebuking those who hotly pursue me; *Selah*. God sends his love and his faithfulness."

A soft, even humming sound came from the bed. Vera stopped. Agatha had fallen asleep with a slight smile on her face. "Psalm 57:1–3," Vera finished. She marked the page and put the Bible on the table, then removed Agatha's glasses and leaned over and kissed her softly. "Sleep well, Auntie."

They tiptoed out of the room and closed the door quietly behind them.

⌒

The following morning, Vera and Alice attended services at Shelton Cove Community Church. It reminded Alice of Grace Chapel. The freshly painted white clapboard building looked old. She loved the traditional designs on the stained glass windows, the tall steeple and the chimes that rang to announce Sunday services.

As they walked inside, she noticed a few differences. Tall, shiny brass pipes extended up the front wall on each side of a large cross. The organ sat off to one side and looked new. Plush, dark green carpet felt luxurious underfoot and absorbed sound. As a result, the sanctuary seemed hushed and peaceful. The pews were padded with thick, dark green cushions.

They sat near the back. Alice settled in, prepared for a traditional service like the ones she was accustomed to. When the worship leaders got onto the platform in front, she knew she was in for a different experience. Two guitarists, a violinist and a flutist began playing. The music was pretty, but very modern. Three singers in front led the congregation, and the words to the music were projected onto a screen behind them.

Alice glanced at Vera, who returned the hymnal to the

pocket in the pew in front of her. She shrugged her shoulders and looked up at the screen.

Alice didn't attempt to sing. The song was unfamiliar, and she wasn't a musician like Louise. She enjoyed listening and silently reading along with the other worshippers. The lively music made her smile. It called for the people to praise the Lord in the words of a Psalm. Alice wished she could remember it to teach the ANGELs at Grace Chapel. The preteen girls in her Wednesday night group would love the song and the lyrics.

Before the message, the worship leader invited the congregation to greet each other and welcome visitors. The room became noisy as parishioners left their seats and wandered around. A young man shook Alice's hand and bid her welcome. He moved quickly on. A tall, slender woman, dressed stylishly in black slacks, a turquoise silk tunic and pointy, spike-heeled, black dress shoes came up to Alice and Vera.

"Vera Jamison!" She drew Vera into an exuberant hug.

"Suzanne," Vera said hesitantly. "It's nice to see you."

"I knew it was you. I told Larry I was sure that was you sitting back here. How are you?"

"I'm fine. Suzanne, this is my friend Alice from Acorn Hill. We came to see my Aunt Agatha."

"I know. I told Larry that was why you'd come." She shook her head. "Poor old thing. Such a shame. I think her accident rattled her brain, you know? Reggie says she can't remember him sometimes." Her voice lowered. "We had to put Larry's mother in a nursing home. I just hate seeing them get old."

"I'm sorry to hear about his mother," Vera said.

"Oh, it's all right. They take good care of her. I tried, you know. I just couldn't handle things. It's better this way. She's up there with Larry." She pointed toward the front of the church. "We take her out to eat after church. Why don't you come with us?"

"I'm sorry. I promised Reggie we'd have lunch with him."

The instruments started playing again, and the people scrambled back to their seats. Suzanne said, "Later," and hurried away. She slid into a pew next to a tall, distinguished-looking man with wavy, salt-and-pepper gray hair. A short, stooped lady with a red pillbox hat sat next to the man. His mother, Alice assumed.

Alice liked the preacher. He talked about making choices, even when they go against popular opinion, and he used Rahab, out of the book of Joshua, as an example. She had exhibited courage in defying the authorities and helping Joshua and the Israelites. God saved her family and blessed her for sheltering His people.

It struck Alice that she had come with Vera to help decide Agatha Jamison's future. As the preacher offered a closing prayer, Alice prayed that Vera would have the courage and wisdom to make the right choice for her aunt, and that her aunt would have the grace and courage to accept whatever was to come next in her life.

⌒

Sunday afternoon, Jane slipped the skin off of a ripe tomato and cut the tomato in small chunks into a large soup kettle. Nearby, several tomatoes bobbed in a pan of scalding water to loosen their skins.

Sterilized canning jars in a variety of sizes sat inverted on clean towels. Louise sat at the kitchen table, dicing sweet peppers.

"I'd better hurry and get these finished. Craig will be here in half an hour to measure the pumpkin." Louise shook her head. "I still can't believe all this fuss. I should have tried growing something simple, like cucumbers."

"Mercy. I'm glad you didn't plant them. With your success, we'd have to open a pickle factory."

Louise laughed. "I saw you try to chase down Patsy Ley at church last week. When she saw you coming with a sack of vegetables, she took off."

"I only wanted to help. She usually puts up vegetables and pickles."

"Yes, and you gave her two whole sacks several weeks ago. She must have had her fill."

Jane sighed. "I hate to have good, fresh produce go to waste. I've offered vegetables to everyone in town, I think. I'll have to give the rest to Samuel for his hogs, I suppose." She finished the tomatoes and picked out a large onion to peel.

"What are you going to do with your pumpkin, Louise?"

"I don't know. My thoughts never went beyond keeping it alive and producing at least one decent pumpkin. What do you think I should do?"

"I'd give it double or triple doses of whatever you're feeding it, then enter it in a weigh-off. Those who know about such things, like our guests on Friday, seem to think it stands a chance of winning."

"I don't know. The logistics of transporting it boggle my mind. Honestly, Jane, growing such a magnificent pumpkin is very satisfying, but I don't intend to repeat this next year, so wouldn't it be unfair to enter against those who try every year?"

"By that reasoning, I shouldn't enter the Harvest 10K Run because I might compete against people who race all the time."

"That's different. You're racing for charity, to help others, not to win a prize."

For a moment, Jane stared at her sister, speechless. Her motives weren't as altruistic as Louise implied. Jane planted her fists on her hips, still clutching a paring knife and a chunk of onion, and faced Louise. "You're missing my point. You grew those pumpkins from seed and nurtured them through spring frosts and extreme heat in August. You pruned and trained and weeded and handpicked bugs off the plants. You've done everything any gardener or professional farmer would do and perhaps more. You deserve to win as much as Delmer Wesley or Harry Gladstone or anyone else."

Jane thought about a few people in Acorn Hill who bragged about their expertise in the vegetable garden, people like the irritating Norman Traeger, who thought he knew all there was to know about agriculture. She raised a respectable garden and entered a few items in the fair each year, but she claimed no special prowess. She tended a garden for the pure joy of watching things grow and the pleasure of serving fresh food to their guests. "I'd like to see Norman Traeger's face when you win a prize for the biggest pumpkin in Pennsylvania."

Louise smiled. "That would be something to see. I've heard him lecture you on what he thinks you're doing wrong and I've heard him giving advice down at Fred's Hardware. He told the Bellwoods that they were making mistakes in raising their field crops. Can you imagine? Sam and his sons have college degrees in agriculture and very successful farms. I doubt Norman has any formal training. But that's off the subject. I'm not likely to have the largest pumpkin."

"You never know unless you enter. Think about it."

"I did check on the contest. It's the first Saturday in October. I can't go off across the state and leave you alone to run the inn."

"You most certainly may. I'm perfectly capable of handling things. Besides, Alice will be back. If we get desperate, I'll call someone to help. So you have no excuse."

Louise diced the last strip of pepper and scraped it into a large bowl with the other peppers, celery and carrots she'd chopped. "That's just one obstacle. There are plenty of others."

"Nothing that we can't handle," Jane said. She nodded her head once. As far as she was concerned, that settled it.

Chapter Thirteen

A mile past Agatha's house, Vera drove through a stately stone entrance with a discreet sign announcing the Madison Golf and Country Club. Fancy wrought-iron gates stood open, but Alice guessed the club required membership. The long, wide brick driveway passed beneath overhanging maple trees bordering expansive manicured lawns to a large brick building similar to Agatha's home.

Off to one side, golf carts were parked along a pathway. A valet in crisp white pants and a white polo shirt stepped forward to open Vera's car door. As she thanked him, another young man opened Alice's door.

"Thank you," she said. She had a fleeting thought that perhaps she should tip him, but Vera came around and he stepped back. Vera looked as if she'd been visiting country clubs and using valet service all her life.

As they climbed the wide steps to the massive oak double doors, an attendant stepped forward and opened one of them. "Mrs. Humbert?" he asked.

"Yes."

"Mr. Jamison is awaiting you in the lounge."

"Thank you, Walter."

Alice was surprised and impressed that Vera knew the man's name, then realized he was wearing a name badge. She thanked him as well. He responded with a nod and a polite smile. "You're welcome. Enjoy your lunch."

Golden hardwood paneling lined the library walls. Soft light from amber-and-bronze wall sconces glowed against the wood, creating an atmosphere of warmth and serenity. The building was both beautiful and finely crafted, but Vera didn't appear to be particularly impressed. Noting Vera's confidence and poise, Alice realized her friend had stepped back seamlessly into a world of privilege in which she was at ease. Alice felt strangely off-kilter.

They entered a lounge where people sat at small tables talking and laughing. At the far end, large windows provided a view of a fairway with golfers evaluating their next shots. Alice had golfed a few times in college and enjoyed the outdoor exercise, but Acorn Hill had no course and she'd had no one to golf with. She wondered if Vera played. There was a nice public golf course in Potterston.

The tall, husky man with thick sandy-blond hair who rose from a stool by a window table made Alice think of a Viking. He set down a coffee cup and sauntered toward them. Vera's eyes lit up. "Reggie!"

When the man grinned, his tanned face creased into deep wrinkles. As he and Vera hugged, Alice saw the obvious affection between them. She searched her memory for references to Reggie and Shelton Cove. She'd heard mention of both over the years, but knew very little. It surprised Alice to realize that she and Vera had been friends for more than twenty-five years, and in all that time Vera rarely talked about her past.

"Reggie, this is my friend Alice."

"It's nice to meet you, Alice." Reggie's large, weathered hands enveloped hers. He gave her a warm smile. She couldn't help smiling back.

A uniformed maître d' approached them. "Your table is ready, Mr. Jamison."

They followed him to the dining room, where they sat at a table overlooking the golf course, a small pond and the Delaware River beyond.

"Do you still serve the Sunday buffet?" Vera asked as their host handed them leather-bound menus that looked liked books.

"Yes, ma'am."

"It's wonderful," she told Alice. "It was always fun driving over for it years ago. Afterward, my father liked to play a round of golf."

Alice set down her menu. "I'll have it too."

A waiter took orders for coffee and tea, and the threesome filed over to the buffet. It looked delicious. All the items had small placards. Alice surveyed the abundant array of offerings: Black Forest ham, beef Wellington, rosemary roast squab, wild salmon and a wide variety of salads, fresh fruits, breads and pastries. She wondered how she would manage to choose.

"There's a fabulous dessert bar too," Vera whispered to her.

"Oh my. It's a good thing I'm famished," Alice said, picking up a plate.

She insisted Vera go first. Then she went through, picking tiny portions, until her plate was filled. She followed Vera back to the table. Reggie didn't offer to say grace, so Alice said a silent prayer. Vera did the same.

When Alice raised her head from prayer, the waiter, who'd been standing quietly beside their table, took the swan next to her plate and gave it a single shake, transforming it into a linen napkin, which he draped across her lap. Alice was charmed. She knew how to fold napkins in creative ways. Jane had taught her and Louise. They set a beautiful table at Grace Chapel Inn, but they let the guests unfold their own napkins.

She took a bite of beef and Yorkshire pudding. It was tender and succulent.

"Want to go out on the river this afternoon?" Reggie asked. "I have a new power yacht that needs trials."

"I'd like to see Aunt Agatha this afternoon," Vera said.

"You could visit her at dinnertime."

"All right. Would you like to go for a boat ride, Alice?"

She swallowed a bite of spinach soufflé. "I'm happy to do anything you'd like," she said. "This is wonderful. I'll have to remember everything to tell Jane. My sister is a professional chef," she explained to Reggie. "We serve gourmet breakfasts at our inn, but not this kind of extensive menu."

"I always thought this was more of a Sunday dinner than a brunch," Vera said. "We won't need more than a snack tonight. We can stop at the store later and pick up a few things." Vera had eaten only a few forkfuls.

"Reggie, what's going on with Aunt Agatha? You called me to come help. That's why I'm here. So let's talk about her situation."

"You saw her last night, didn't you? It's obvious she needs to be in a facility where she can be taken care of."

Vera sighed. She poked at her salmon with her fork. "It looks that way." She looked up. "You said you visited an assisted living center and talked to them?"

"Yeah. Nice enough place. She'll have her own apartment. It's small—nothing like what she's used to, obviously—but it's sufficient. She doesn't need all that space to rattle around in. She only uses a couple of rooms now."

"True, but they're her rooms."

"I'd take you to the place, but I've got a buyer coming tomorrow. Unless you want to wait until Tuesday, you can go on your own."

"We'll go tomorrow," Vera said.

"So what about that ride? It's a perfect day for it."

"All right, as long as we're back early enough to spend time with Aunt Agatha."

They finished up and agreed to meet at the marina. Alice hadn't realized that the boatyard together with the marina next to Agatha's home was the family business— Vera's family's business.

The Shelton Cove Yacht Club shared the driveway that led to the Shelton-Jamison Boatworks and Marina. The stand of evergreen trees from Agatha's property spread out around the upper end of the yacht club, hiding it from view. As they drew up alongside the building, Alice craned her neck to get a full look at the amazing three-story, gray weathered-cedar mansion. The red roof had multiple levels and angles that extended on and on, finally disappearing into the trees. The combination of towers, grand arches, gingerbread trims and green-and-gray striped awnings over the windows gave the building a fanciful appearance.

"What an amazing building. It looks old."

Vera stopped the car and looked over at the clubhouse. "Eighteen fifty-three to be exact," Vera said. "My great-great-grandfather built it. He was a Shelton. I grew up in that house."

"Oh, Vera, how remarkable. When did it become a yacht club?"

"When my parents retired, they moved to a retirement village in Florida. I didn't want the house, so the company acquired the house and land when my parents sold their part in the boatyard. The club leases it from the company."

"You had no desire to come back here?"

"Are you kidding? All our friends and our church family are in Acorn Hill. I never really liked the house. Too big and dark inside. I liked playing in the towers, but we hardly used most of the house."

Alice loved her family's home in Acorn Hill, which her great-grandfather had built. She loved being surrounded by family history and knowing her ancestors had lived their lives in the same house. That gave Alice a sense of belonging and security and comfort. She'd always considered it a large home, but this house made Grace Chapel Inn look small.

Vera drove on, passed the marina and parked in front of the long, tall building that housed the boatworks.

"We'd better take our sweaters," she said as they got out of the car. "It can get chilly out on the river."

Alice took her sweater and followed Vera around the side of the boatworks. In front, the building extended over the water. A large opening and hoists allowed for boats to pull right into the work area. Reggie met them and unlocked the entrance gate that blocked the way to the private docks.

At the end of the dock, a gleaming white, sleek yacht bobbed gently on the water as the slow current in the cove lapped against it. Reggie went up a set of steps first, then helped Alice climb aboard.

The Nest Egg was a fifty-foot luxury yacht with teak decks and rails. Vera helped Reggie cast off. Then he climbed to the flybridge while she and Alice went inside the salon to explore. The boat moved from side to side beneath Alice's feet. She grabbed the handhold on top of the built-in cabinet beside a blue leather settee to get her balance. The boat accelerated slowly. Alice was surprised how smoothly it moved through the water, even when they crossed the wake of other boats.

The designer salon was furnished with the finest, butter-soft leather furniture and mahogany tables and cabinets. Forward of the salon, the galley had a small refrigerator, stove, microwave oven and a trash compactor. The dark-blue granite countertops matched the furniture.

They moved aft and found two staterooms below deck. The master stateroom had its own bathroom, or head, as Vera called it. Alice was surprised at how roomy and comfortable the craft was.

"You could live on this boat," Alice said.

"It certainly has everything you'd need, doesn't it?" Vera ran her hand over the smooth railing as they walked around a side deck to the front of the boat.

They held onto the bow rail and looked ahead. The boat created a curl of wave in front of the prow as it cut through the water. The wind ruffled their hair. The fresh air and misty spray felt exhilarating. Alice raised her face and breathed deeply, enjoying the experience.

"Wonderful, isn't it?" Vera said, smiling. She looked happy and perfectly at home standing on the bow of the luxury yacht.

"Do you miss this?" Alice asked.

Vera was silent for a moment, then inhaled and closed her eyes. When she opened her eyes, Alice saw a bit of indecision in her wrinkled brow.

"I didn't think so, but then I've been away for so long." She tilted her head to catch more of the spray. "I wonder if Fred would like to take a cruise vacation or come here for a visit. He doesn't care much for boats. He gets seasick." Vera turned away from the water. "Let's go up to the flybridge and see how Reggie's doing."

Without another word, she went aft and climbed the ladder to the upper deck.

A large canvas canopy covered the entire area. Vera explained that it was called a Bimini Top. They went forward to where Reggie sat at the helm in a leather captain's chair. In front of him was a bank of dials and the controls. He slowed the boat and set a control to idle, then swiveled around and leaned back.

"Have a seat."

Vera had Alice sit up front in another captain's seat. She took the auxiliary cushioned bench seat behind them.

"What do you think?" Reggie asked, looking completely confident that the boat would impress anyone who came aboard.

"Beautiful. You've really steered the company into the luxury craft business, haven't you?" Vera said.

He shrugged. "We take on one or two a year, but our reputation is growing," he said. "I'd love to return to the days when we built barks and steamers for river commerce. Those were the days. But our bread and butter still come from refits and repairs. Here . . ." He stood. "Take the wheel."

"I haven't steered a boat in years," Vera protested.

"This baby steers itself. Come on."

"Well, okay." Vera moved into the captain's chair and took the wheel. She slowly advanced the throttle. The boat accelerated smoothly.

For a few minutes, Vera looked ahead intently as she maneuvered the yacht. When the river widened, she sat back and relaxed.

Alice heard the low hum of the engine and Vera and Reggie's voices, engaged in a discussion about boats. She didn't try to join the conversation. Rather, she slipped into a pleasant reverie, taking in the surroundings and marveling at the magnitude of God's remarkable creation.

So much water, ever flowing toward the sea, and yet the huge body of water came from small trickles of springs and snow runoff from mountains far from this spot. It struck her that trying to comprehend how that could happen and continuously flow without stopping was like trying to comprehend the vastness of God. The river was like a droplet of water in the stream of God's power and presence. Amazing.

Chapter Fourteen

The last guests had checked out by the time Craig came to the inn. Just thinking about the Kramdens made her cringe. Very nice people, but Jane's garden was not a playground for children.

"It looks larger, but not significantly," Craig said. He took a long cloth tape measure out of his pocket and unrolled it, handing one end to Jane, who stood on the other side of the giant pumpkin.

When he finished with his measurements, he called out the results, which Louise jotted down in her notebook.

"We had two pumpkin growers visit Friday morning," Jane said. "They did a different calculation, using three measurements."

"Yes, I've read about that. It may be more accurate. What did they come up with?"

"Nine hundred eighty-eight pounds," Louise said.

He took a piece of paper out of his pocket and unfolded it. "Well, according to my chart, it now weighs about nine hundred ninety-eight. Since Friday, that's an additional ten pounds, give or take a few ounces. That's probably pretty close to their finding. So what did they think of your pumpkin?" He rolled up his tape and put it in his pocket with his weight graph.

"They were impressed," Jane said. "One of them seemed disgruntled to find such a large pumpkin."

"Especially one raised by an amateur," Louise said. "The other man was helpful. He's the one who measured it."

"I saw the grumpy one sneak into the garden in the dark. The other man caught him and made him leave. Later we found a split in the stalk. Do you suppose the man tried to sabotage the pumpkin?" Jane asked.

"Where is the split? Let me take a look."

Louise showed Craig where they had mounded dirt on top of the split stalk. He gently brushed the dirt aside and squatted down to look. He prodded, then re-covered it with dirt and checked along the stalk for other breaks. He examined the stem.

"It looks fine. Splits like that are common and don't really stop nutrients from getting to the pumpkin. I don't see any vine borers or bugs."

"We found a squash beetle yesterday," Jane said. "I'm surprised we don't have an infestation on the pumpkin plants."

Louise went looking through Jane's flowers. "Here's a strange creature that looks like an elongated lady bug, but it's yellow, instead of red. Is this a squash beetle?"

Craig went over and examined the bug, which was busy

feeding on a goldenrod flower. "No, but here's why you don't have more," he said.

"Aha. Of course," Jane said. "We have leatherwings. They're fierce-looking bugs, aren't they?"

"Ugh. Don't tell me they're beneficial," Louise said, eyeing the long, dragon-like beetle.

"Very. They dine on harmful garden insects."

"Those little soldiers may have helped your garden, which is looking very fine," Craig said, surveying the greenery and bright flowers and herbs. "Particularly your pumpkins, Louise. For some reason, all your growth went into the huge pumpkin, but the others look healthy as well."

He stood, one hand on his hip, the other rubbing his day-old scruff of beard as he stared at the giant pumpkin. "Fred and I were talking, and we want you to enter this in the weigh-off in Baskenburg. Fred offered his truck and trailer to haul it. I figure we can arrange some way to move it. That'll be the trick."

"That's kind of you, Craig, but I can't ask you and Fred to go to all that trouble and then give up your weekend to drive such a long way. I doubt if I have a chance."

"Sure you do. Think of it as representing Acorn Hill. We've never had anything this large grown in a garden. You don't have to decide right now, but we need a little time to rig a hoist to get this on the trailer without damaging the great pumpkin. Think about it."

"All right, I will."

"Oh Jane, don't compost or till in your garden remains this year. If those squash beetles have laid their larva on anything, they'll winter over in the compost and you'll have a real problem next year. Best thing to do is bag it all and haul it to the dump."

"Oh great. Thanks for the warning. I had planned to turn it all under."

Louise stood looking over her pumpkin patch. "It's hard to believe the season is almost over. I'll be sorry to see it end. I never dreamed growing something could be so satisfying." She sighed. "And so time-consuming. I'm glad I had this experience, because I don't intend to plant a seed ever again."

"All the more reason to enter your pumpkin in the Baskenburg Weigh-off," Craig said, tucking his gloves into his back pocket.

Jane picked several large tomatoes and gave them to Craig. They started walking toward the gate.

Louise turned to follow them. "We'll see," she said. She was curious to find out if her pumpkin could compete against the other giant pumpkins, but she hated disappointments. It would be bad enough for herself, but she didn't want Craig and Fred to be disappointed too.

Agatha looked lost in the bank of pillows propping her up in bed. Her shock of white hair, combed but sticking out at all angles, accentuated her pale, ashen complexion. Her sky-blue eyes nearly matched the blue in the flowers Vera had sent. Vera leaned over the bed rail and gave her aunt a kiss on the cheek.

"Reginald took you out on the new yacht this afternoon?" Agatha said, more a statement than a question.

Vera smiled. "Yes. I'm sure we look a mess. We stood on the bow and got pretty wet."

"Your color gave you away," she commented. "Your cheeks are red. I knew he'd want to show off his new boat."

"He's running trials. It handles beautifully," Vera said.

"Of course. Reginald is a true Jamison. Boatbuilding is in his blood. That's good. I was more concerned with the bottom line, but he has a board of directors now to worry about all that," she said, waving a feeble hand in the air. "Did he convince you to put me away?"

"He didn't even try, Aunt Agatha. I have an appointment to talk to the doctor and therapist tomorrow and to look at this center they're suggesting. After we check out everything, I'll come talk to you some more."

"Sit down, Alvera."

Vera pulled a chair close to the bed and sat down.

"There's a brown envelope on the table. Would you hand it to me, please?"

Vera picked up the manila envelope and gave it to her aunt. It had the name of a law firm stamped in the corner.

"This is for you. I had my lawyer draw it up. It gives you my medical power of attorney. I'm still sane enough to make my own decisions, but I'm getting old. I trust you, Alvera. Don't let me down." She handed the envelope back to Vera.

Vera took it and held it, staring at her aunt. "Does Reggie know you're doing this? He's very concerned about your welfare, you know."

"I know. Reginald is a good boy, but he doesn't understand there's more to life than being comfortable and safe. I want to live, Alvera. Going into one of those nursing homes isn't living. It's just existing until the Lord decides to take me home."

Alice had visited two assisted living centers in Potterston, and they provided small, but very nice apartments with staff to help and lots of social events. The residents had seemed happy and active. Agatha might actually like such an arrangement if she gave herself a chance, but a negative attitude could make life miserable too. Vera had her work cut out for her.

They stayed for a while. Agatha wanted to hear more from the Psalms, so Vera opened Agatha's old Bible.

"Read Psalm forty-six to me," Agatha requested. She folded her hands together in her lap and leaned back against the pillows.

Alice loved the Psalms and the beautiful language in them, so she closed her eyes and listened to the reading.

"Psalm 46:1–5," Vera said. "God is our refuge and strength, an ever-present help in trouble. Therefore we will not fear, though the earth give way and the mountains fall into the heart of the sea, though its waters roar and foam and the mountains quake with their surging. There is a river whose streams make glad the city of God, the holy place where the Most High dwells. God is within her, she will not fall; God will help her at break of day."

Agatha will see the river of God, thought Alice. It would make all the rivers of the world seem like trickles and it would make everyone glad. Then all the trials and storms Agatha still had to face would be insignificant. How glorious that would be. She glanced over and caught the old woman's gaze. She could see by Agatha's nodding agreement with the message of the Psalm that the elderly woman had the hope of future glory.

Jane's feet beat the pavement coming down Chapel Road early Monday morning. She topped the hill. Her lungs burned and her heart pounded hard against her chest.

One hundred yards from the driveway she slowed her pace. In half a minute, she turned and loped along the driveway, then jogged in place behind the inn, slower and slower to bring her pulse down gradually. She looked at her watch in the dim morning light. She'd shaved a minute and a half off her best time. Bending down, she stretched one leg back. She'd learned the hard way the importance of stretching before and after a race.

Me-ye-owl. Meowl. Yeowl, screeched through the morning air, coming from the direction of the garden. Jane ran to the gate, jerked it open and nearly tripped over a streak of something dark, the size of a small dog, that raced past her, out of the garden. She looked to see what it was, but it was already gone. Across the garden, something moved. Peering through the dim light, Jane saw a head poke up out of the leaves in the pumpkin patch and two luminous eyes stared at her. As she made her way through the garden, she realized Wendell was sitting in the middle of Louise's pumpkin patch.

Meow, the cat beseeched in his most beguiling voice.

"When did you come, Wendell?" Jane reached down and picked up their black-and-gray-striped tabby. Then she saw a bright red spot on his paw. "What is this?" She held up his paw and looked at it. She couldn't tell if he'd gotten it caught on something or gotten into a fight with whatever streaked past her.

"Let's go inside and see what's wrong."

Wendell let out another pitiful meow and let Jane carry him to the house. She got out a bottle of diluted hydrogen peroxide and cleaned his paw. A scratch appeared as she did so.

Louise came into the kitchen while Jane was tending to his paw. "What happened to Wendell?"

"He scared up something in the garden by your giant pumpkin. Whatever it was went shooting past me when I opened the gate. He got a little scratch, so he must have confronted it."

"Wendell did? That's amazing. He's rarely attempted to chase anything."

"He's been out watching you in the garden every day. He must feel proprietary about your pumpkins."

"Well, Wendell, I think you deserve a special treat for that. How about some real tuna for breakfast?" Louise said, reaching into the cupboard for a can. She opened it and flaked half of the contents into his bowl.

Jane put him down. He barely favored his paw as he walked to his dish.

"He doesn't seem concerned about his injury. I guess we don't need to baby him."

"Perhaps not, but he's my hero," Louise said. "Imagine him protecting my pumpkin patch." She shook her head.

"We need to check the garden after breakfast and see if the invader did any harm," said Jane. "So what'll it be for breakfast? Looks like we have tuna or squash."

"No thank you. Toast and tea will do for me."

"That rhymes. Forget the tuna. I just made a batch of zucchini bread with nuts and raisins," said Jane.

"That's what I meant. Zucchini toast and tea. I'll even do the toasting."

"Good. In that case I'll run up and change. Be back in a jiff." Jane made her way to the back stairs, leaving Louise to fix breakfast.

Chapter Fifteen

I can't stand seeing Aunt Agatha in such poor health," Vera said, sorting through the clothes in her aunt's large walk-in closet. She pulled out a dress and held it up. "Most of her clothes aren't suitable for the new life she'll be facing." She hung the dress back on the rack. "I suppose we could go shopping."

"What about this muumuu?" Alice said, holding up a flowing, Hawaiian print caftan. "The colors would perk her up."

"As well as everyone else in the center."

"That's good. It's slip-on and loose. Does she have any others?"

"I think she used these as house dresses," Vera said, holding up another roomy gown.

"Those will do nicely. How about toiletries? Does she wear makeup?"

"Yes. Bright rouge and red lipstick and penciled eyebrows. Maybe that would make her feel better."

"It's worth a try."

They sorted through her toiletries drawer, taking out a supply of makeup and foundation. Vera found a portable magnifying mirror. "I don't know if she's strong enough to apply these things herself, but we can doll her up a little."

"What about shoes? Does she have some comfortable slippers or house shoes?"

Vera opened a cupboard. "Here. There are a dozen pairs in here. Most don't look like they've ever been worn. I wonder which ones she'd like the best."

"Take several pairs. We can always bring them back."

They packed two suitcases with Agatha's things and put them in the car to deliver after Vera's appointment with Agatha's doctor.

The doctor looked at the power of attorney papers and handed them back to Vera. He leaned back and rested one foot on top of his opposite knee. They were sitting in a small lounge area for visitors at the nursing home where Agatha was recovering from her postsurgery pneumonia. It was late morning and the lounge was empty except for them.

"According to Mrs. Jamison's chart, her broken hip has healed well. She should be getting full physical therapy right now, but the pneumonia set her back a couple of weeks. The longer she goes without therapy, the less likely she is to regain full mobility," he said.

"She seems terribly weak," Vera said. "Is that from the surgery or the pneumonia?"

"Both. There's no doubt surgery is hard on a patient her age, but we see elderly folks come through with flying colors all the time. Your aunt seems to resist our efforts to build her up."

"Excuse me," Alice said. "Might I interject an observation?"

"Alice is a nurse at a hospital in Potterston," Vera explained. "I asked her to come because she has so much experience working with surgery patients."

"I'd appreciate any insight you can provide," the doctor said.

"When we first visited her, Mrs. Jamison seemed disoriented. As you said, the surgical trauma, on top of the injury, is very hard on the elderly. She seems to have gotten the idea that your treatments are attempts to put her in a nursing home permanently. Perhaps Vera can persuade her to cooperate more. She told us that she has fought the intravenous medications and she won't swallow the pills you've prescribed. Perhaps she would drink some high caloric nutritional milkshakes."

"We can try that. If you will talk to her, Mrs. Humbert, that might help."

"I'll try. Assuming her condition improves enough to leave here, what, in your opinion, needs to happen? Could she return home if she has a caregiver?"

"Mr. Jamison indicated that her home is unfit for a person with mobility problems. She'll never be able to handle stairs again. Could those problems be resolved?"

"I don't know," Vera said.

"We have a wonderful facility in Shelton Cove. Why don't you go talk to the administrator."

"We have an appointment to see him this afternoon," Vera said.

"Good." He closed Agatha's chart and stood, indicating the appointment was over.

"We may want to talk with you again this week."

He took a business card out of his shirt pocket and handed it to Vera. "Here's my office number. My receptionist can make an appointment for you, if you wish."

"Thank you, doctor."

The doctor left the room, his footsteps heavy and purposeful as he strode down the tiled hallway.

"Well, that was quick," Vera said. "But I'm not sure that I learned anything new. Did you?"

"Actually, we learned that your aunt's surgery was a success. With the right motivation and help, she can get up and walk. So the trick is to appeal to her spirit of independence. But she still may need to move into an assisted living center. She's too fragile at this point to live alone."

"Let's stop by her room before we leave," Vera said.

They passed aides who were wheeling patients to the

dining room for lunch. At Agatha's room, an aide was helping her stand and get her balance with a walker. She had on
a hospital robe over a hospital gown.

"Hello, look at you," Vera said. "You're ready to take a
walk."

"They want me to walk to the dining room. I don't know
if I can make it. I haven't walked that far since I've been here,"
she said. "I'd rather eat in my room. It makes me ill watching
people drool and spill their food all over themselves."

"We'll go with you," Vera said. "May we?" she asked the
aide.

"There, Agatha. You won't be alone," the aide said. To
Vera, she answered, "You certainly may. We encourage family
members to go to meals and other activities with the
patients."

"You run along, dear," Agatha told the aide. "My niece
and her nurse friend can help me walk."

"I'm supposed to stay with you," the aide replied.

"Is it a requirement?" Alice asked. "Otherwise, we'll be
happy to help her."

"Just stay at her side in case her knees buckle."

"We'll be your private guards," Vera teased her aunt.
"I'm not sure if we need to protect you or everyone else.
You won't speed, will you?"

"Oh, go on," Agatha said, giving her niece a glowering
look that came across as an affectionate glance. Vera laughed.

"You see what I have to put up with?" Agatha said to Alice.

"And you love it. Shall we go?"

Alice walked on one side, and Vera walked on the other, just far enough back to support Agatha if she stumbled. She took one halting step, moved the walker forward, then took another step. It took five minutes to go down the hallway to the dining room, about seventy feet away. At the doorway, Agatha looked around.

"Over there," she said, pointing to a small table that seated four. It had a single occupant. "She's not so bad."

The lady, dressed in street clothes, had a walker parked beside her. Her hands were shaking as she reached for her water glass. By the time Agatha and her escorts made it to the table, the woman had managed to get the glass to her lips—although a good bit of the water had spilled out—and returned it to the table. She looked up when they approached and she smiled.

"Agatha," she said, beckoning for them to sit down. Her smile made her eyes sparkle. "One of these lovely girls must be your niece. Hello, dears."

"Hello. I'm Alice. This is Vera, Agatha's niece. How nice of you to call us girls."

"Well, you are certainly younger than I, but up here..." she tapped her head with a shaky finger, "I'm only twenty-nine.

That's how I feel inside," she said, patting her chest above her heart.

"That's Lillian Vickers," Agatha said. "She and I played bridge together, back when we were young. And you're not twenty-nine anymore."

"Oh, sit down, you old lady, you. I know how old I am, but I'm not going to let that stop me and neither should you. I just pretend that walker contraption there is a skateboard," Lillian said. "I told my grandson I'd race him when I get out of here."

"Pshaw! As if they'd let you skateboard in the halls of that old people's home." Vera helped lower Agatha down onto a chair across from her friend.

Alice sat across from Lillian. Vera took a seat to her right. A woman with a hairnet and disposable gloves brought two trays of food and set one in front of Agatha and one in front of Lillian. "Looks like you've got helpers today," the woman said, then hurried off to get another tray.

Agatha scowled. "Good thing I can feed myself. Otherwise I'd starve in here." She pushed aside her tray.

Alice noticed several uniformed staff who were helping patients eat. She turned to Lillian, pointedly ignoring Agatha. "Are you moving into a retirement home?"

She sighed, then sat up a little straighter. "Yes. I'm going to Briarhurst. My son is making the arrangements." Lillian's lower lip betrayed her distress. "He came by this morning with papers for me to sign to sell my house." She was silent for a moment. "I hear they treat you like a queen there. Not like here. Not that I'm complaining, mind you. They do their best here, but this is not a residential home. This is rehab, although some people live here, bless their hearts."

"They've got pill pushers at that home, just like here," Agatha said.

"And a good thing," Lillian said. "Then you don't have to worry about what time it is or if you already took your pills. My memory isn't what it used to be, you know. Neither is yours, I'm thinking."

"My mind is as sharp as one of those needles they keep poking in my arm. I am not going into that home, no matter how nice you say it is." She glanced at Vera.

"I wonder if the doctor knows you're capable of being independent?" Alice said softly.

Agatha gave her a startled look. "What do you mean?"

"I was thinking about my own experience, working in a hospital. I have patients who come straight from the recovery room. I imagine you were groggy and disoriented from the anesthetic they gave you. You know, sometimes it can take weeks for that to work out of your system. I don't like to hurt people, but I have to make them cough, sit up, stand up, walk—all the things that are so hard those first few days."

"Hard. You can say that again," Lillian said.

"It's for their own good. Getting better requires deter-mination and courage, you know? Then they progress from intravenous feedings and ice chips to broth to soft foods, then finally to real food like your lunch. If they don't progress, they don't improve very quickly. I've had patients who rip out their intravenous tubes and feeding tubes and refuse to eat. But once they are determined to get better, they make amazing strides."

"Are you talking about me?" Agatha asked, raising her chin defiantly.

"I don't know. Am I?" Alice replied. Agatha stared at her. Alice gazed back, trying to convey true sympathy for her condition.

"You think it'd make a difference?" Agatha asked.

"Yes. I do."

"Vera, would you say a prayer for us, so we can start eat-ing?" Agatha said. She bowed her head and closed her eyes.

As Alice bowed her head, she caught Lillian looking at her. The older lady winked, then bowed her head and shut her eyes while Vera thanked the Lord for their meal.

"I'll be out in a minute, Louise. I want to check my e-mail before I go out to the garden. I sent a message to my old friends and coworkers in San Francisco, looking for sponsors for the Harvest race. I want to see if there are any replies."

"Take your time. I'll go on ahead." Louise went through the kitchen, collected what she needed, then hurried out to the garden while Jane was absorbed with her e-mail. Wendell followed Louise and sniffed around, looking for whatever he'd encountered earlier when Jane found him.

Louise retrieved a trowel from the shed, then went to the pumpkin patch.

She saw the mess before she got there and nearly dropped the paper sack she was carrying. The smallest of the three pumpkins was split open and the vine and leaves scattered. She looked beyond it to her giant. Leaves were strewn, the umbrella leaned at a precarious angle, but the pumpkin seemed to be intact.

She stepped up to it carefully. A scratch marred the surface. The split stem that had been buried was uncovered, but not cut through. Looking around to make sure she was alone, Louise opened the sack she was carrying and took out a jar. She knelt down and poured the contents around the base of the plant's stem, then worked it in with the trowel. She put the jar back in the sack and set it out of the way, beneath a bunch of leaves where Jane wouldn't see it. As she stood to go back to her pumpkin, the side door of the inn opened. Louise started, but quickly regained her composure and returned to the pumpkin.

Jane went first to the shed, then came out carrying two

rakes and a large black plastic yard bag. She looked around at the carnage. "What a mess! Is your pumpkin all right?"

"The big one just has a scratch. But the little one is split open."

Jane went to the big one first. "I think it's all right, Louise. The skin looks like it's toughened, so the scratch probably didn't breach the pumpkin. We'll have to watch it, but surface cuts can heal. Let's give it additional shade. We can attach some old blankets to the umbrella and make a tent."

"Good idea. Did you see this one? Whatever attacked the garden got to this one first."

Jane went over to the smaller pumpkin. It had split wide open and dirt had been tossed all over the pumpkin, the leaves and the path as if something had been digging or scuffling. "Wendell must have surprised it. I wonder if a raccoon invaded the garden, Louise. I haven't seen any around this summer, but they like ripe fruit and vegetables. And where there's one, there's a family of raccoons."

Louise looked around. Considering the damage from one animal, she pictured the complete destruction of Jane's garden. Although Jane harvested daily, an abundance of produce remained. "If it's a raccoon, it'll come back. What shall we do?"

Jane pushed up her three-quarter-length sleeves as if

preparing to do battle. She pivoted around, surveying the garden. "First we clean up this mess, then we pick everything in the garden. That won't protect your giant, though. Let's call Craig. Maybe he'll have an idea."

"I'll call him, but don't start cleaning up that mess. Take care of picking your vegetables first. I'll be right back."

"All right. While you're at it, invite him to dinner. I was going to call Fred too. We have leftover ham and tons of vegetables to go with it."

"I'll call them both." Louise retrieved her sack, then rushed into the house, knowing that her sister would have everything finished before she got back if she didn't hurry.

"Don't you look lovely today," a voice said from the doorway. Vera stopped brushing Agatha's hair and looked up. Alice looked over her shoulder. A tall, stocky woman with a cheery smile and friendly brown eyes stepped into the room. She had on tan pants and a blue smock that Alice assumed was a uniform.

"Gracious me, look at you after so many years," she said to Vera. "I'm so glad you've come to help your aunt. Mrs. Agatha's my favorite patient around here, but I don't get to spend much time with her."

"This is Olivia Martino," Agatha said. "Maybe you remember her husband. He worked at the boatyard for years. He helped me keep the business solvent through those first two years after George died."

"I do remember. How nice to see you again," Vera said.

"Olivia came by every week to see if I was all right."

"Mr. and Mrs. Jamison saw us through some hard years. Least we could do to help out. Your aunt's a good lady."

"Yes, she is." Vera took Agatha's hand and squeezed it gently. "I'm glad you're here to keep an eye on her ... and make her behave." Vera winked at her aunt.

"As if I could do anything else," Agatha said. "Olivia is deserting me, though. She's going to retire."

"Congratulations," Alice said.

"I don't know if I'm going to like retirement," Olivia said. "I've been in nursing for thirty-five years. But I've got things I want to do, like needlepoint projects, a stack of novels to read, boxes of pictures to put into albums for my grandchildren and a family story to write for them. There's never enough time."

"It sounds like you have plenty to keep you busy," Vera said.

Olivia shrugged. "For a few hours a day, perhaps, but I have to be active. I'm thinking about doing home health care. They're always looking for people. Maybe I'll come visit you, Mrs. Agatha. I can help you put on your makeup. You look so pretty today. Especially with that colorful gown. You look like you're ready to go out on the town.

Maybe I'll take you out for tea or we can have it at your place. I'll even bring the treats. I love to cook, but it's no fun cooking for one. Well, I'd best get back to work before they come looking for me. Nice seeing you, ladies."

Vera and Alice bid her good-bye.

"You have all kinds of friends in here, Aunt Agatha. I'm surprised you're not out in the halls, visiting."

"I would be if I could just get around better."

"We'll come take you for a nice long walk tomorrow. We're going to go now and let you rest."

"You're going to see what to do with me, aren't you?"

"You want me to help, don't you?" Vera asked.

Agatha lay back against her pillows and closed her eyes. "I suppose you must. I can't stay here. They won't let me go home. You might as well order my coffin. You can bury me in this caftan."

"Please, Aunt Agatha, don't talk like that," Vera said. "You're going to get better."

"The doctor doesn't think I will. Reginald doesn't think I'll get better. I can't walk by myself without that silly walker, or take a shower without some nurse helping me. Do you know how humiliating that is, Alvera? Sometimes I wish Jesus would come take me home. George is waiting for me up there in heaven. Your mother and father, rest their souls, they're waiting for me. What do I have here? Just a bunch of old bones that don't work anymore. You're going to leave and go back to that place with your husband, and it's right you should. I'm just a burden. To you. To Reginald. He's trying to get someone to take care of me and he has to keep that business going. How else will I pay my doctor bills?"

"Mrs. Jamison, did I hear you right? Vera told me you had spunk and an independent streak. Are you giving up?"

Agatha opened one eye and looked at Alice. "Are you goading me?"

Alice tried Louise's trick and raised an eyebrow, but didn't reply.

"I'm tired, so you'd better leave now." Agatha closed her eyes.

"We'll come back at dinnertime," Vera said. She leaned over and gave her aunt a kiss. Agatha lay still, breathing noisily as if she were snoring. *Well,* Alice thought, *I'm not sure the makeup and dress helped much, but at least Agatha's still willful enough to have the last word.*

Chapter Sixteen

*T*his looks like one of those sprawling Cape Cod estates," Vera said as she pulled in to the visitors parking at the Briarhurst Retirement Village.

The white clapboard buildings were trimmed in blue and had blue tile roofs. American flags, the Delaware flag and a variety of state and foreign flags flapped merrily on poles along the street in front of the buildings. People meandered along the walkways of extensive lawns and gardens. Some used walkers and wheelchairs, but many were walking about, dressed as if out for a game of tennis. Families sat around picnic tables. Children played tag and did cartwheels on the manicured lawns.

"It's lovely," Alice said as they walked up a sidewalk bordered by red and white geraniums and chrysanthemums in riots of color. "Not what you'd picture as a typical nursing home. I wonder if your aunt has ever visited here."

"I don't know, but the beauty wouldn't sway her, I'm afraid. If it meant leaving her home, she'd turn down an invitation to live in the White House."

"I think I understand. I'd hate to move out of my home. Other than my years at college, I've never lived anywhere else."

A sliding glass door opened automatically at their approach. The commodious reception area looked like a fancy hotel lobby. Off to one side, people milled about in an inviting lodge-style room. Bookshelves flanked a massive rock fireplace. At one table, four women played Scrabble. At another, two men played chess, surrounded by a group of observers.

"May I help you?" a pleasant young woman asked.

"We have an appointment with the administrator," Vera said.

"I'll show you to his office."

They followed her down a carpeted corridor. A few potted plants and pleasant landscape pictures decorated the hallway. She stopped at a door, knocked, then opened it when a voice bade them enter.

A man in casual business attire stood and greeted them. "I'm Barney Johnson," he said, holding his hand out toward both of them.

"I'm Vera Humbert." She shook his hand. "This is Alice Howard."

"Welcome. Please sit down." He gestured toward two chairs in front of his metal desk.

A large, framed aerial map of the town, the river and the retirement village hung on the wall behind him. A photograph of a woman and three teenagers hung on the opposite wall. The office was simple and functional. It appeared that the decorating budget had been reserved for the public areas.

"I understand that my cousin, Reggie Jamison, has spoken with you concerning our aunt, Agatha Jamison," Vera said. "She may need to move into an assisted living residence. She's named me caretaker of her physical well-being, so I'd like to find out more about your facility."

"Certainly. We have a wide range of possibilities here. We are a retirement community, so our residents must be over fifty-five. Our accommodations range from garden homes to condominiums, apartments and both limited- and full-care facilities. In the limited-care facility, the apartments have kitchenettes. However, there's also a full-service dining room with professional wait staff. Our residents can choose among a variety of options. Mr. Jamison indicated that you're interested in our limited-care apartments. Would you like to see one?"

"Yes, if we could," Vera said.

He took a set of keys out of his desk and stood. "If you'll follow me, we can go out the back." He held the door for them, then led them down the hallway to an outside door.

He took them in a motorized cart. They followed a paved path to a two-story building with a view of the river on one side and one of the woods on the other. He parked and escorted them inside.

Near the entrance was a nicely decorated room with a wide-screen television in one corner and a baby grand piano in another corner near a large fireplace. The room had one occupant, a woman with a tote bag and a purse. She sat perched on the edge of a chair, as if expecting someone. The marble-tiled floor had no carpet so that people with walkers and wheelchairs could navigate without obstruction.

"This residence is for our mobile patients who do not require full-time nursing care. Some use walkers or wheel-chairs, but they can get around on their own." Barney turned to the receptionist at the front desk. "I'm going to show Mrs. Humbert the facilities."

They walked down a brightly decorated hallway. He pointed out a library with filled bookshelves, reading areas and two computer stations.

Farther down the hall he took them inside a large room. "This is the dining room," he said. It looked like an elegant supper club, with white linens and a fresh flower arrange-ment on each table. "We require our residents to eat at least one meal a day here. We encourage them to socialize. I assume your aunt is able to get about?"

"I'm not sure. She's using a walker right now, but she isn't very strong."

"She might need our nursing facility then."

They went into an elevator to the second floor, then down a hallway and around a corner to another hallway. He stopped at a door and unlocked it.

The L-shaped apartment had no interior partitions. The larger side had a big window looking down over a courtyard with a fountain and a garden with paths through it. The inside wall had a small refrigerator, stovetop, sink and cupboards. There was a bathroom in one corner with a tub equipped for the handicapped. Vera looked around without comment, but Alice could see her difficulty trying to imagine her aunt moving into such a small space after living in a mansion most of her life.

"Do you have anything larger?" she asked.

"We have one- and two-bedroom units, but none of them are available right now. This came open unexpectedly. If you want it, we need to reserve it right away. We have inquiries daily."

Vera stood in the middle of the empty room, frowning, rubbing her chin, looking around. The sudden availability could be God's provision. How would Vera know for sure? Alice tried to picture Agatha's furniture crammed into the room. Her bedroom was larger than the entire apartment.

"I'll have to think about it," Vera said.

Barney nodded. "I realize it's hard to envision your aunt living in a small apartment, but we have a very qualified, caring staff and a wide range of activities for our residents. We have a spa on the premises, a beauty parlor, an art studio and various classes, lectures and movies. Your aunt would adjust."

He dropped them off at Vera's car. She said good-bye, but was silent all the way back to town. She parked in front of the Blue Claw Diner and they went inside and found a table.

"I'm sorry to be so quiet. I don't know what to say."

"It's all right. You've had a shock. I know you're distressed thinking about your aunt and what to do for her."

"I am. I'm not really hungry, but we have to eat. Maybe a lobster roll will help my mood. I guess I want to put off facing Aunt Agatha as long as possible."

"I'm sorry. Making life-changing decisions that affect you is hard enough. I can only imagine the pressure you're feeling," Alice said. "Would you like to pray about it?"

"Yes, please."

After they gave their orders and the waitress left, they bowed their heads. Alice prayed, "Dear Father, we thank You for the meal we are about to eat and for the abundance and grace You give us. You know all about Agatha's condition and the problem of her future. You know the responsibility and love Vera feels for her aunt. You love Agatha and You know what's best for her. Please give Vera wisdom, guidance and peace in this situation. Reveal Your plan for Agatha, whether this opening is Your provision for her or not, and help Vera calm her aunt's fears and anxieties. In Jesus' name. Amen."

"Amen." Vera raised her head and looked at Alice.

"Briarhurst is a wonderful place, but I just cannot believe in my heart that it's right for my aunt. She's ready to give up. I'm afraid that's what she'd do in an assisted living center. I can't let that happen. When I was young, Aunt Agatha always treated me like a grown-up and let me help whenever she worked at a homeless shelter or put on a charity affair."

"She was a big influence in your life," Alice said.

"Yes. She taught me life was about helping others and she lived by that code. My mother was sweet and beautiful, and she did what she could to support charities, but she didn't like to get dirty. She tried to teach me to be a proper lady." Vera laughed. "As you can imagine, I wasn't very good at it. Aunt Agatha encouraged me to follow my heart when I wanted to be a teacher and go to a state university instead of Avonwood College, where my parents went. My poor mother thought I was throwing away my life.

"When I wanted to marry Fred and move to Acorn Hill, Aunt Agatha stood up to my parents and supported my decision, even though it meant moving away from Shelton Cove. I can't turn my back on her now. There has to be a different solution, even if I have to move her to Acorn Hill to live with me."

The garden looked decimated. Most of the plants had been pulled or stripped. Baskets and sacks of vegetables were lined up in rows, ready to be hauled to the house. Only the potatoes and Louise's pumpkins remained to be harvested. Marigolds, asters and goldenrod still added color to the emptied plot. Jane looked at Louise and laughed. Louise looked up to see what was so funny.

"You should see yourself," Jane said. "You have twigs and leaves in your hair, and your shirt and pants look as if you've been making mud pies."

Louise wiped her brow with the back of her garden glove and left a new smear. "You don't look so tidy yourself," Louise said, laughing. "I'm just glad I didn't have piano lessons this afternoon."

A truck rumbled up the driveway. Fred made a tight turn, then backed up to the garden gate. The back of his truck was filled with lumber and a large roll of heavy-gauge chicken wire mesh. Fred and Craig got out and came back to the garden.

"Afternoon Jane, Louise," Fred said. "We're ready to box in your pumpkins. That umbrella has to go."

Jane went over and rolled down the umbrella, then started pulling and twisting it out of the ground. "It's in there to stay."

Craig went over to help her.

"What are you planning to do?" Louise asked Fred.

"We'll build a frame over the patch and cover it with tarps and your blankets," Craig said.

"There's going to be some cold weather tonight," Fred said. "Shouldn't get down to freezing, but no sense taking a chance. I'm giving you the supplies you need to keep this beauty safe."

"Then we got all this produce harvested in the nick of time," Jane said. Fred's weather predictions came true most of the time, although temperatures rarely dropped below the forties until late October. "If you would be so kind, you men can help us carry it all in."

Craig grabbed a basket. "A pleasure. Just tell me where you want it."

"On the back porch for now. We'll take it in later."

Fred picked up a basket and carried it to the porch. Then he returned and pulled several lengths of board out of his truck and laid them out on the driveway. Craig helped him unload while Jane carried the umbrella to the shed.

"I appreciate your helping us get our produce in, but you don't need to go to all this trouble for my pumpkins. I can't let you give it to me. I say we let nature take its course."

Fred leaned against his truck and crossed his arms. "You have a winner there, Louise. No one from Acorn Hill has ever been in a position to win a pumpkin weigh-off before and it might not ever happen again. I'd be mighty proud to have a picture of you and that pumpkin with its big ol' ribbon to hang in the hardware store. I can just see it now," he said, raising his hands as if framing the picture. "Lloyd'll put up a sign outside town . . . Welcome to Acorn Hill, Home of Louise Smith's Prizewinning Giant Pumpkin."

"Surely you jest," Louise said.

Craig rubbed the shadow of beard that covered his chin. "What did you plan to do with your pumpkin now that it's grown so large, Louise?"

"Plan? Nothing. I thought we'd have enough for a few pies and perhaps a large jack-o'-lantern for the front yard. Now I hear that the giant pumpkins have such a high water content, they become mushy when they're ripe, so it's destined for the dump."

"In that case, I'd like to purchase it," Craig said.

Louise looked dumbfounded. "Whatever for?"

"The seeds from a pumpkin this large are valuable. Especially if the pumpkin becomes a weigh-off prizewinner. I can reuse the fencing mesh at the nursery, so that's no expense."

"If you can haul that pumpkin out of here and dispose of it, you're welcome to it. The seeds won't cost you a thing."

"You went to a lot of work to raise it. And it won't do me much good if you don't enter it in the weigh-off," Craig said.

"He has a point, Louise. I say you should take it to Baskenburg," Jane said.

Louise threw up her hands. "All right. We'll take it to Baskenburg, but you'll have to figure out how to get it there."

Craig grinned. Fred stepped away from the truck and took out a tool box. "First order of business . . . we have to keep it safe and growing for another week and a half, until it's time to move it. Let's get this frame built. I calculate we can finish it before that dinner you promised us, Louise."

"This seems like a lot of trouble for a pumpkin," Louise muttered as she moved the blankets out of the way.

"That's the price of fame," Jane said, grinning at her sister. Knowing her sister wasn't fond of gardening, she was proud of Louise for her persistence and diligence. She wasn't averse to a little teasing though.

The men laid out boards in a grid pattern and fastened them together using Fred's nail gun. In no time, they had four lengths of fencing a few inches taller than the giant pumpkin. They carried the lengths into the garden.

"We'll try not to damage the plant, Louise, but we've got to secure this so the garden robbers don't burrow under."

Jane and Louise helped the men move vines and trim off unnecessary branches, then guide the boxed frame into place. Once it was secured with stakes and wire, Jane left Louise with the men to finish the project while she went to the house to start dinner.

As she washed vegetables and cubed a mix of eggplant,

carrots, beets, kohlrabi, potatoes and onions to bake and glaze, she watched the progress out the kitchen window. Fred and Craig covered the frame with the wire mesh, stapling it in place, and Louise helped spread out the large blue plastic tarp, then cover it with the old blankets.

With any luck, the pumpkins would be safe from the cold and the critters. Jane didn't normally pray for plants and animals, but she wanted Louise to experience the full glow of success, even if the pumpkin didn't win, so she uttered a little prayer, asking the Lord to watch over Louise's pumpkin patch until the weigh-off.

Chapter Seventeen

hew, I'm glad that's over," Vera said, setting her
purse on the table in Agatha's large kitchen. "How about
a cup of tea?"

"Sounds good to me," Alice said. Agatha's kitchen
looked like one that might be seen in a popular home decorating magazine. The stainless steel appliances appeared
new. The combination of apricot and red décor as well as
the gold and tan granite countertops had to be recent. The
cupboards had pull-out shelves and dividers. "Jane would
love this kitchen. Is your aunt a gourmet cook?" she asked.

"Heavens no. I doubt she knows a spatula from a whisk.
She had a cook for years. From the food in her pantry, I'd
guess she eats out a lot, except for breakfast. She has her
traditional oatmeal, only I see she uses the instant variety
now." Vera filled a bright red electric teapot and turned it
on to heat.

"That kind of lifestyle must get expensive." Alice
couldn't imagine eating out meal after meal. The idea left
her cold. Although she enjoyed an occasional meal at a

restaurant, Alice would ordinarily prefer to share a meal with her sisters.

"She brings home a doggie bag of leftovers, so she gets two meals. Aunt Agatha is pretty frugal when it comes to spending money on herself, but she likes her home to be modern, and she doesn't need to worry about finances. She has more than she'll ever need."

"It looks like she redecorated the kitchen recently."

"No doubt," Vera said. "Every time I visit, something has changed. She loves variety and it keeps her occupied."

"Would she be up to more remodeling?"

"I suppose, but what's the point if she has to move?"

"What if she didn't have to move?"

"She'd love that, but how? What are you thinking?"

"Let's look around after we have our tea. A few changes might make this house elderly-friendly."

"All right. I feel so torn, between Aunt Agatha and Reggie, and trying to please them both. Reggie is the one who will be on hand. If Aunt Agatha needs something, she'll call him. Just because she's been independent doesn't mean she can remain that way."

"I know, but let's explore the possibility."

"Thank you, dear friend. You can't know how much your company cheers me."

Alice was glad she didn't have to make the final decisions.

Her father's sudden death had been a terrible shock, but perhaps the Lord had spared him from facing declining health and periods of pain. As a nurse, she could have cared for him at home to a point, but some things require the care available at a professional nursing home. She was grateful that she and her sisters had been spared making such difficult decisions and that their father had been spared the dependency.

Vera was eager to look around, so they carried their tea with them.

They tackled the main floor first. Off the kitchen were a large pantry lined with empty shelves, and a utility room with laundry appliances and a chest freezer. Off the hallway leading from the kitchen to the front door was a large, walk-in butler's closet. Inside were cleaning supplies and household supplies. "Did your aunt have a butler?"

"Yes, when I was little. I wasn't allowed in his closet, which made me curious. I was disappointed when I sneaked in here to see what he was hiding." She looked around, as if she thought she had missed some treasure all those years ago and it might still be there.

"What's on the other side of this closet?"

"My uncle's study. We'll have to go around to see it."

She led Alice to the front, then around the back side of the sweeping stairway. A doorway at the end of the hall opened to an office with dark, heavy mahogany furniture.

Floor-to-ceiling bookshelves lined one wall, and deep pigeonholes with rolled charts and maps lined part of another. A world globe sat on a library table. Vera pulled out a map. A puff of dust billowed up. She put it back without unrolling it. "What a fascinating room," Alice said "What's right above us?"

"I'm not sure. Let's go see."

They ascended the stairs. At the top, straight ahead, above where the closet and study would be, was a doorway.

Vera pushed open the door and they entered a luxurious dressing room with comfortable chairs and a wall of floor-to-ceiling mirrors. Another door went off to the back, which Vera explained led to a bathroom large enough to accommodate full skirts.

"Aunt Agatha calls this the Ladies' Necessary," she said, grinning. "I always thought it should have a brass plaque with that label on the door. When they entertained a hundred years ago, the women could come up here to fix their hair, repair their gowns and gossip." Vera set her mug of tea on a small table and sat in the low-back upholstered chair next to it. Alice sat in the chair on the other side of the table.

"Aunt Agatha held a ball here for the yacht club when I was in college." Vera looked around. "I remember all the ladies gathering, talking about who was dating whom and who'd broken up and how unsuitable some young lady's date was. I remember thinking it was a good thing that Fred hadn't come or they'd have been talking about him, which would have been highly unfair since they didn't know him as I did."

"Didn't you invite him?"

"Oh yes. I invited Fred to the ball, but he had to work. Silly me, I was upset that he didn't skip work so he could escort me to the ball. Then, when he didn't come, I compared him to the guys from my set. They were so sophisticated in their tuxedos. They had impeccable manners and talked about politics and yachts and international races."

"Somehow, I can't picture Fred hobnobbing with the yachting crowd," Alice said. She couldn't picture Vera as a social butterfly, either. Her friend was down-to-earth and completely without guile or pretensions.

"He hated it. Fortunately, he liked me enough to put up with my friends." Vera sighed. "Up to a point, anyway. I almost lost him because of my social set."

"That's hard to believe. Fred wouldn't judge you for your friends," Alice said.

"You're right. He didn't judge me. I judged him."

"Surely not. I've never known you to judge anyone," Alice said. She looked around the powder room, trying to picture Vera as a young woman, all dressed up, surrounded by socialites in beautiful gowns.

"To get back to your aunt and the house, what do you think she'd say to taking out part of this room?"

"Are you thinking we could install an elevator here?"

"Exactly. I've known families who have done that. They make small lifts for homes. They aren't cheap, but it would pay for itself in a matter of months, considering what your aunt would pay at an assisted living center. She'd need to have a live-in companion. The nurse at the rehab center—the one who's so fond of your aunt—might be interested in such a position. Agatha wouldn't need constant attention, but she'd need help with bathing, getting in that big bed of hers and generally having someone around in case she needed help. I have a feeling that if she thought she could come home when she's more mobile, she'd start getting better quickly."

"It'd be worth checking out. Where would I begin?"

"We could look for elevator companies. It would help if we had a computer to look on the Internet."

"Reggie has one in his office. I'll ask him if I can use it. Oh, I hope this'll work. What else would we need to do?"

"We can make a list of all the changes you'd need to make. I think I'd find out about the possibilities before you mention anything to Agatha."

"Yes, of course. I won't say a word. We mustn't tell Reggie either. I can't wait to start. First thing in the morning."

"There, that's the last of them," Louise said, putting a swirl of buttercream frosting on a pumpkin spice cookie Tuesday morning. She handed it to Jane, who piped the outline of a pumpkin on top of the cookie.

Jane arranged the cookies on a large round platter. "I hope the children like these. Maybe it will give them a taste for pumpkins."

"Beautiful," Louise pronounced. "I predict they'll love them."

"Now to get the garden ready." Jane removed her apron and washed her hands. "Let's go put up the corn stalks."

"I'm right behind you," Louise said, tying a blue paisley bandanna around her neck. "How do I look?"

Jane gave her a once over. Louise had worn her only pair of jeans and a flannel shirt, and that she'd borrowed from Jane. "You look like you're ready for Halloween," Jane teased.

"It was your idea to dress like farmers for the school-children."

"Yes, and you have on the right clothes. Maybe after we roll around in the corn stalks, you'll look more the part."

"No thank you. I'll let you do that."

Louise thought about feeding the pumpkins, then decided that would have to wait. The children were due to arrive within the hour, and she wouldn't have time to uncover the pumpkins and feed them.

Jane handed her a couple of small pumpkins. Then she piled colorful dried gourds and Indian corn in a basket, which they carried out to the garden.

"Somehow, this seems backward. First we carried all this in and now we're bringing it back out," Louise said.

"Yes, but it'll look terrific for the children," Jane responded.

Sam Bellwood had left a pile of cut, dry corn stalks by the garden gate. Jane brought gardening gloves and twine from the shed. They sorted through the pile, separating the stalks into piles.

"If we use six per bundle, we'll have enough for two corn shocks by the garden and several for the front yard," Jane said.

Louise held the stalks together while Jane tied twine around the middle. When they had two shocks ready, they arranged the bottoms of the bundles so that they'd stand against the fence on each side of the garden gate. They piled the small pumpkins, winter squash, bright yellow, green and red gourds and multicolored dried corn beneath the shocks. Louise had to admit, it made the garden look festive. After they'd harvested most of the produce, the garden looked abandoned except for her pumpkins and Jane's flowers.

"Let's move the rest of the corn stalks, so the children don't destroy them," Jane suggested.

"Good idea." Louise grabbed a handful and carried

them around to the shed. Jane followed with the remaining stalks.

They'd just finished when a school bus pulled up to the curb in front of the inn. High pitched squeals and laughter erupted into the midmorning air.

"Everyone line up single file," a teacher ordered.

"Are we ready?" Louise asked.

Jane looked at Louise, then down at her clothes. She grinned. "Yup, and now we really look like farmers."

Louise looked down at her shirt and jeans. Bits of dry corn shucks clung to her clothes. She tried to brush them off, but they wouldn't budge. Jane's clothes were covered too. She reached up and pulled a piece of dry corn silk from Jane's hair. "We look like a couple of hayseeds," she joked.

A line snaked its way around the driveway toward them. A teacher led the way, with three helpers herding what looked like a group of lively jumping beans.

"Hi, Mrs. Smith," a youthful voice yelled. Bill Green was a kindergartner and one of Louise's beginning piano students.

"Hello, Mrs. Smith," Mandy Gardner, another of Louise's five-year-old piano students, called and waved. She grinned and showed a gap where her front tooth had come out. Her twin sister waved too. When she laughed at something, she showed an identical gap.

"Hello," Louise called back, but she didn't want to contribute to a disturbance. Jane had gone to speak with the teacher in charge. Louise didn't recognize her, which surprised her. She thought she knew most of the school staff. She went over to join them.

"We have snacks for the children and they can play games on the lawn while we take small groups into the garden," Jane said.

"Perfect. How many children can go into the garden at a time?"

Jane looked at Louise. She raised an eyebrow. "Five or six? How many children are with you?"

"We have twenty-nine."

They divided the children into five groups. The parent chaperones started a game of Duck, Duck, Goose, while the teacher accompanied Jane and Louise and six kindergartners into the garden. They lined up along the path, standing before the covered cage.

Louise took one side of the blankets and tarp and Jane took the other. Together, they lifted and pulled the covering back, revealing the giant pumpkin.

"Wow! I can't believe it!" a little boy burst out. He put his thumbs and forefingers together to make circles and stared through them as if they were binoculars. Louise and Jane exchanged amused glances.

"*That's* a pumpkin?" another child exclaimed. "Are you going to make a jack-o'-lantern with it?"

"Probably not. It's too big," Louise said.

"Sure is. It's so big it would cave in," Bill Green said sagely. "That happened to my friend last year. Just went *shmoosh*," he said, making a face and smacking his hands together to emphasize his point.

"Can I sit on top of it and get my picture taken?" a little, dark-haired beauty asked. She gave them a toothy smile, as if already posing.

"I'm sorry, but no one can sit on it. It's still growing and it's not that strong."

A woman stood off to one side, holding a camera. "You can stand there and I'll take your picture," she told the child. To Louise she said, "I thought I'd take all of the children's pictures, if you don't mind."

"Not at all," Louise said.

One by one, the children posed next to the wood-and-mesh cage while the woman took pictures. She wanted the children posed just so, but the children were getting restless, so Jane stepped in to speed up things.

Out on the lawn, the other parents had their hands full with exuberant children running, shouting, pushing and yelling.

After the first group filed out, before the second group

entered the garden, Jane had all the children sit down on the grass, then she got the treats and passed around pumpkin cookies and small cups of apple cider. For a few minutes, the children were subdued as they ate their snacks. On cue from their teacher, a chorus of *thank-you*'s arose and grew louder and louder, as if someone had a volume controller and was raising the sound. The children were laughing and shouting and having a great time hearing their own voices.

Louise said a silent thank-you to the Lord for sending the raccoons to the garden. Because of them, the pumpkins got cages and were safe and protected from nighttime visitors, frost and rambunctious children.

Chapter Eighteen

Sounds of power saws, sanders and nail guns echoed and reverberated off the metal building and the cove in the warm, clear air. The marina looked deserted, but the boat-yard was a busy place at ten o'clock Tuesday morning. Alice followed Vera up a set of outside stairs at the rear of the long, tall building. At the top of the stairs, she opened a door leading into a small, dim hall. Vera knocked on the second door.

"Come in," they heard. Vera opened the door and poked her head inside.

"Morning. Are you busy? I was wondering if I could use your computer for a little while to go on the Internet?"

"Morning, Vera, Alice. Sure. Come on in." Reggie stood and moved from behind his desk. "Did you get over to the nursing home?" he asked.

"I wouldn't call it a nursing home, but yes, we visited there yesterday," Vera said. "If that's what you're calling it, no wonder Aunt Agatha is so upset."

Reggie winced. "I'm afraid I hadn't thought of that," he said. "I'd call it a five-star resort if it would make her happier. So what did you think?"

"It's a lovely facility. The campus is larger than I expected, but the assisted living apartments are small."

"I'm not sure what constitutes big enough. She doesn't use most of that mausoleum she calls home now."

Reggie was right about Agatha's house. Most of it was covered in cloth. Still, Alice understood the older woman's desire to live in her own home, where she was surrounded by familiar rooms, furnishings and memories.

"What we need and what we cherish aren't necessarily the same thing, Reggie. At least not to a woman," Vera said.

Reggie shook his head. "Bunch of sentimental mush, if you ask me. You know how to get your mail?"

"Yes."

"Good." He smoothed his hair back and put on a baseball cap. "I'll be down at the dry dock if you need me. Just leave the computer running when you're finished."

"Thanks."

"No problem. If you want to wait around, I'll take you to lunch at the yacht club."

"We can't, but thanks for the offer. We have things to do."

"Suit yourself." Reggie left them alone.

"Pull up a chair, so we can look together," Vera said.

They searched and found a nearby company that sold and installed home elevators. They also found a local company that serviced local shut-ins with supplies. Agatha would be able to get meals delivered, a visiting healthcare aide and eldercare transportation to wherever she needed to go. By the time they finished searching, Vera had a long list of numbers to call for information and help.

As they drove out past the yacht club, Vera didn't even glance toward the wonderful, fanciful building. She drove into town and parked downtown in front of a medical supply store.

"I thought we could check here first, then find someplace for lunch."

"Fine with me," Alice said. She wondered if Vera was avoiding her cousin or the house in which she'd grown up. Alice was sure Vera had enjoyed showing her around Agatha's house, but she hadn't displayed any interest in her own childhood home.

"Hello. I'd like some information about home healthcare options," Vera told the young female clerk.

"Sure. Let me get Lennie to talk to you." She turned and called through a doorway to the back, "Dad, could you come up front please?"

A tall, slender man with sandy-blond hair appeared. He was smiling. When he saw Vera, his smile faltered. "Vera Jamison?"

"Hi, Lennie. I didn't expect to see you here. How are you?"

"Good, good. And you?" He stared at Vera as if seeing a ghost. "You look great."

Vera smiled. "Thanks. So do you. And this lovely young lady is your daughter?"

He glanced at his daughter, who was entering data in a computer. "Oh. Yeah. That's Zoe." His daughter nodded and smiled at the visitors. "Come on back to my office," he said, opening the door for them.

Vera introduced Alice and explained to her that she'd known Lennie since high school. He offered them chairs and coffee. They declined the drinks, but sat down. He leaned against his desk to talk to them.

"You still married to ... a ... Fred, wasn't it?"

"Yes. We still live in Acorn Hill."

"Wow. I'm single at the moment. For the third time." He shrugged. "Just can't seem to settle down. How long have you been in town?"

"We got here Saturday night. I'm here to help decide how to care for my Aunt Agatha. She broke her hip a month ago and is having a hard time recovering."

"That's too bad. You moving her into Briarhurst?"

"Not if I can help it. That's why I'm here. To see what's available so she can live at home."

"That can be a tough way to go. She'll need lots of care. Are you moving back here, by chance?"

"No. We'd have to find a live-in companion."

He shook his head. "That usually doesn't work out. It's hard to get good long-term help, you know. I can recommend a homecare agency. She could have someone come by daily to help her, but she'd still be living alone. Is she still at the big place next to the yacht club?"

"Yes. We'd have to make some changes, like installing an elevator."

"That would help, and we can supply lift chairs, scooters, portable potty chairs, bath stools, walkers and all kinds of aids to make homecare easier. Here's a brochure of available resources around Shelton Cove. We have a fairly large retirement population, so there are options if she decides to stay at home." He paused and looked at Vera. "Just between you and me, I wouldn't recommend keeping her at home. Not unless you want to move in with her to care for her. If you do that, I'll be happy to help you all I can."

Vera stood. "Thanks, Lennie. You've given me a lot to think about." She held up the brochure he'd given her. "I'll read through this."

He pushed away from the desk and stood, looking down at Vera, who was several inches shorter than he. "Let me give you my cell phone number, just in case you have any questions." He took a card out of his pocket and scrawled a number on the back of it, then handed it to her.

"Thanks." She took the card and slipped it into her purse.

Lennie walked them to the front of the store. He glanced at Alice, then back at Vera. "Would you like to go to dinner while you're here, just for old time's sake?"

"We won't be here long," Vera said. She smiled and said good-bye and reached for the doorknob.

"Don't hesitate to call me anytime, night or day," he told her. "I know a lot of people. I can help you with your aunt."

Vera smiled and said good-bye, then sailed out the door. Alice got the impression she couldn't leave soon enough.

"Old boyfriend?" Alice asked after they got into the car.

"Not really. We went to school together. He asked me out, but I never accepted. Lennie thinks he's a lady's man, which is probably why he's been married several times."

Vera drove through town, then turned south. She continued for a few miles until they crossed a bridge over a tributary. "I saw this place from the boat Sunday. It used to have good food. We can stop there for lunch."

Alice didn't say anything, but she thought it interesting that Vera seemed to be avoiding places where she might run into old acquaintances or reminders of her past.

Jane removed the last jar of Italian-spiced, stewed tomatoes from the canner and turned it upside down on a towel on the counter. That made three-dozen jars, half in quart sizes and half in pint jars. That would get them through the winter with a few jars to spare. She set aside some pints to give away. They were just the right size for a meal for two people.

Removing the canner from the stove, she was pouring

the scalding water into the sink when someone knocked on the back door. The steam from the water made it hard to see.

"Come in," Jane called, setting the empty pot on the counter. She pushed wisps of damp hair back off her forehead with her sleeve and removed her hot pad mitts.

"It's me," Ethel said, stepping into the kitchen. She had an envelope in her hand. "Oh my, you've been busy."

"Yes, and I have some jars for you to take home."

"Wonderful. And I have something for you," she said, holding up the envelope, which looked thick. Jane couldn't imagine what was in it, but Ethel looked particularly pleased.

"I was just going to take a break and have a cup of coffee. Would you like to join me?"

"Yes, thank you. I don't suppose you have a little something to go with it. I've been so busy, I missed breakfast this morning."

"Auntie, you mustn't skip meals. That's not good for you."

She dismissed Jane's concern with a wave of her hand. "I had a piece of whole wheat toast with peanut butter, but that was early."

"I have just the thing," Jane said, putting a large slice of oatmeal-apple strudel on a plate. "If you'll get a couple of mugs, I'll pour our coffee."

Ethel slipped the envelope in her pocket and took two mugs out of the cupboard and set them on the table, then sat and waited for Jane.

"Louise's pumpkin is causing quite a stir, isn't it?" she said after Jane sat down.

"It certainly is, and she's been helping me in the garden. That's why I have all the canned tomatoes. Since Sunday, Louise and I have put up chutney, salsa, marinara sauce and these stewed tomatoes. I've made relish and I still have green tomatoes ripening in the basement."

"That hasn't left you much time for this race you're training for, has it?"

"I've been able to get out and run almost every day. I'm not doing as much fund-raising as I'd like, which is too bad. It's such a worthy cause. I can't feel too upset, though. People are giving, just not through me."

"Well, I knew you were busy with guests and curiosity seekers, so I took it upon myself to campaign for you." Ethel pulled out the envelope. "Lloyd helped me. We went around City Hall. Then I contacted folks in the surrounding towns, and I even went to Potterston and to the hospital. I knew Alice would have helped if she could, but she's gone, so I stepped in. Here. Open it," she said, passing the envelope to Jane.

Jane accepted the envelope. It was sealed. Jane opened the envelope and pulled out a wad of money and papers. "What is this?" she asked, giving her aunt a questioning look. She opened one of the papers. On it, Lloyd had pledged to sponsor her for the Harvest Run. She opened a second one. It was a pledge from Bella Paoli, Lloyd's secretary.

There were more. Cash folded in a piece of paper had a note from the police department. A pledge from Justine and Josie Gilmore with a note that they'd be rooting for her at the finish line brought a lump to Jane's throat. She blinked, surprised that the gesture from her aunt and her friends had affected her so much. She didn't consider herself sentimental, but this genuinely moved her.

"Thank you, Aunt Ethel," she said, smiling at her aunt. "I don't know what to say. I'm touched and grateful for all the support."

"It's the least I can do, since I'm not up to running the race myself. Besides, I like fund-raising. I'm good at it. So you do the running and I'll do the asking. Besides, I heard the track team was trying to drum up support around town. That makes it hard for you, because everyone wants to encourage them, but you need encouragement too."

"I just got a big dose of it. I'd better train a little harder, so I can give all these sponsors a real run for their money."

"You just do the best you can. That's all anyone can do."

"Thanks, Aunt Ethel. I'll give it my best. Will you hang on to this for me and keep track of it?"

Ethel smiled proudly. "I'll be happy to manage your pledges. Anything else I can do to help you?"

"There's one more thing you can do, if you would."

"Certainly. What is it?"

"You can take a plate of goodies to City Hall as a

thank-you. And I'll make a plate just for you," Jane said, standing. "Such generosity deserves a treat."

"I know you know these verses by heart, Mrs. Agatha, because you quoted them to me fifteen years ago. I listened to you. Now you listen to me. The apostle Paul says you've got to get up out of that bed and get moving."

Alice and Vera heard the voice scolding Agatha as they neared her room. They stopped outside her door to listen.

"You got me up and moving when I was ready to quit," the voice continued. "Now it's your turn. Listen to what Hebrews 12:1–3 says. You even have it marked here in your Bible. 'Therefore, since we are surrounded by such a great cloud of witnesses, let us throw off everything that hinders and the sin that so easily entangles, and let us run with perseverance the race marked out for us. Let us fix our eyes on Jesus, the author and perfecter of our faith, who for the joy set before him endured the cross, scorning its shame, and sat down at the right hand of the throne of God. Consider him who endured such opposition from sinful men, so that you will not grow weary and lose heart.' Now I gotta tell you, I see you lying here helpless 'cause you've lost heart. Are you going to let Mr. Reginald get his way? Not if you're the same Mrs. Agatha that helped me see the light."

The door opened and Olivia Martino stepped out

carrying Agatha's old Bible. She nearly ran into Vera. She stopped and blushed.

"I'm sorry. I wasn't looking," she said. "And I didn't mean to jump all over your aunt, but I feel so frustrated."

Vera put her finger to her lips. "Shhh. Come here," she said quietly. She walked down the hallway to a small alcove with chairs.

"So what was all that about?" Vera asked.

"I lost my patience and scolded her. Your aunt just won't listen to reason. It's like she's given up. She's always been so strong for everybody else, I can't stand seeing her the way she is now. Today is my last day. I won't be here to watch over her, and I'm just afraid Mr. Reggie is going to put her away. He's a good man, mind you, but he can't take care of her."

"Could you?" Vera asked. "I mean if you had the right equipment and a place to do it, could you handle her?"

"I . . . well, I suppose I could. Yes. There's nothing wrong with her that some good nutrition and a dash of hope wouldn't cure. I don't know about that house of hers, though. It's so big, and all the stairs and everything. Course, I've spent little time anywhere but the kitchen."

"You said you want to do some home nursing. What if you just had one patient? It'd mean you'd have to live with her. Would you be willing to come by and talk to me about her future?"

"Yes," she blurted out. Her eyes misted up. "You don't

know how I've been praying for the Lord to show me what He wants me to do."

"It might not work out," Vera said. "I probably shouldn't have said anything yet, but I don't have much time."

"Are you going to tell Mrs. Agatha now?"

"No. In fact, I think we'll let her alone for a while. You've given her a lot to think about. Let's keep this just among Alice, you and me for now. But keep praying. We need the Lord's blessing if this is going to work out."

"My knees will be raw from praying," Olivia said. "When can I come?"

"How about this evening, around seven? We're staying at my aunt's house."

"Seven's fine. Thank you. I knew you were an angel coming to answer my prayers when I saw you brushing her hair. Now I'd better get back to work. I still have five hours before I retire." Olivia stood and hurried away.

"Well, what do you think?" Vera asked Alice as they watched the nurse leave.

"She loves your aunt and she feels as though she's ordained to help her. With her experience and her faith, that's compelling. I just hope I haven't suggested something that can't happen. I'd hate to see your aunt have to give up her home and have her friend disappointed."

"I feel the same," Vera said. "Let's go see if we can open some doors."

Chapter Nineteen

*Y*our aunt's pans look brand-new," Alice said that evening as she poured beaten eggs into a frying pan.

"I can understand that. With the yacht club dining room next door and the country club up the street, she probably doesn't use them. She'd rather swing a hammer at the boatworks than cook a meal, although I doubt she's done either recently."

They heard rapid knocking on the side door. Vera went out to see who was there.

"Reggie, come in."

"What in thunderation do you think you're doing?" he asked, his voice loud enough to be heard next door.

"I have no idea what you mean, but come into the kitchen. We did some food shopping and we're just fixing a bite to eat. Will you join us?"

"I . . . I came to . . . oh, what's the use. Yeah, I'll join you. We need to talk."

Vera appeared in the doorway, Reggie behind her, towering over her. He removed his baseball cap and scratched his head.

"Alice, Reggie's going to join us for dinner. Could you add a few eggs and more ham to the pan?"

"Sure. Hi, Reggie."

"Evening, Alice." He turned a kitchen chair around and straddled it. "Hope I'm not putting you to any trouble."

"No trouble at all, as long as you don't mind breakfast for dinner." She flipped the sliced potatoes, onions and sweet peppers that were frying in a separate pan.

"Smells good."

"This is one of my sister's easier frittatas."

Vera popped four slices of artisan bread from the local bakery into the toaster.

"So what did you want to talk to me about?" Vera asked her cousin.

"I talked to Barney Johnson, from Briarhurst. He said you weren't impressed with their facility."

"I didn't say that. I simply thought the apartment he showed us was awfully small." Vera turned to face her cousin and leaned against the counter. "Honestly, Reggie, can you see Aunt Agatha living in that tiny place? Have you ever seen her bedroom set? That alone would take up the entire apartment."

"Can't say I have. I rarely go upstairs in this museum."

"Then you need a tour. Maybe you'll get a better idea of what we're asking her to give up. We'll take you after we eat."

Reggie frowned, clearly not pleased with this turn of events.

Alice cooked the eggs and added the potato mixture, ham, diced tomatoes and grated cheese. Vera buttered the toast, and they served the simple meal with a green salad and fresh apple cider.

Vera said a prayer, thanking the Lord for their meal. Reggie bowed his head with them, but Alice got the impression he wasn't used to praying.

"One of my favorite parts of fall," Vera said, raising her glass. "We stopped at the cider mill. I couldn't believe it's still there. I haven't been there in twenty-five years. Its cider is every bit as good as I remember."

"They're still using the old steam engine to run the press," Reggie said. He swallowed his cider in two or three gulps. "Got any more?"

Vera took a jug out of the refrigerator. "If we have any left over, I'll take some to Aunt Agatha tomorrow."

"I saw her this afternoon," Reggie said. "She wasn't happy to see me, but she looks better. Got more color, I think."

"Good. Olivia Martino's been encouraging her. You remember Olivia?"

"Yes, I still see her around. I apprenticed under her husband. She used to stop by with his lunch. She made a mean Italian-sausage grinder. Best I ever had. She'd bring two, so I could have one."

"She's coming by here in an hour. Maybe we'll hold off

on the tour until then. She's retiring, you know? In fact, today was her last day."

"I can't imagine her sitting around doing nothing. She's too industrious for that," Reggie said.

"Exactly. She's looking for homecare work. She adores Aunt Agatha, you know."

"Yeah. Aunt Agatha and Uncle George took good care of the Martinos. Course, the Martinos were good to them too."

"I might as well tell you before Olivia gets here: I'm checking out options that would allow Aunt Agatha to stay in her own home."

"Here? She can't take care of this place. She can't even get around in it."

"Not the way it is, but with a few changes she might be just fine. Especially if she has a live-in companion who's an experienced caregiver."

"Olivia?"

"Precisely. She could take care of the house as well as provide care for Agatha. In addition, there are agencies that supply equipment for handicapped people. We can get lift chairs, walkers, wheelchairs, all kinds of equipment. If the doctor prescribes it, we can even get help from her insurance and Medicare." Vera looked at Alice. "I told you Alice is a nurse. She's had some experience with elderly people. She thinks it's feasible."

Reggie frowned. "What would it take?"

"The most important step would be installing a home lift or a small elevator and handrails in bathrooms—that sort of thing. Although one of the rooms on the main floor could be converted into a bedroom, a lift would enable her to stay in her own room, where she's most comfortable."

"I suppose you have an idea where you'd do this?" Reggie asked.

"We were looking at the butler's closet and part of the study. They're back to back, and there's a large powder room upstairs. We didn't check out the third floor."

"Somehow, this all sounds like work for me," he said.

"We can hire a contractor. I found a company where we can get a nice elevator and they can have one available within a few days."

Reggie sighed. "Assuming all this is possible, I suppose I could spare several guys to do the labor. We don't have a current contract. I have a couple of refits coming in next month, but we're slow right now."

Vera grinned. "I think it's possible, but you'd know better than I would."

"You haven't told Aunt Agatha any of this, have you?"

"No. I don't want to get her hopes up if it won't work out."

"All right. We'll see." He finished his supper. "You got anything for dessert?" he asked.

"As a matter of fact..." Vera got up and took their plates to the sink. "I bought an apple pie and a slab of sharp cheddar cheese at the cider mill. We'll save it until Olivia comes." Vera put a kettle of water on to boil.

"Don't suppose you have coffee."

"Sorry. You can have a cup of tea with us or a glass of milk."

Reggie made a face. "Guess I can settle for a glass of milk. Might have to have two pieces of that pie, though."

"If it will put you in an agreeable mood, you can have half of the pie," Vera said.

Reggie nodded. "I just might go for that."

Vera smiled. "You're a good man, Reggie Jamison."

"Don't know about that, but I never could win an argument with you or Aunt Agatha. Teaming up the two of you isn't fair. Can't say I always agree with you, but I have to admit, you've been right before. Like when you rejected Gerald Weatherwax. I never told you, but I'm glad you didn't listen to me all those years ago. Weatherwax got disbarred, you know. I don't know what he's doing now, but he was involved with a bunch of shady schemes over the years." Reggie shook his head.

"I never seriously considered Gerald. He was your idea."

"Not one of my better ones. He seemed like an all right guy. His dad was our lawyer. They had big plans for Gerald going into politics. He was keen on you, you know. Begged me for an introduction." Reggie shrugged. "You'd brought Fred to one party and I could see he wouldn't do, or so I thought. I figured you needed to date someone from our own set. Then you broke up with Fred and got engaged to Derrick, and everyone was happy about that. Your dad was ready to bring him into the shipbuilding business. I figured we'd end up being partners some day. I couldn't believe you'd just walk away and give all this up. You'd own half the business now if you'd stayed."

"But I do own half a business—a hardware business with Fred," she said. "I don't expect you to understand, but truly, my cup runneth over."

"I'm glad," he said. "I keep busy, but it gets lonely. Maybe it'd be a good thing to have Aunt Agatha nearby. I need a good argument with her once in a while to keep my blood pumping."

"I talked to Mrs. Agatha before I left today," Olivia said as they climbed the stairs to the second floor of Agatha's house. "She told me I'd better come visit her every week or she'd send Mr. Reggie after me."

"She did, huh?" Reggie said. "Sounds like she's feeling feisty this afternoon. I saw her too. I thought she looked better."

"Maybe your scolding worked," Vera said to Olivia.

"Oh dear. I hope so. I felt so guilty after I was so bossy to her," Olivia said.

"Bossy? You? I don't believe it," Reggie said.

"But I was."

"You spoke the truth to her," Alice said. "Sometimes the truth is hard to hear, but it's good for us. Especially if we take it to heart."

"What do you think of this idea of having her come back here, Olivia?" Reggie asked.

"I think it would be better than putting her in a home. I know Briarhurst is a nice place. I went out there and applied for a job. They take good care of people and treat them with respect. They wanted me to work the night shift, though, and I didn't want to be out driving at night."

"If you took care of Agatha, it'd be around-the-clock care," Alice said. "That could be restricting."

"She'd never let me coddle her. If I ever needed help, I know lots of trained people I could get to fill in, but I don't expect I'd need it. Mrs. Agatha's a fighter. Soon as she gets the idea she might be able to come home, she'll get better real fast. And we get along real good, she and I."

They rounded the top of the stairs and Vera led them to Agatha's room.

"Are you ready for this?" Vera asked. She opened the

door and flipped on the light, then stood back and let Olivia and Reggie enter.

"Oh my." Olivia chuckled. "Yup. That's my Mrs. Agatha. Put her in this room and she'll be up dancing a jig in no time."

"If that doesn't beat all," Reggie said, standing in the middle of the room, turning around and around. "I should have figured. She always argued with me about decorating the yachts we built. She wanted bright colors. I guess I can see why. How in the world did Uncle George ever sleep in here?"

The three women laughed at Reggie's question.

"You're right about her furniture, Vera. All this really wouldn't fit in that apartment at Briarhurst."

"Then you'll help me fix up this place for her?"

"I'm probably crazy, but let's see if it's feasible. If . . . if you're willing to go to work for our aunt," Reggie said, looking at Olivia, "we'd have to make up a contract. Then we'd have to figure out Aunt Agatha's finances, so we can maintain this place. She's got the money, though."

"We can set up a trust fund or something," Vera suggested.

"Well, we can talk more about that later. Okay? Now perhaps you'll show me where you want to put the elevator."

Vera took him to see the *Ladies' Necessary*, then downstairs to the study.

"This place offers some engineering challenges," he

said. "I think we could put an elevator here, though. It could open to the hallway."

"This is wonderful," Olivia said. "I can make some of the rooms into activity rooms for Mrs. Agatha, and the enclosed porch is perfect for her to get some sun in the wintertime. We can put plants there to make it cheerful. Maybe she'd enjoy doing some scrapbooking with me."

"She could put together a history of the family and the boatyard," Vera said. "She knows more about it than anyone else."

"I'd like to move all these charts to the yacht club," Reggie said, opening an old one. "This goes back to the early 1900s. Maybe we could create a chart room in one of the rooms there."

"Grandfather had a chart room," Vera said. "Sometimes I hid there to get out of sitting with a bunch of ladies having tea."

"How long has it been since you've been in the house?" Reggie asked.

"Not since Mom and Dad moved out." Vera shrugged. "No reason to go in there."

"I remember exploring the towers when we were kids. The yacht club doesn't use the whole house. Would you take me through the old place? We might be able to utilize more of it."

Vera shrugged as if it didn't matter to her. "I suppose, if there's time."

"I've got time. You don't leave until Sunday, right? How about Friday."

Vera hesitated for a moment. "All right," she said. "I guess I can do that."

Wednesday morning was perfect. Something about the angle of the sun and the crisp, early morning air gave clarity to the brilliant colors surrounding Fairy Pond. Jane tried several different locations for her easel until she found a spot with a view of the pond with rocks and branches reflected in the water, and several wrens enjoying a morning bath. Getting out her acrylic paints, she blended her background colors and began spreading paint with a palette knife over the canvas. At home, she often painted with oil paints, loving the depth and richness they created, but today she wanted to capture the scene in one sitting, without having to wait for layers to dry.

Concentrating, she blocked the outside world from her thoughts. She loved the sense of isolation that came with painting a scene. The narrow view and her canvas became the entire world for a brief time, and she could pour her heart and soul into capturing a moment in time, apart from the bustle and problems of life. As she applied color upon color, the richness and variety of God's creation amazed her anew.

A sudden noise sent the robins flying as the canopy of trees and the water magnified the sound of pounding footfalls. A lone figure broke into the scene, a jogger in running shorts and a T-shirt. Jane could hear his breath heave as his arms and legs moved in harmony. Peace and stillness shattered by sound and action.

As the runner exited her scene, another jogger came into view. Suddenly, in her mind's eye, she saw the race. Dozens of racers in colorful shorts and sweat suits and a variety of clothing would run and walk through her scene.

Mixing a new batch of flesh color, Jane added vertical lines and angles, sharp and straight—motion against the backdrop of languid lines and the smooth blues and purples of the water and soft, warm greens, yellows and hints of red in the trees and bushes.

She worked quickly, dabbing and slashing and swirling the paint onto the canvas, trying to capture as much from the vision in her mind as from the scene in front of her eyes. Finally, she sat back and looked with a critical eye at the finished painting. The total effect made her smile. Not a masterpiece, perhaps, but the sensations of peace and disruption, stillness and action were there, just the way she'd seen and felt them. She'd painted Fairy Pond many times, in every season. This painting might become her favorite.

Glancing at her watch, she realized the morning had slipped away from her. In a few hours, she would be the figure breaking the silence of Fairy Pond, along with Eleanor Renda and perhaps the entire high school cross-country team. She packed up her paints and headed home.

Chapter Twenty

*A*lice and Vera were ready to leave Agatha's house Wednesday morning when Reggie arrived with a full team of tanned, rugged-looking men in jeans and T-shirts. Some were unshaven and had tattoos adorning their arms. Alice thought they'd look intimidating if Reggie weren't leading them.

"We want to see if your renovations are possible," Reggie said. "You showed me where the elevator might go, but take us through everything you have in mind so we can look at structural issues. We might as well get a full list of what's needed. Then we can decide which supplies we'd need and whether we can do it."

Vera took the men to the butler's closet in the hallway.

They measured and tapped on walls, talking about studs and sixteen-inch centers and rough-cut lumber. Alice and Vera listened as they discussed the original materials, which were not the standard sizes available now, and whether they would need to add weight-bearing beams and all manner of terminology foreign to Alice.

They descended to the dark, cold basement. In the dim light of a bare bulb, they measured some more and checked floor joists. The scruffiest of the men rattled off codes and mathematical equations that meant nothing to Alice. Vera was listening intently. "Do you understand what they're saying?" Alice asked.

Vera shook her head. "Not really, but it sounds impressive, as though they know what they're doing. Considering the boats they've built, I'd trust them to do the job right."

One of the men suggested a system of ramps to get into the house. They decided to go with a more expensive elevator than the one the women had discussed. The new one would go from the basement all the way to the third floor.

"All right. We'll estimate everything, then see how much we can do. I know moving her into Briarhurst would be expensive, but her house could be sold if necessary," Reggie said.

"She'd hate that. See what you come up with."

Reggie closed his notebook. "Give me the number of the elevator company. I should have a rough estimate by tomorrow morning. We'll talk some more then."

"Good. I'd love to have this settled before I have to leave, one way or the other. I don't know how much longer they'll keep her in the nursing facility."

Vera gave Reggie the phone number. Then he and his crew left. Vera looked at Alice.

"I feel like I've been through the ringer. What if this can't work?"

"At least your cousin is agreeable to trying. Don't borrow trouble," Alice said. "Wait and see what he can do."

Vera nodded. "I don't want to disappoint Aunt Agatha. I know I'd hate it if someone insisted I had to move out of my home."

Agatha was sitting in a chair, dressed in her bright red-and-purple caftan. She had on a pair of lavender slip-on shoes. Her hair was combed, although the back stuck up from lying on it. Her lipstick covered more than her mouth, her eyebrows peaked like two tepees and she was frowning like a thundercloud.

"Aunt Agatha, you look beautiful!" Vera said, smiling delightedly.

"You look lovely, Agatha," Alice echoed. "Do you feel better?"

"I suppose," she said, but her glower said otherwise.

"What's wrong?"

"I'm so mad I could just spit nails," she said. "Poor Lillian. Her son told her she couldn't go home, even to make sure they pack her things properly. He wants to have an estate sale and get rid of everything. She collected fine porcelain vases from all over the world and he wants to sell them off, just like that," she said, trying to snap her fingers.

"What does Lillian say?" Vera asked.

"She tried to talk to him, but he won't listen. What can she say? She's helpless. She's been crying all morning. I hate it," Agatha said. "Lillian and her husband used to go cruising with George and me. We went up the coast to Maine and Prince Edward Island before George died. Her husband died the next year. She and I took a cruise to Greece a year later, to honor our husbands. They loved the sea, you know."

"I know," Vera said.

"Her husband would take that boy of theirs to task, let me tell you. He wouldn't put up with this. Neither would George."

Vera took a deep breath. Alice could see she was holding back, wanting to say something about her plans, but knowing it was too soon. She gave Alice a helpless look.

"I'm sorry, Aunt Agatha. I wish there was something I could do."

Agatha gave Vera a sad, resigned smile and patted her hand. "I know, dear. I know. I've been praying. I don't know how the Lord can make this better, but I just know He can. If you would, you can pray for my friend too."

"I will. I definitely will."

Jane was out on the lawn stretching, one leg extended back as far as it would go, when Eleanor pulled up, parked at the curb and got out. The track coach was dressed in a navy blue workout suit. She still had a whistle hanging around her neck. She opened the back of her car and shed her cover-up suit down to running shorts and a sports top.

"Hi," she said, shutting the door and turning around. "Ready to run?"

"Yes. Do you want to stretch out first?"

"I just did stretches with the kids." She did a couple of twists and leg extensions. "I should be good to go."

Jane straightened, bounced on the balls of her feet a couple of times, then nodded. "Up or down?"

"Let's start up and see how fast we can take the hill. Ready?"

This woman meant business. Jane got into a starting position. "Ready."

"Go." Eleanor took off like a shot. Jane ran after her, giving it her all. She was amazed to pass Eleanor on the last stretch of the hill and top it just a hair ahead of the track coach. She slowed to a medium pace.

"Good run," Eleanor said, catching up. "Let's see if we can keep a nice pace." She accelerated slightly, but nothing like the initial push.

Jane caught her easily and set her pace to match, step for step. They ran in silence for half a mile. Jane's ponytail swung side to side. Eleanor's short hair bobbed slightly. For a few seconds, Jane considered cutting her own hair, but then discarded that idea. The race would only last a short time. It would take years to grow back her hair.

"You've got a good sprint, especially uphill. Can you sustain it?" Eleanor asked.

"Not at this pace," Jane said, glancing over at her partner. Eleanor didn't even look winded.

"What's your goal for this race?"

"To finish?" Jane said, half joking. "I just want to do my best. They're expecting contestants who run marathons all the time. I haven't run a race since high school."

"But you walk and jog regularly, so you're in training all the time. I teach others how to train, but I don't do much of it myself. I do laps on the school track every day. That's only part of a good training regime. We have two and a half weeks. Let's attack this to turn in a good time."

"I'm game. I need all the help I can get."

"All right. We don't have to run the full course every time we work out. We'll work to build stamina and speed. Hills are important, since the course has several. If we can work out together Monday, Wednesday and Saturday, we can work by ourselves the other days."

"I can do that. What's the best workout when I'm alone?" Jane asked.

"Two things. At least once a week, work out on the long

hill. Run it several times, increasing your speed each time. A couple of days, do track workouts. Come to the school and run laps. Do consecutive lap sets, increasing your speed on each set. Run four laps at moderate speed, then three laps at a faster pace, then two fast laps and finish with one lap at top speed. Walk a lap between each set."

Jane nodded. "I can do that. Do I need someone to time me?"

"No. It doesn't matter so much how fast you run, but that you're pushing your limits. You can judge that by your heart rate and breathing. Don't exert so much that you cramp up or hurt yourself. This Saturday we'll run a hard three miles. That will get our bodies into a race mode."

"I appreciate this, Eleanor. I had no idea how to prepare for the race."

Eleanor laughed. "I can feel the strain, just trying to keep up with you. I don't often get to run with a partner anymore. I miss the competitive challenge. But you're doing a fine job on your own."

"*You* feel the strain?" Jane said, laughing. "I'm about to die." She couldn't believe her good fortune. She'd never imagined having an actual coach help her. She could picture crossing the finish line ahead of Carrie Gleason. Wouldn't that be something? She didn't care if that put her in first place or second to last. Beating Carrie would be enough.

"The figures look reasonable," Reggie said. "I got a quote on the elevator and the more expensive materials. Our accountant ran the figures and confirmed this is the way to go, if..." Reggie stopped and looked across the kitchen table, strewn with paperwork, at Vera.

"It all sounds wonderful to me. What are the problems?" Vera asked.

"We need a firm commitment that Olivia Martino will move in and care for Aunt Agatha for at least one year. If she does that, our costs will come out about the same as if she moved into Briarhurst. If she stays more than a year, the costs drop dramatically."

"Let's call her and talk about details."

Reggie grinned. "I knew you'd feel that way." He glanced at his watch. "She should be here any minute."

A car pulled into the driveway and stopped under the *porte cochere*. Vera hurried to the door to let in Olivia.

"I'd feel better coming through the back door to this place," Olivia was saying as they came into the kitchen. "I can't be coming and going through the grand entry."

"Of course you can," Vera said. "But there is a back door. A lane circles around to the kitchen. It has room for trucks to park and turn around for deliveries."

"Mr. Reggie, I came as soon as I could," Olivia said. She set her purse on a counter and walked to the table.

Reggie stood and held out his hand toward an empty

chair. "Please sit down, Olivia. We appreciate your coming on such short notice."

"I know you're in a hurry to figure out how to care for poor Mrs. Agatha." She sat and looked at Reggie expectantly.

"I've estimated all the work and supplies we'd need to bring this house up to standards to provide for someone who is handicapped, like Aunt Agatha. We would install an elevator, special hardware in all the bathrooms and handrails along the walls. She already has an intercom system, which can be set to monitor. With my crew and the available supplies, this house could be ready for Aunt Agatha in two weeks."

A big smile bloomed on Olivia's face, plumping her cheeks like rosy apples. "That's wonderful!"

"We have one problem that must be solved or it won't work."

"Oh." Her smile faded. "Is there something I can do to help?"

"Yes. This entire plan depends on your being willing to commit to living here and caring for Agatha for at least a year. Have you thought about it? Can you do that?"

"Yes. Oh, this is an answer to my prayers, Mr. Reggie. Miss Alvera, I love your aunt and I'd do it just for her. But this will help me so that I won't have to go back to work."

Reggie frowned and rubbed his chin. "This'll be more restrictive than a job. Agatha can be demanding. If she has trouble getting around, she'll require a lot of help."

"I know. I've worked with elderly people and people with mobility problems for years." She glanced at Vera and Alice. "You've seen the people in the rehabilitation center. Some of them get better and move on, but a lot of them stay there in the nursing home wing. We have to give them lots of attention. I can do that. I'd give her space to be independent too."

"I know that'll mean more to her than anything," Vera said. "We can hire extra help when needed and she has a cleaning service, so you won't have to do any of that. What about cooking for the two of you? Do we need to hire a cook? You'll need transportation to take her to the doctor and shopping and to her social events. She'll want to do as much as possible," Vera said.

"Mrs. Agatha and I can get along just fine with the two of us. Transportation shouldn't be a problem, and with Mr. Reggie right next door, I can call him if I need anything, but that would only be in an emergency," she added, patting his hand. "I'm willing to sign a paper saying I'll stay for a year, if that's what you want."

"You haven't asked what we'll pay or if you'll have any time off," Reggie said.

"My husband worked for you for forty years. I know you'll give me a fair wage. Whatever you think is right is fine with me. But there's still one person who has to approve."

"Aunt Agatha," Vera said. "I have no doubt she'll get up and jump for joy when we tell her."

"Please ask her if all these plans are all right. I don't want to work for her unless she wants me."

"She will. How long before you can move in?"

"I could move in pretty soon. Just give me a few days. I'll try to rent out my house after I move in here."

"Good," Reggie said. "I'll get my crew and we'll move your stuff. You can have the entire third floor, if you like. Look it over. You can use Agatha's furniture or put your own up there. We'll talk to Aunt Agatha first thing tomorrow morning and find out from the doctor how much time we have to get ready. I want the elevator installed before she comes home. We'll call you tomorrow."

"Maybe I should come with you when you talk to her, so I can reassure her and make sure this is her decision," Olivia said.

"Meet us at the center at nine o'clock, then." Reggie stood. "I'll see you ladies in the morning."

"Mr. Reggie turned into a fine man," Olivia said as he walked out the door.

Vera smiled. "Yes, he did. And I'm relieved that Aunt Agatha will be in such good hands with you and Reggie. She was so sure he wanted to put her in a nursing home. All he wants is for her to be safe and well cared for. She'll be thrilled."

Chapter Twenty-One

*H*ave any of you entered the Harvest 10K Run that's coming to Acorn Hill?" Jane asked the ANGELs in the Assembly Room at Grace Chapel on Wednesday night. Alice had led the preteen-aged group of girls for years. Jane had promised Alice she'd fill in for her while she was gone.

"My whole family's entered," Bree Brubaker said. "My dad doesn't have to travel that week. Mom and Clinton and I jog every day to get ready. I don't think we can run the whole way, though, but Mom says that's all right."

"My mom and I are helping at a water stop," Sissy Matthews said. "My brother and my dad are running."

Several of the other girls were involved in some way.

"Who wants to win the race?" Jane asked.

Three girls raised their hands.

"It sounds like the race will be lots of fun," Jane said. She wasn't sure what she was looking for from the girls, since she was trying to figure out her own motivations. She knew she wanted to beat Carrie. If she came in ahead of her former track teammate, she'd be happy. And surely that was

a legitimate goal. "The Bible talks about racing. Does anyone know what it says?" she asked.

"Yeah, it says we should run to win," Sarah Roberts said.
"My dad tells me something like that about my homework
sometimes."

"That sounds like my dad," Sissy said. "He watches football and basketball, and he's always yelling about scoring
and winning."

"I looked in Scripture and I found other verses about
racing." Jane lifted a slim stack of pages on which she'd run
off a number of quotations, then passed out one page to
each girl. "This is the one you're referring to, Sarah. 'Do you
not know that in a race all the runners run, but only one
gets the prize? Run in such a way as to get the prize.' That's
1 Corinthians 9:24. There'll be prizes for the winners of
this race. It would be fun to get a prize. What kind of a race
is the Bible talking about, though?"

"Does it mean we should work hard to do our best in
everything?" Kate asked.

"No, it means we should run to follow Jesus," Sissy said.

"The next verse says, 'Everyone who competes in the
games goes into strict training. They do it to get a crown that
will not last; but we do it to get a crown that will last forever.'
So I think Sissy is closer to the truth, although we have to
work hard to do our best. That's why we train for a race. Has
anyone ever won a prize for something?" Jane asked.

"I won a prize for spelling the most words right," Sissy said.

"Do you still have the prize?" Jane asked.

"No way! It was a candy bar. I ate it."

Everyone laughed at her answer.

"That's what the Bible verse means. In life, we compete to win prizes that don't last. Like a candy bar. I won a trophy for bowling once. After a few years, it didn't mean much sitting on my bookshelf, except that I had to dust it. I think a candy bar would have been a better prize."

"Yeah. Hey, I know. We could give everyone a prize after the race. We could give out candy bars," Bree said. "Then everyone would be a winner."

"That's a wonderful idea, except we might have over a hundred entrants. That's a lot of candy."

"What if we gave out cookies with a Bible verse," Linda Farr suggested. "I'm not entering the race, so I could hand them out at the finish line if my mom says it's okay."

"I can help too," Lisa Masur said. "I can't run," she said, lifting her leg. She had a soft boot cast on her foot, the result of a torn ligament.

"Excellent idea. I knew you girls would come up with something fabulous. Miss Howard will be home by then. You could come over to the inn and make the cookies. We could put the cookies in plastic snack bags with the verse attached. Here's a list of Bible verses I found about running and racing. Let's look them over. Then you can decide which verse to use."

"'. . . Forgetting what is behind and straining toward what is ahead, I press on toward the goal to win the prize for which God has called me heavenward in Christ Jesus' (Philippians 3:13–14). That's a good one," Kate said.

"Psalm 119:32 would be terrific," Sissy said. "'I run in the path of your commands, for you have set my heart free.'"

"I like this one," Bree said. "'It is God who arms me with strength and makes my way perfect. He makes my feet like the feet of a deer; he enables me to stand on the heights.' That's Psalm 18:32–33."

"Wait, this is one we should use," Sarah said. "It's my grandma's favorite verse. She quotes it all the time. Isaiah 40:31, 'But those who hope in the Lord will renew their strength. They will soar on wings like eagles; they will run and not grow weary, they will walk and not be faint.'"

"I think we should use all of them and put them on different bags," Jenny said.

"Me too," Kate agreed. "My mom can print them out in fancy letters. She does that with notes she puts in sacks when she takes food to people who are sick."

"All right. Kate, you take care of printing the verses—if your mother agrees. I'll get the ingredients for your cookies.

Maybe we could meet at our house next Wednesday night to prepare the cookies and the bags. So girls, not all of us are running *the* race, but how are we running *a* race by doing this?"

They looked at her with blank expressions. Clearly, she hadn't conveyed the point. "If we help others, are we doing what Jesus did?"

"Yes, that's why we do secret ANGEL projects," Lisa said.

"That's exactly right. Why don't you do it out in the open so everyone can see you?" Jane asked.

"That wouldn't be any fun. Then they'd know we did it and not why we do it," Bree said.

"We do it to make people feel good and to help them," Jenny added.

"We want them to know Jesus loves them," Kate said. "Miss Howard said Jesus knows we're doing it and He smiles when we help others."

Alice lived what she taught and she'd passed it on to the girls. "You're all correct," Jane said. "That's the race Jesus gives us, to run after Him, to live and treat people the way He did, isn't it?"

All of the girls agreed.

Jane served refreshments and afterward the girls helped her clean up. Then they went upstairs to find their parents, who'd been in the Wednesday night prayer service.

"Good morning, Aunt Agatha. You're looking chipper this morning," Reggie said Thursday morning, giving Agatha a kiss on her cheek. She was sitting up, dressed in a bright-green muumuu and slippers. Her hair still needed attention. It looked like she'd tried to comb it. The front had been brushed, but the back was matted from lying on it. Her lipstick was crooked.

Agatha frowned. "Are you here to talk me into moving into that old people's home?" she asked, glaring at him suspiciously.

Reggie held his hands over his heart. "You wound me, Aunt Agatha. I'm innocent."

The sight of the tall, broad-shouldered man becoming subdued under the gaze of the diminutive elderly woman impressed Alice. She'd seen Vera's capable cousin in his club, captaining his yacht, leading his rugged crew of employees around Agatha's mansion. She expected him to master any situation, but Agatha had the upper hand, even in her incapacitated condition. Vera might have been able to convince her, but even that was doubtful. Alice suddenly realized that Agatha would not have gone to an assisted living residence without giving her consent and cooperation. So why had she called Vera with such desperation? She must have realized she needed help.

Vera gave Agatha a kiss just as Olivia entered the room, smiling at those visiting the old woman.

"Good morning, Mrs. Agatha. And a fine morning it is," she said. "Have you talked to her yet?" she asked Reggie.

"Not yet. We were waiting for you." He sat on the edge of the bed, changing the dynamic. He still seemed an imposing figure next to his aunt, but he no longer appeared intimidating. "We have good news for you," he said. He looked at Vera and nodded.

Vera pulled up a chair in front of her aunt. She put her hands on Agatha's withered hands and smiled. "You won't be moving to Briarhurst. You'll be returning to your own home."

"How can I go home? I can't climb the stairs. I can't cook my meals. I can't even take a bath without help."

"That's where I come in," Olivia said. "If you don't object, I'd like to work for you and take care of you in your home. That means you'll have to have me for a housemate," she said. "But it's up to you. Mr. Reggie could find someone else, I'm sure."

Agatha gazed up at Olivia, searching her face. For a moment, Alice thought she might be disoriented. If that was the case, the plan might not work.

"You'd give up your freedom to take care of an old lady like me?" Agatha asked. A tear broke free from her eye and trickled down the corner of her cheek. "What an angel you are." Agatha reached up a shaky hand and touched Olivia's arm. Then she looked from Vera to Reggie and back. "Do you mean it? How can that be?"

"Reggie is installing an elevator, Auntie. You won't have to use the stairs. The bathrooms will be equipped so you can use them. And Olivia is a great cook. As you get stronger, you can do as much as you want, but she'll be there to help you."

Agatha stared at Vera for a moment. She pursed her lips. Then a deeply distressed look entered her eyes. "This is terrible. I can't. I told Lillian I'd move to that home so she wouldn't have to be alone. I can't let her down."

Vera, Reggie and Olivia stared at Agatha in stunned silence. Agatha stared back, her expression filled with pain.

"Olivia, you know Lillian. What's wrong with her?" Alice asked.

"She's just been diagnosed with Essential Tremor and she has a few other things related to age. They've started her on medications to help control the tremors. There's no cure. It's not life-threatening, but it is debilitating."

"It's embarrassing. She puts on a good front, but she's mortified when she has those tremor attacks," Agatha said. "She gets depressed and doesn't want to be around people."

Alice glanced at Olivia. She could tell by the woman's thoughtful expression that they were on the same wavelength.

"Lillian's an easy patient. She doesn't demand attention and she has the sweetest disposition. Most of the time she can get around with a cane or walker, but she needs care. She's a good friend of yours, isn't she, Mrs. Agatha?"

Agatha's chin was firm and determined. "My closest friend."

"Do you suppose she'd want to come live with us? We'd have quite a time, the three of us," Olivia said. She looked toward Reggie, who nodded.

Agatha's eyes lit with hope. "Do you think it could work?" She raised her hands to her cheeks. "Oh my, yes, we'd have a delightful time. Is it possible? Are you sure, Olivia? I don't want to be a burden."

"I'm sure. This is a blessing for me, Mrs. Agatha."

Agatha's face wrinkled into a thousand little lines as she grinned. "Oh, I do want to go home. I was so afraid. This is your doing, isn't it Alvera? Thank you."

"Actually Alice saw the possibility first. Reggie figured out how to make it work. And I'm sure we all like the idea of Lillian's joining you."

Agatha turned to Reggie. "Learning your father's trade, building all those yachts taught you valuable skills. He'd be proud of you. But what about that rapscallion son of Lillian's? What if he refuses to let her come."

"Does Lillian's son have her power of attorney?" Reggie asked.

"No. He has her signature on a real estate agreement to sell her house, but that's all."

"Then I don't see that he can stop her. I'll be glad to talk to him and reassure him. I'll mention cost-effectiveness. That should convince him to cooperate."

"Bless your heart, Reginald Jamison. Your mother would be proud of you too. If Lillian lives with me, she won't need that house." Agatha frowned. "We need to hurry. He's going to sell all her possessions. We have to stop him. I have lots of room for her things."

"Let's go talk to Lillian, Aunt Agatha." Reggie clapped his hands together.

"Get that metal contraption for me." She pointed to the walker, then pushed to try to get up. "Well, don't just stand there, Alvera. Give me a hand. You wait and see. In a couple of weeks, I won't need that thing."

Vera got on one side and Olivia got on the other and helped Agatha to stand and grab the walker.

"I'll look forward to that day," Reggie said. He looked at Vera and Olivia and winked.

Jane parked in the high school lot and turned off her lights. At 6:30 Thursday morning, the sky had lightened to a steel gray. She shivered. A sweatshirt wouldn't be enough cover in a week or two.

She locked her purse in the trunk, slipped her keys in her pocket, picked up a small flashlight and headed around the school buildings to the football field and track. Eleanor had suggested that she run laps. The best way to use the track was to get there before school.

As she'd expected, the track was deserted. Start at a moderate pace and increase speed with each set, Eleanor had said. Jane squatted down and stretched out her right leg, then her left. She went through a series of warm-up exercises, then started out jogging around the track, loping easily. The cold penetrated her sweatshirt. She held her arms crossed, rubbing them as she ran. One lap. A figure emerged from behind the bleachers and started running behind her. She glanced back. The figure was clad in a sweatshirt with the hood up and sweat pants. She couldn't tell if it was a man or a woman.

She heard the thud, thud, thud of the runner's feet, beating the ground twice to her once, running hard toward her. Her heart pounded. She felt the adrenaline pump through her veins. She considered running off the track to her car. She reached in her pocket and grabbed hold of her small flashlight. The feel of the small metal tube gave her a sense of security. Then reason returned to her mind. *This is Acorn Hill*, she thought.

The footsteps caught up to her, came alongside her. The figure was a few inches taller and broader in the shoulders than she was. The figure glanced over at her and smiled.

"Hey, Jane. Getting ready for the big race?" He fell into step next to her, matching her step for step. His legs were longer than hers.

"Hank Young. Did you try to scare me on purpose?"

"Scare you? Why would I do that? You didn't think . . . Hey, I'm sorry. It never occurred to me that you didn't recognize me when you looked back."

Jane gave him a withering look. Sometimes she thought Hank lived on a different planet from the rest of them, his head in the cyberclouds of the Internet. He was a whiz at anything technical, but naive when it came to life in general. He looked at her with wide-eyed innocence, and she couldn't help laughing. "You have your hood on."

He looked up. "Oh." He pulled the hood off. "Sorry. But there's no one around here to worry about."

"I realized that. I wasn't really scared. Well, maybe for a few seconds, but then I thought better of it."

"Good. How's the Web site doing?"

"Fine. We're going to have to add a page for Louise's giant pumpkin, though. It's become a huge attraction."

"Huge, huh?" He laughed.

"Yeah. So how's the computer business? Are you keeping busy?"

"I've got contracts in Potterston and all over the state. It's great. I can work and never leave Acorn Hill."

Jane realized she'd completed four laps. "I've got to walk now for a lap," she said, slowing.

"Okay. I'll see you later." He waved and sprinted off.

Two women came onto the track, talking as fast as they walked. Behind them, a man in shorts and a T-shirt jogged on, wearing a headset. He quickly passed the women and Jane. By the time she rounded the track and started a faster set of laps, a handful of high school athletes had shown up for an early workout. Jane completed her sets, winded and overheated, but feeling like part of a community of exercise-conscious residents. Although she hadn't carried on a conversation with anyone other than Hank, everyone had greeted her with a smile of camaraderie. She wondered if all of them were entering the Harvest 10K Run. The track had seemed congested enough. She couldn't imagine running with a real crowd.

Chapter Twenty-Two

era stood at the foot of the steps to the Shelton Cove Yacht Club and silently stared up at the remarkable mansion, as if she'd been frozen in place. Alice wondered what she was thinking about the house where she grew up. Vera's expression gave away nothing.

Reggie stood on the other side of her, waiting patiently, as if he understood the emotions swirling through his cousin.

The weathered, gray cedar siding, the towers and the red shingles of the roof made Alice think of mansions she'd seen above the beaches of Newport, Rhode Island.

Finally, Vera took a deep breath and they climbed the steps to the entrance. The door opened and three people came out. They were dressed to go sailing in casual clothes, deck shoes and light sweaters. They smiled and greeted Reggie, said hello to Vera and Alice, then went on down the steps, except for one of the men, who held the door for them to enter.

The encounter seemed to relax Vera, who'd been tense all morning. Inside the entry hall, arched doorways led in three directions. Laughter could be heard from the left.

"They kept most of the rooms the same," Reggie said. "They extended the dining room by putting tables in the library, so they could seat more people, but all the bookshelves are still there. Now they house trophies and sailing memorabilia."

They went toward the laughter and stepped into a bright, elegant room with large mirrors in between posts of rich, golden wood paneling. A mural of an Atlantic shoreline dominated one wall above a long sideboard. Several round and oval tables occupied the room. A party of eight was eating breakfast at one table. One of the ladies called to Reggie. They went over and Reggie introduced everyone.

"Vera!" A woman jumped up and enveloped Vera in a warm hug.

Vera hugged her back, but without the enthusiasm of the other woman. "Georgia, how nice to see you," she said, ending the hug.

A man stood. "Alvera," he said, holding out his hands. He took her hands and leaned over to kiss her. She pulled back, barely allowing him to brush the side of her cheek.

"Hello, Derrick. How are you? You're looking well." She smiled politely and removed her hands from his grip.

Derrick arched one eyebrow. He was tall and dark-haired and had a sophisticated appearance. His white sweater with blue trim was monogrammed. His white shorts were sharply creased. "You look lovely, as always. If anything, you've grown more beautiful," he said.

"And you haven't lost any of your charm," she replied, putting her hands in the pockets of her khaki slacks. She did look nice, Alice thought. Her blue eyes held warmth and friendliness and a spark of humor. Alice had never considered the fact that Vera's natural poise might have come from the society in which she'd been raised.

"Anyone like to join us for a set of tennis this afternoon?" Derrick asked, looking at Vera, then her companions.

"Unfortunately, we already have plans," Reggie said. He turned to Vera. "We'd better get on with our business."

"Bye. Nice to see you again," she said as she allowed Reggie to lead her away.

"Sorry," he said when they were out of earshot. "I didn't think about your running into him. He never married, you know."

"I'm sure that had nothing to do with me," Vera said.

Reggie grinned at his cousin. "I don't know. I think you broke his heart."

"Or his pride. I suppose that isn't very charitable of me, but he said some mean things about Fred." Vera turned to

Alice. "I dated him after Fred and I broke up. Everyone expected me to marry Derrick."

"Including Derrick," Reggie said.

"I'm glad you and Fred got back together. Is that why you hesitated before coming in?" Alice asked. She didn't want to pry, but she had been curious. She and Vera had become friends when Vera accepted a teaching position in Acorn Hill and moved in with her grandmother, a long-time member of Grace Chapel and friend of Alice's mother. Alice knew a romance had blossomed between the new school-teacher and Fred Humbert, the young man who'd returned to Acorn Hill to manage the hardware store. She'd learned that the couple had known each other in college, but she'd never heard much about their lives before Acorn Hill.

"Some of it, I suppose. I'd rather remember this house the way it was when I was a child than to see what it's become. Besides, that last year was stressful. My parents wanted me to marry Derrick. When I broke up and insisted on marrying Fred, they had a hard time accepting my decision. I think they believed I was going to Fred on the rebound."

"You never cared much for the social scene, although you played the part well in college," Reggie said.

"I enjoyed socializing in college. I think we were all spreading our wings and feeling independent. It was excit-ing and frenetic."

"Frenetic? There you go, sounding like a schoolteacher. I remember you could still find time to party."

"I do prefer a good book."

He reached over and ruffled Vera's hair. "Which is why you're the teacher and I'm the carpenter."

"Carpenter? Far from it," she said, smoothing her hand over her hair. "Not that there's anything wrong with carpenters, but I'd call you a designer and a craftsman."

They went up to the top of the front tower to a circular room with seats beneath the windows all the way around. "This is my favorite place," Vera said. "I used to come up here to read and daydream about adventures in other times or places. No one would bother me."

"I knew I could find you here, but I preferred to go out in the dinghy. That's where I did my daydreaming," Reggie said. Alice could almost see them as children, living out their daydreams in their own ways.

They left the tower and went down a hallway on the main floor that opened up to a round anteroom that rose three stories high. A wide spiral stairway wound upward, with a landing at each floor. To the outside were stained glass windows that cast a rainbow around them. Reggie opened a double door on the left.

"This is the ballroom, where Vera danced the night away," Reggie said. "They still hold balls here."

Vera stepped inside and looked around. Her eyes

sparkled. Alice followed her gaze as she pointed toward a carved figure of a cherub playing a horn on the frieze that circled the room between the picture rail and the crown moldings. All around the room were similar cherubs playing various instruments.

"I loved this room for the angels. Mother had a huge tree brought in here every Christmas and she decorated it with angel ornaments. When I was ten, she let me help decorate. She would have a chamber orchestra play for her charity parties. I always had to dress up to make an appearance at the beginning of the party. Then I was sent upstairs."

"That must have been hard, knowing there was a party going on down below," Alice said, still trying to understand why Vera hadn't wanted to visit this lovely old house.

"Oh no. The doors were always left open so people could wander from the ballroom to the refreshment area that was set up in the parlor. When I was little, I'd sit on the stairs and watch from up above. My father would bring me a plate of dainty desserts and punch, and he'd sit with me until he saw mother down below looking for him."

"What a wonderful memory," Alice said.

Vera nodded. "Mother would pretend she didn't see me. Then later, she'd come upstairs with one of the party favors and she'd give it to me, then tuck me in bed. My room is up there," she said, pointing up the circular stairway. "There's also a sitting room, where the ladies would gather to chat, like the Ladies' Necessary at Aunt Agatha's."

They wandered up the staircase. The bedrooms had been redecorated as guest rooms for visitors from other yacht clubs or for occasions like weddings. Vera's room looked like a luxurious hotel room. She frowned, then turned and left without a word. She walked down a hallway farther back into the house, with Reggie following. He hadn't said much. Just let Vera wander.

They came to a locked door at the end of the hall. Reggie took a key out of his pocket. "The club doesn't use the rest of the house," he explained, unlocking the door.

They stepped into a dim, cold hallway with older, worn carpet on the floor. Their footsteps echoed as they walked down the hall.

"When I was little, this was my Grandma Lindsey's wing when she'd visit from Acorn Hill. I remember her holding court with her old lady friends." Vera laughed. "I suppose they were about my age, but they seemed ancient. I was in awe of them."

"I remember," Reggie said. "I had to put on a monkey suit to come have tea with a bunch of old ladies. I hated it."

"And we'd sneak out after a while and go down to the cove. Remember, you tore your good pants on the old rowboat and I lost my gloves."

Reggie laughed. "Boy, did we get in trouble, but it was worth it."

"I remember your grandmother," Alice said. "Louise and I adopted her, since our own grandmothers died before we were born. She came to our tea parties and helped with the church choir and the social committee. When Mother died, she organized the ladies at the church to bring in meals and help us take care of Jane. We'd have been lost without her."

"I loved the short time I lived with her before Fred and I got married. She adored Fred, which helped convince my parents to accept him. They didn't dislike Fred. They just didn't think he was the right fellow for me."

"They were certainly misguided about that," Alice said.

"We all were," Reggie said.

Back on the main floor, as they went toward the front section of the house, Vera commented, "I don't know what you'd use these rooms for now, unless the club opened it as an inn or rented offices to members."

"That's not a bad idea," Reggie said. "Maybe I'll move my office into this study. It'd be a lot quieter. A lot of your parents' furnishings are still here. Is there anything you'd like to take? If you'd like some of the furniture, we can have it shipped."

Vera looked around the study. A large carved desk and chairs and bookshelves occupied one end of the room, and a heavy brown leather couch and chairs were arranged around the fireplace.

"It's all set for your office, Reggie. I don't want anything. I have my memories and I don't have to dust them."

Alice smiled inwardly. Vera didn't care for housekeeping. Although she kept things clean, she didn't pay much attention to clutter. Whenever she was expecting company, she'd say she needed to "redd-up" the house. Now Alice realized she was probably raised with a housekeeper and there would have been a massive cleaning campaign before each of her mother's large affairs. Alice had always loved Vera's casual approach to her home. It had the homey atmosphere where you could sink into an easy chair and relax. That was not the way Vera had grown up. She'd purposely turned her home into a refuge where she could relax and be her unpretentious self.

"It's nearly lunchtime. I'd be happy to spring for lunch," Reggie suggested.

"How can we refuse such a generous offer?" Vera said.

Reggie showed them to a table on the large sun porch overlooking the cove and the river to the east. Out on the water, boats with rippling sails unfurled rode the breeze. All manner of craft from rowboats to yachts bobbed in the water. A jet ski raced past, weaving in and out between the boats, scaring the fish.

"It was a lot quieter here when we were kids," Vera said.

"Maybe you'd like to jet ski this afternoon."

"No thank you. I want to make it back to work in one piece."

"I nearly forgot. You're still a schoolteacher, aren't you? Have you thought about retiring?" Reggie asked.

"Retire? And do what? I love teaching."

Alice found it difficult to reconcile her friend Vera, a beloved Acorn Hill teacher, with the girl who grew up in Shelton Cove amid the wealthy yachting set.

Alice gazed out at the deep, blue water. This may have been Vera's life, but no longer. The Vera she knew was humble, down-to-earth and seemingly unsophisticated. At her childhood home, Vera's favorite memories had to do with reading and playing with her cousin and spending time with her father and mother and aunt. She remembered the parties, but commented on them as an observer, not a participant. Alice suspected that Vera had always longed for a simpler, quieter life than the one she knew as a child, and she'd found it with Fred in Acorn Hill.

Chapter Twenty-Three

"There. That's my dad," Vera said, pointing to a faded color photograph in a large album. The pictures were mounted with corner tabs on black construction paper. Alice and Vera sat on a floral print couch in Agatha's parlor Friday evening, surrounded by albums.

The picture in question showed Vera at about eight years of age, dressed in a plaid flannel nightgown, her knees up under her gown, hugged to her chest. Beside her, a handsome, elegant blond man in a black-and-white tuxedo sat balancing a plate of food, feeding her an hors d'oeuvre. He was smiling at his daughter, who was making a silly face at the camera.

"That must have been Uncle George taking the picture. He always had his camera with him. I doubt if my parents had this one. Mother wouldn't have approved."

"Of the snack?"

"No, of my face. She used to tell me my features would be permanently deformed if I kept making such faces." Vera laughed. "I did it a lot. I think I did it to tease my mother.

She never raised her voice, but she'd give me that glare. You know what I mean."

The next picture showed a good-looking young man, whom Alice recognized as Fred. "That was taken shortly after we got back together."

"I didn't know you had broken up with him before your engagement. That's when I met you, after you and Fred got engaged at Fairy Pond. I thought that was so romantic."

Vera sighed. "It's a miracle Fred and I managed to get married. I almost let my family and peer pressure persuade me that Fred was wrong for me and that I'd hurt him in the long run if I married him." She shook her head.

"You weren't from Acorn Hill. How did you meet?"

"As you know, Fred and I met at college. I majored in education, but I needed math credits and math wasn't my best subject. My professor recommended a tutor. Guess who? It was Fred. He was two years ahead of me, majoring in business and economics. With his help, I actually discovered I liked math. Then we saw each other at church. We became friends, studying together and going to church together."

Alice nodded. "That's a good solid basis for a relationship. Fred's so thoughtful and steady, he must have been very attractive."

"Cute too. That didn't hurt," Vera said, grinning. She

looked through the album and found one of her standing next to Fred. He had on a suit. She wore a beautiful dress and heels. "Fred held down two jobs to pay for college, so there wasn't much time or money for dating. I found out later that he went without lunch for a week so he could pay for our date. Then I invited him to a Christmas dance at our house. Poor Fred. I was crazy about him, and I wanted my parents and friends to meet him. He went just to please me. He hated it. All the guys wore tuxedos. Fred wore his Sunday suit. I know he was embarrassed. My parents were polite, but the evening didn't go well. I was disappointed. I didn't ask him to do things with my friends again."

"That must have been hard. You'd known these friends for a long time, hadn't you?"

"Years and years. And they were nice people. It was just . . . different. We didn't move in the same circles. My parents made sure to point that out. They came up to college for parents' weekend and attended church with us, then took us out to dinner at a really posh restaurant afterward. Dad grilled Fred on his plans for the future. Fred didn't seem to mind, but I was mortified. Following all that, they encouraged me, privately, of course, to date someone from our social set."

"Like the boy Reggie tried to set you up with?"

"Yes." Vera laughed. "I wasn't even tempted. He might

have impressed the guys—he played sports and drove a brand-new, bright-red Lincoln convertible. Poor Fred didn't even have a car. Then Fred graduated and got a job across town from college. He worked overtime to get established. I hardly ever saw him. We argued about it. Fred insisted he needed to establish a strong work record so he could get ahead and provide for a family. I wanted him to spend time with me. I wanted to be more important than his job. Besides, my family owned a lucrative business. Fred could have worked for them, but he wouldn't even apply."

Vera thumbed through several more pages of pictures. "I tried to understand his need to work hard and his refusal to work for my family, but I wasn't very successful. I decided my parents might be right. Maybe Fred wasn't the guy for me. The next week a friend invited me to her home for the Thanksgiving holiday. I told Fred I'd be busy, even though I knew he'd be alone, and I went to Connecticut with my girlfriend. When I got back, Fred was gone. He'd moved. I couldn't believe it."

"Is that when he moved back to Acorn Hill?"

Vera nodded. "But he didn't tell me. I was crushed. I got a letter from him. In it he said he'd been offered a job in Acorn Hill that could be a real opportunity. The owner of the business hired him as manager with the possibility that someday he could buy the business. I knew about Acorn

Hill from Fred and from my grandmother. I'd visited her one summer."

"I think I remember her bringing you to a church potluck once."

"That's right. I thought Acorn Hill was a nice town, but it didn't have a lake or a river. No boats. I didn't believe I could be happy away from the water. Fred called and asked me to come visit Acorn Hill, to see if we could work on our relationship. I told him I didn't want to live in Acorn Hill. I said if he would come back and try to be part of my life, then we could talk. He actually got angry. I couldn't believe it. He told me I had to choose between him and my society friends. I said, if he loved me, he wouldn't ask me to choose." Vera shook her head. "I was so self-centered and shortsighted that I couldn't see he was offering me a chance at a new life of my own. I hung up on him."

"I remember there were a couple of single gals at church who were interested in Fred, but he never dated as far as I know," Alice said.

"He told me later that he believed I was the one for him and he was saving up for a house. He intended to have something to offer me before he tried again. But then I met Derrick Dalton. You met him at the yacht club. His family moved to Shelton Cove from Boston. He came for the summer. We hit it off immediately. We liked the same things.

He even liked my favorite ice cream, pistachio. He was everything I thought I wanted. Smart. Friendly. Charming. Ambitious. My parents adored him. He transferred near me for graduate school. We talked about the future. Everyone thought we'd get married after he finished school."

"So how did you and Fred get back together?"

"When I got my degree, I rented an apartment near the school where I was teaching and I guess I got a dose of reality. Mom and Dad weren't paying my bills. I had to watch my pennies. Then I saw how Fred had struggled to pay his bills and complete college, and my respect for him grew. I finally understood how much he'd sacrificed for the future. I became more and more disillusioned with the social life my parents enjoyed. I realized that Derrick really didn't share my faith. He encouraged me to go to church because it looked good, but he would have been happy for me to represent him there while he played golf. He said he was making business contacts. In contrast, I remembered how Fred had refused a chance to go sailing because it would have meant missing church.

"One Sunday after services I was confused and disillusioned, so I called my grandmother in Acorn Hill."

"Ah, God guided you in that decision."

"I believe so. It was June when I arrived. Everything was blooming. I'd forgotten how pretty the town was with its cozy homes and modest places of business. I took Grandma out to eat at the Coffee Shop. While we were waiting to be served, Fred came in. He saw us, of course, and came over. He and my grandmother had become friends. I couldn't believe it. He ate with us, and afterward Grandma raved about what a wonderful Christian he was and how he'd made great improvements to the hardware store.

"With Grandma's blessing, Fred and I spent the afternoon together. The next weekend he came to see me. I fixed a picnic lunch and we went to the park. I was so nervous, I ate more than I should have and got a stomachache. Fred was so sweet and concerned. He really made me feel cherished. It didn't take long to figure out I was making a huge mistake with Derrick and that I still cared for Fred."

"Oh dear. What a different life you would have lived if you hadn't made that visit."

"I know the Lord gave me that feeling of disquiet about my relationship with Derrick. It was very humbling to know God cared that much about me, to guide me when I was trying so hard to please others. I'll never forget the day I told my parents. Mother cried. Father tried to talk sense to me. He advised me to take time to pray about it. I told him I had been praying about it. I talked to Aunt Agatha and she advised me to follow my heart."

"Somehow, I can see her saying that," Alice said.

Vera nodded. "So I broke up with Derrick. He was furious and accused me of playing him for a fool. From his reaction, I don't believe his heart was broken. More likely I hurt his pride. Then I applied for a teaching job in Acorn Hill, praying that something would open up if it was God's will. I couldn't believe it when I got a call that same week. The fifth-grade teacher had just given notice. Her husband had been transferred unexpectedly. So I moved in with my grandmother in Acorn Hill. And you know the rest.

"We got engaged at Fairy Pond and later we had a simple ceremony in the church we'd both attended at school." Vera flipped several pages and found their wedding pictures. She looked lovely in a simple white gown. Fred looked handsome wearing a suit.

"Fred's a lovable guy."

"He sure is. And I can't wait to get home and see him. It's been fascinating to see Shelton Cove and what's happened to some of my old friends, but I don't miss it at all. It was worth coming here to learn that. Especially since Aunt Agatha will be well taken care of. Reggie may not always understand the way a woman thinks, but he's good to her." Vera closed the photo album. "Olivia is coming over in the morning to start getting the house redd up for Aunt Agatha's return. I'm thinking we can help her tomorrow—if that's all right with you—then leave things in her capable hands. We could go say good-bye to Aunt Agatha and be back in Acorn Hill by dinnertime."

Alice smiled. "I think that's a fine idea."

⌒

Jane shoved the peeler down the carrot, shaving off more than the outer skin. She gave the carrot a turn and shaved it again.

"There won't be anything left of that poor carrot when you get done peeling it. What's wrong?"

Jane looked up, startled. Louise stood in the doorway watching her. She looked down at the carrot and the peels in the sink. She'd done in three carrots without realizing she was taking out her frustrations on them.

"I didn't want to leave any skin on them," she responded. "I guess I got carried away."

Louise came over and looked in the sink. "I'd say you're right. Know anyone with a rabbit?"

Jane laughed. "No, but they'll compost, so it's no loss. I have lots of carrots."

"True. Tell me what the carrots did to deserve such punishment." Louise took two plates out of the cupboard to set the table.

"Add a plate. I heard from Alice. They're coming home early. She'll be here for dinner."

"Good. I've missed her." She reached for another plate.

"I talked to Carrie Blankenship, the race coordinator, a little while ago. I wanted to clear it for the ANGELs to give out cookies at the end of the race. It was their idea and I figured it'd be a nice thing to do. Well . . . it seems they have rules about who can do what. As if the finish line isn't on public property. Now I wish I hadn't even called her. Just let the girls do it. I was trying to be nice."

"Did she say no?"

"Not exactly. She said they had to be careful about what people offered the race participants at these events. I told her the girls just want to give out cookies." Jane shaved another strip off a carrot.

"So can the girls pass out cookies or not?"

"If the cookies have the ingredients listed, or at least the amount of carbs and sugar and whether they contain nuts. They have people with diabetes in the race and they have to be careful about people with food allergies."

"That sounds reasonable. Can you do that?"

Jane sighed. "Yes. I have a computer program that tells me all that information if I enter the ingredients. It's not that." She set down the peeler and carrot and turned, wiping her hands on the towel tucked in her belt. "Of course I want to make sure our cookies don't harm someone. It's her attitude that gets to me. She always has to have the upper hand. There's always some objection to anything I suggest. She has to win."

Louise raised an eyebrow. "Always? How would you know that?"

Jane hung her head. "She used to live in the area. That's why she picked Acorn Hill. She was on the cross-country team a year ahead of me. We raced together."

"Ah. I'm beginning to get the picture. I think I remember her. She used to do a victory dance when she crossed the finish line, sort of like the football players on television when they get a touchdown."

Jane nodded grimly. "That's her. So it wasn't just my imagination. She really was a show-off. This may not be very Christian of me, but I want to beat her so badly I can taste it." Just admitting it made Jane feel small and ashamed, but she couldn't help it. She felt like a high schooler again, talking to her big sister, who'd been like a mother since their mother had died after Jane's birth.

Louise's eyes softened with compassion and she opened her arms. Jane fell into her sister's hug. "I've been embarrassed to admit my feelings, even to myself," Jane said against Louise's shoulder. "I should be above such pettiness."

"Don't be ashamed of wanting to win. The Bible admonishes us to run for the prize. I'm not sure it means a 10K race, but wanting to do your best is a good thing. Maybe Carrie beat you in all those high school races, but she was older, and perhaps running was the one thing she excelled at. Maybe her finish line posturing was exuberance that she did well. Who knows what's in her heart? Sometimes when I catch myself thinking disparaging thoughts about someone, I try to say a prayer for that person. It usually turns my attitude around, and that's what you're really battling."

"I haven't prayed for her or for the race to be a success. I'll do that. But I'm still going to try to beat her."

Louise smiled. "And I'll be there rooting you on. You are a winner, you know. Someday you'll have a golden crown to prove it."

"Maybe. If I get my attitude straightened out. Thanks, Louie. I don't know about a crown, but I'm certainly blessed. And I will put the nutrition values on those cookies, on the back of the Bible verses the girls picked to go with them. Maybe we'll give away some apples, too, for those who can't eat the cookies."

"I don't know if this is good or bad, but you'll get a chance to work on that attitude problem. Your nemesis has booked a room here for the race weekend. She's coming Friday afternoon."

Jane's eyes widened. "That may be more of a challenge than a chance." She picked up a carrot and carefully, gently, ran the peeler down it, removing a thin strip of skin.

Chapter Twenty-Four

Until Fred, Vera and Craig showed up Sunday afternoon with a harness contraption, the pumpkin weigh-off hadn't seemed real to Louise.

The men unloaded lengths of wide heavy-duty straps with chains and hooks on the ends and carried them into the garden. Next they dragged out a heavy tarp and set it near the pumpkin cage. Vera went over to talk to Louise, Alice and Jane, who stood at one side of the cage, watching.

"When Craig came by the store with the equipment to get the pumpkin ready to move for next weekend, I thought I'd come over to see what they're going to do," Vera said. They watched the men lift the tarps off the pumpkin. "I think it's larger than when Alice and I left last week."

"It's still growing, but not as fast," Louise said. "Jane and I tried to measure it yesterday. We came up with one hundred and sixty-six and a half inches, which is larger than last week."

"If you're not all field-tripped out, will it still be all right for me to bring my class to see it?" Vera asked.

"Yes. If you'd like, bring them Friday morning and watch the men move it. That should be quite a sight."

"Good idea. We'll give you a royal send-off," Vera said.

Louise turned to watch the men remove the cage they'd built to keep out raccoons. "How are you going to get that equipment under the pumpkin?" she asked.

"We'll have to rock it side to side," Craig said.

"Like the way we make a hospital bed with the patient in it," Alice said.

"I hope you don't have any patients this large," Fred said, "but I expect it's basically the same idea. We'll slide the tarp and winch straps underneath one side, then roll it over and pull them through."

Louise wondered how they would accomplish that, even with all of them pushing and pulling.

"Don't worry about the pumpkin," Craig said, as if he'd read her mind. "I called in reinforcements."

A truck pulled into the driveway and parked next to Craig's truck. Sam Bellwood and his oldest son Caleb got out.

"Howdy," Sam said, coming into the garden. "Looks like we got here just in time." The two men looked so much alike, no one could mistake they were father and son. Sam stood an inch taller than Caleb, but both men were tall by any standard. They came over and grabbed the sides of the cage. With all four men helping, they lifted it away from the pumpkin patch.

The women folded the tarps and blankets while the men carried the cage to the far side of the harvested garden.

"We need to be very careful of the stem," Craig said, moving to the head of the giant pumpkin. "It's brittle by now. Louise, if you could help us free it up," he said.

Louise went to the main vine and removed leaves and tendrils that were caught on other vines and tendrils. Jane helped her loosen the vine connecting the giant pumpkin to the main plant.

They carefully lifted and adjusted the vine while the men rolled the pumpkin to one side. The sand underneath helped cushion it. As the men offered directions, Alice and Vera folded the ends of the straps and carefully arranged them beneath the pumpkin, pressing the chain and hook down into the sand to prevent them from harming the pumpkin, then they did the same with the tarp. Alice and Vera stepped back.

"Ready?" Craig asked.

"As ready as we can make it," Alice said, holding up her crossed fingers.

Louise held her breath as the men slowly rolled the pumpkin back. She glanced at Jane, who was likewise holding her breath. Jane caught her gaze and gave her a reassuring smile. She let out her breath. "It's going to work," Jane said.

"I hope it works for Craig's sake. He's put a great deal of time and energy into helping me," Louise said.

"Watch the stem," Craig said. "We're going the other way now. Alice and Vera, get ready to pull the straps and tarp through."

The men grunted as they pushed and pulled. Trying to roll a thousand-pound pumpkin slowly was a strain, even for four strong men.

"It'd be easier if this baby was perfectly round," Sam said. He was turning red in the face. "Pushing one of my bales of hay is easier than this."

"Hold it there for a second," Alice said. "We've almost got it." They pulled the tarp through and up over the pumpkin, giving the ends to the men, who held the pumpkin with the tarp.

"Hang on a little longer," Vera said. She and Alice dug into the sand and freed the straps. They spread them out, so they crisscrossed in the middle and fanned out like spokes in a wheel.

"That should do it," Alice said, standing back. "Let her down gently."

The men repositioned the pumpkin, letting it roll back slowly to its original place.

"How did the stem do?" Craig asked, coming to examine it where it attached to the pumpkin.

"Fine," Jane said. "Great job, guys. Now what?"

"We'll put the cage back over it and keep it under the

blankets at night to protect it. We'll cut it free Thursday night and load it to move Friday morning."

"How will we transport it?" Louise asked.

"Fred is lending us his truck with a heavy-duty trailer. We'll strap it on," Craig said.

"I reserved two rooms in Baskenburg," Louise said. "I think I got the last two rooms in town. Evidently, this is a very popular event."

"Good. It'll be just you and me," Craig said. "I promised we'll take lots of pictures. By the way, Jane, there are other categories, if you want to send something. They have tomatoes, long gourds, cantaloupes, watermelons and squash."

"If they had a category for the smallest or lightest or maybe the best-tasting vegetables, I might have a chance," Jane said. "They're looking for size and weight, aren't they? Most of my vegetables are the miniature varieties. I prefer them for flavor and cooking."

"How do you plan to lift this giant out of the garden?" Alice asked.

"I thought we'd bring my front-end loader over," Sam said.

Louise frowned. She'd seen his loader at their farm. It was very large. "How will you get it into the garden?"

Sam looked around. "The gate's not wide enough." He walked over to examine the back of the fence, where it bordered the field behind their yard. "I could come in this way. We'd need to take down part of the fence and remove a couple of posts here."

Louise glanced at Jane, who showed no reaction, but Louise was hesitant. She'd already disrupted her sister's garden enough. She shook her head. "I'm not sure that's a good idea."

"We can put it back when they're done, Louise," Jane said.

The men looked at each other helplessly.

"Let us think about it," Fred said. "We'll come up with a solution."

"Yeah. We'll think of something," Caleb said.

"Trust us," Craig said. "Just be ready to go Friday morning."

"All right. We'll see," Louise said, crossing her arms to emphasize her determination. She intended to be in the garden early Friday morning, to keep any damage to Jane's garden to a minimum.

"How's the training coming?" Alice asked Jane as they stripped beds Monday morning.

"I'm doing better since I started running with Eleanor. She's a terrific coach. I've enjoyed getting to know her a little better too." Jane had been out early for stretches and a short workout. After school, she'd meet Eleanor to run together. "It's interesting to think of her and Vera as college roommates. They're very different."

"The serious student and the athlete. Vera was a bit of a tomboy growing up, though."

"Really? I suppose that doesn't surprise me. She likes to exercise. The two of you walk all the time."

"True, but our walking isn't all that athletic," Alice said. She tossed a handful of linens in the laundry pile. "We talk as much as we walk."

Jane laughed. "Well, I'm glad that you were so successful in providing for her Aunt Agatha. You and Vera make an invincible duo. And I'm sure you were both praying about it." Jane picked up the pile of sheets and towels. "I'll take these downstairs."

Jane heard the phone ringing as she descended the stairs. She hurried, but Louise had picked it up before she got there.

"Oh dear. All right, I'll tell her," Louise said into the phone. "Take care of yourself and get well." She said good-bye and hung up. "That was Eleanor Renda. She sounds awful. They had a track meet out west of Harrisburg. She said it was cold and foggy. She caught bronchitis, so she won't be able to run today."

"Poor Eleanor. I'll have to make her a batch of chicken soup as soon as we're finished cleaning."

⌒

It was still dark outside when Louise entered the kitchen Friday morning. Jane was standing at the sink, washing vegetables.

"Good morning."

Jane set a zucchini on the drain board and turned to her. "Morning. How come you're up so early?"

"I couldn't sleep."

"I never can before a trip either. What time will you leave?"

"Not until this afternoon. Am I crazy to do this? We have a full house this weekend."

"Alice is here. We'll be fine. I wish we could go with you." Jane reached for two coffee cups. "Want some coffee?"

"Yes, please."

Jane poured two cups and handed one to Louise. "What time are they coming to load the pumpkin?"

"Not until nine. That'll give me time to help serve breakfast." Louise stirred her coffee.

"We have lots of time before that."

The door from the hall opened and Alice came in. "Morning," she said. "I didn't realize you were up, Louise. Have you been out running already?" she asked Jane.

"No. I'll go later, after the pumpkin is loaded. The water's hot. Have some tea." She thin-sliced the zucchini and an onion on a cutting board.

"Can I help you? What's on today's menu?" Louise asked.

"Zucchini and mushroom frittata with gorgonzola, acorn squash latkes, plus plum and pear compote and apple fritters. If you'd like, you can slice a loaf of cinnamon bread and wrap it in foil to heat."

Jane got her coffee, which was getting cold, and sat at the table. "I'm curious to see if our former guests enter pumpkins in the weigh-off. Harry Gladstone was nice, but I'd love to see you beat Delmer Wesley. You have to call and keep us posted, Louie. We want to hear every detail."

"I'll let you know, but I'm not expecting to win anything. I'm doing this for Craig and Lloyd and Fred. I just don't have that competitive streak," Louise said. She saw the blush of red on Jane's cheeks and wished she could recall her words. Poor Jane was supersensitive about the upcoming charity run against her old schoolmate. Personally, Louise was much more concerned about Jane's race and her rival's coming to stay at the inn the next weekend than she was about the pumpkin weigh-off looming ahead.

Chapter Twenty-Five

*C*raig's here," Jane said, poking her head through the dining room doorway, where her sisters were clearing the table. One couple was still eating breakfast. "Excuse me," Jane said to their guests. "It's likely to get noisy around here. We're about to load my sister's thousand-pound pumpkin onto a trailer, and a busload of schoolchildren will be arriving any minute to watch."

"My goodness. We don't want to miss that. Is there a good viewing spot?" the young man asked.

His wife set down her napkin. "I'm just finished. Let me get the camera."

"I'll get it," the man said, dashing from the room. They heard him racing up the stairs two steps at a time.

"There's no hurry. I'm sure it will take a while. You can go through the sunroom. The garden is off to the right at the back of the house. The children will be on the lawn," Jane told the wife. "Is there anything else I can get you? More coffee?"

"Oh no, thank you. Our breakfast was delicious." She stood, then headed for the doorway.

Jane hurried to the kitchen with her sisters. "I have cookies and apple cider here for Vera's class when the time comes. Let's go watch." Jane removed her apron and hung it by the door as she grabbed her windbreaker. The nights had turned cold. There'd been a suspicious sheen of white on the grass when she first got up.

Craig turned the rig around and backed up to the fence. Jane wondered how he planned to move the pumpkin. Louise had been adamant about not moving the fence.

Craig entered the garden and began removing the blankets covering the pumpkin cage. Fred and Sam showed up and went to help him.

Jane heard the deep rumble of a large engine. She looked around in time to see Caleb Bellwood coming along Chapel Road, driving a large flatbed truck with an excavator secured in back. Caleb carefully maneuvered the truck into position near the garden as a school bus drew to a stop at the end of the driveway. Jane saw Vera and a crowd of young students ready to descend from the bus. The children ran across the yard. Jane stepped out on the lawn to stop them. She didn't want them near the heavy equipment.

Vera came over to the sisters, who were standing in the middle of the lawn between the children and the garden.

"Wow! You really know how to put on a show," Vera told Louise. She laughed at Louise's stunned expression.

"This is really something, isn't it?" Jane said, joining her own laughter with Vera's.

Carlene Moss came striding across the lawn, followed by Lloyd, Ethel and Craig. Caleb climbed out of his truck and made ready to off-load the excavator.

Movement at the side of the house caught Jane's eye. She glanced over. The inn guests stood watching from the corner of the house. It looked as if half the town had joined them. Rev. Thompson and Henry and Patsy Ley were walking from the direction of the church. Carlene's camera clicked several times in succession. Louise's pumpkin was a celebrity.

"Louise may shoot me later, but we brought streamers and signs to decorate the trailer," Vera told Alice.

Alice chuckled at the image that popped into her mind of Louise and Craig driving down the road with streamers flying and cans rattling like a car with "Just Married" written across the back. "Louise doesn't have a violent bone in her body, but she may wish she did," she said.

Alice looked at the crowd of school kids. Two chaperones were talking with them, keeping them contained. So much energy.

Louise went over to the huddle of men to learn what

they planned to do. She found them in a huddle. They talked, then pointed to the garden, then talked some more.

Jane joined Alice and Vera. "This could take a while. Let's break out the cookies and cider now."

"All right. I hope we have enough."

"I have plenty for the kids, but I'm not sure about the rest of the town. I made extra though. Let's go see what we have."

Louise stayed outside "to keep an eye on the fence," she'd told Alice and Jane.

"We can pour the drinks outside," Jane said, taking a stack of paper cups out of the pantry.

Alice arranged frosted pumpkin cookies on a tray. Jane pulled a square plastic container out of the refrigerator.

"I made these apple-cranberry bars last night for us and our guests. Let's pass these out now and I'll make more this afternoon."

Alice glanced out the window. "Caleb is going back to the excavator. We'd better get outside." She picked up the two trays of goodies. Jane opened the door and followed her with two jugs of cider.

Grabbing handholds, Caleb hoisted himself up into the cab of the big machine. It rocked side to side when it rumbled to life. The sound of the engine drowned out their voices. Alice beckoned to several of the students to help pass out cider and cookies. Then she did the same. Caleb was missing out on the treats, but Alice suspected he was enjoying himself, commanding that big machine as he moved it into position.

The machine's long arm slowly unfurled and stretched out and up, then pivoted and swung over the fence until the bucket hovered a few feet above the pumpkin, its stem now neatly removed. When it stopped, the crowd let out a collective sigh.

Craig, Fred and Sam entered the garden. Louise started to follow them, then changed her mind and went back to the yard. The men rocked and moved the pumpkin to the center of the blue tarp beneath it, then wrapped the tarp over the pumpkin and raised the hoist straps. It took a bit of maneuvering, but they finally attached all the chains and hooks over the teeth of the excavator's bucket.

"Stand back," Sam yelled.

The men stepped back away from the pumpkin, but stayed in the garden, ready to move in if needed. Caleb raised the bucket a few inches. The chains grew taut. The pumpkin moved. The crowd gasped. Alice looked around. Louise was watching with pursed lips. Everyone stared at the pumpkin and the giant arm above it.

Inch by inch, the big arm rose, then stopped. Fred and Sam went over to check the pumpkin. Craig stood far enough away to watch and tell them if anything was amiss. They tested the straps. When they were satisfied, they stepped out of the way. Sam gave Caleb a thumb's up signal.

Alice could see Caleb shift a gear. The wrapped pumpkin package began to rise. It dangled and swayed like a giant blue wrecking ball.

"Oh, I can't look," Louise said, turning away from the sight, but she turned back a second later.

When the pumpkin dangled ten feet off the ground, the arm slowly extended, stretching out toward the far fence and the trailer parked on the other side. Sam stood to one side, giving Caleb hand signals. The pumpkin rocked and bobbed on the end of its tether. Craig and Fred went out to stand on either side of the trailer. The other men surged forward, ready to help do whatever was required. Cameras flashed and clicked.

"Move-it, move-it, move-that-pumpkin," the children began chanting in unison. The guests and townspeople took up the cry.

"Move-that-pumpkin. Move-that-pumpkin. Move-that-pumpkin," reverberated in the air.

Cars pulled to a stop on both sides of the street and people got out to watch. Alice looked overhead, almost expecting to see a news helicopter, but the sky was clear.

The pumpkin cleared the fence and the arm began to

lower. It swung out, then back, nearly snagging on the top of a fence post.

"Stop!" Everyone screamed. Sam made a chopping motion with his hands and the arm stopped. Alice released her breath. Another inch and the pumpkin would have been impaled on the top of a pointed fence post.

The men gathered around the base of the dangling pumpkin. Caleb climbed down out of his machine and went to investigate.

Alice and Louise went to see what was wrong. Jane stayed with Vera to keep the children from surging forward to see better.

"I need another foot of stretch space, but the arm is extended to full length," Caleb said.

"If I can move my truck, I can get the trailer closer," said Craig.

"Give it a try." Sam clapped his hands together as encouragement.

Craig got in his truck to reposition the trailer. Half of the men stood on each side of the truck, hollering directions as he backed it up closer to the pumpkin. Alice wondered how he would manage with all the help, but he did.

Craig jumped out of the truck and ran back to help Fred position a large pallet under the pumpkin, making sure it was square to the sides.

Sam watched, his hand in the air, holding Caleb off as six men got behind the pumpkin to push it away from the fence. When he got a nod from Craig, Sam yelled, "Lower away!" as he motioned downward with his hands.

"Here we go," Alice said. She held her breath as the pumpkin lowered in slow, jerky motions and the men pushed against the dangling pumpkin to position it.

"Touchdown!" someone yelled.

The blue tarp made contact with the pallet. The trailer moved beneath the weight of the pumpkin as the arm lowered it, until the cables were slack.

Craig and Fred scrambled up onto the trailer and removed the cables from the bucket's teeth. They spread open the tarp and checked the pumpkin for damage. Louise stood next to the trailer, clasping her hands together while the men ran their hands all over the pumpkin. Finally Craig turned toward Louise and the waiting audience. He raised his hands in victory and gave them a huge grin.

"Perfect landing," he yelled. "Not a scratch on 'er."

Cheers, whistles and applause erupted from the backyard, side yard and street.

Louise's shoulders dropped and her hands unclasped. She smiled and thanked the men, then turned to find her sisters.

Looking relieved, she went over to Jane, Alice and

Vera. "I'm never growing anything again," she said. "The stress is just too much."

Alice and Vera laughed. Jane gave Louise a hug. Then everyone crowded around to congratulate her, while the spectators cheered and cameras continued to click.

Slowly, but with a great deal of noise, the crowd dispersed. The schoolchildren descended upon the trailer like a swarm of bees. Vera and her helpers went to supervise. When they stepped away, several minutes later, bright orange and red and purple streamers were attached to the truck and trailer and crisscrossed over the pumpkin, which Craig had secured with straps. A big sign was propped against the back of the pumpkin. *The Monster Pumpkin of Acorn Hill*, it announced.

Alice read the sign and smiled. Louise and Craig would make quite a sight, rolling down the highway with the pumpkin in tow. She wished she could follow along behind to watch the spectacle.

Chapter Twenty-Six

*L*ouise looked about as she and Craig rode in his truck to the pumpkin festival Saturday morning. Evidence of the event decorated every lamppost and storefront. Banners stretched across the street overhead, announcing the Baskenburg Fall Carnival and Great Pumpkin Weigh-off. She'd been too excited to eat breakfast. The cup of tea in her hotel room hadn't helped.

Craig pulled into the Baskenburg fairgrounds where they'd unhooked and left the trailer the night before. She hadn't known what to expect, but at least thirty trailers with huge pumpkins and squash and watermelons had already arrived. An official-looking man had told them where to park.

The fairgrounds buzzed with activity. The colors orange and green predominated, with displays of pumpkin para-phernalia, pots of chrysanthemums, banners, ceramic jack-o'-lanterns and cornucopias filled with gourds and Indian corn. Booths sold pumpkin doughnuts, spiced cider, caramel popcorn, hot dogs and breakfast foods. Vendors offered whimsical wind chimes and whirligigs, bottles of barbecue sauce and fancy pickles, aprons, hats, T-shirts and hand-made jewelry. Off to one side, the seats of a Ferris wheel creaked in place, empty in the early morning hour. All the carnival rides stood still. Colorful flags and banners flapped in the breeze as if to invite would-be riders to join the fun.

They went to a registration table to sign in. Louise filled out an entry form and paid her fee, while Craig moseyed around, looking at the various giant vegetables. He came back as she got a number. Then they went to the trailer and waited. A worker arrived on a forklift. He maneuvered its tines into the palette and lifted Louise's pumpkin as if it weighed just a few pounds. It bounced as he drove over and set it down beside a row of other pump-kins on palettes. An official then attached an entry number to the orange giant.

"That's it. Now we wait. Let's go find some coffee and something to eat. I'm starved," Craig said.

"Me too. We should have eaten breakfast."

"Couldn't. Too nervous," Craig said. "Besides, I love carnival food."

"Me too. Silly, isn't it?" Louise said. They walked over to a booth selling homemade baked goods and coffee.

"Good morning," a lady said. "I saw them unload your pumpkin. Looks like it might be our winner, unless someone shows up later with something even bigger, but they only have forty-five minutes before registration closes."

"Really?" Louise looked around. There were so many huge pumpkins, it was hard to tell which one looked the largest.

"I haven't seen you here before. Is this your first year?"

"Yes," Louise said. "This festival is amazing." She bought a cup of coffee and a square of crumb cake.

"Come back later, after you win a ribbon. We'll have bratwurst with sauerkraut or chili and the best blackberry ice cream you ever tasted."

"That sounds very tempting indeed," Louise said. "I love anything made with blackberries. I'll be back, win or lose."

$\backsim$

"Welcome to Baskenburg's Twenty-Seventh Annual Giant Pumpkin Weigh-off," a voice announced over the loud speaker. "Gather around the weighing station. We'll start with the giant squash."

A small band with accordions, guitars, a banjo and a drummer had set up on a side stage. They played a lively polka. Some of the audience began clapping in time. After a rousing few minutes, the music stopped and the weighing began.

Louise noticed that none of the entries was round.

Some of the vegetables looked like they were covered with warts, but beauty wasn't the point. Only size mattered. The forklift carted one palette after another to the big scale.

Seventeen squash later, the winner, weighing 671 pounds, was announced. An elderly man hobbled up to the front to a polka tune, accepting his trophy before a cheering crowd. He posed for a picture, grinning broadly.

The audience had grown. The big draw of the day would be the giant pumpkins, but there were still lots of other vegetables to be considered.

"You could grow any of these at your nursery," Louise told Craig. "You should try."

He clicked a picture. "And take the pleasure from that old man? I don't think so."

Next on the scale were watermelons. The winner was a beauty at 176 pounds. The music played, and a middle-aged woman accepted her prize as her family cheered for her.

The long gourds fascinated Louise. Jane grew gourds for decoration, but she'd never grown one like these. Louise preferred the bulbous shapes and variegated colors of Jane's gourds. Sometimes she painted them to look like dolls and donated them to fund-raisers in Acorn Hill. These gourds were long and dark green and looked like giant zucchini squash. The winner was ninety-eight inches long, about three feet taller than its grower.

They watched the tomato competition. A large crowd enthusiastically clapped and cheered for every entry, no matter what it weighed.

Louise had to admit that a three-pound tomato was impressive. It also looked tasty.

Finally, after the cantaloupe, they started weighing the pumpkins. Louise heard her name called by someone behind her and she turned around. Reba and Harry Gladstone stood behind them. He had on a bright orange ball cap with a pumpkin on the front and she wore an orange straw hat.

"I was wondering if you'd come," Harry said. "Which one is yours?"

She pointed out hers. "I gave in to pressure," she said, glancing at Craig, who smiled. She introduced them. "Did you bring anything?"

"I brought a squash and a watermelon, but neither one placed." He shrugged. "Maybe next year."

"We do better every year. We come mainly to see friends. The giant growers are great people," Reba said.

"Everyone's been awfully nice," Louise said, looking around. "Are your friends here?"

"Haven't seen them yet, but I'm sure they're here. Delmer wouldn't miss it," Harry said.

"I think he has a big one this year," Reba added. "Good luck."

"Thank you."

The judges started with the smaller pumpkins and advanced to the larger ones. Louise watched the numbers gradually rise on the pumpkin scale. Five hundred. Six hundred. Eight hundred. Nine hundred. So far, none was as large as hers, but she had no idea if Craig's weight estimations were on target.

The forklift brought a huge pumpkin to the scale. Louise thought it looked larger than hers. The numbers whizzed away, stopping on 1,027. Surely that was the winner. She saw Delmer and Genevieve Wesley step up to the scale. The crowd applauded. The man handed them a piece of paper, then scrawled the weight on the pumpkin in black marker. Louise sighed. She chose to be happy for the man, even if he was a grouch. He certainly looked happy now. She thought he glanced her way, but he didn't seem to recognize her. The forklift removed his pumpkin.

The next pumpkin weighed thirty pounds less. The following one looked smaller, but weighed within three pounds of Delmer's pumpkin.

Finally, they brought Louise's pumpkin to the scale. Craig went closer to get a picture. Louise followed him so that she was standing right in front of the scale.

The numbers whirred past eight hundred, nine hundred, one thousand, and finally stopped at 1,040.2 pounds. Louise blinked and looked again. The crowd began to cheer.

"Go get the paper," Craig said, nudging her elbow.

"Oh." She stepped forward and received a copy of the official weight. They'd already marked the pumpkin. Several people congratulated her as she went back to stand by Craig.

"I knew you had a winner," Harry said. "Congratulations."

"They aren't finished," she said.

"None of the rest are even close," he said.

They weighed three more pumpkins. They were all less than a thousand pounds.

"And the winner is . . ." The announcer waited for a drum roll. "Louise Smith of Acorn Hill with a pumpkin at one thousand forty point two pounds. Will the top three entrants come accept your prizes," the announcer said.

The band struck up a victory song that Louise remembered from college football games. In a daze, she went up front. The music stopped and the announcer started with third place. Then Delmer accepted second place. He stood next to her while she accepted the winning trophy. The announcer congratulated her and handed her the microphone. "Would you like to say a few words?" he asked her.

Louise didn't know what to say. She looked at Craig, who was grinning and clapping and nodding encouragement.

"Tell your secret," Delmer said beside her.

"Oh dear." Louise held the microphone near her mouth. "Thank you. I'm stunned to win this competition," she said. "I have to confess, I am not a gardener, but I had exceptional seeds, a sister who knows how to prepare a garden, and a dear friend, our local nurseryman, Craig Tracy, who advised me all the way. They all share the credit for this prize. To all of you who grow these amazing pumpkins every year, you have my utmost respect," she said, looking at the man beside her. "Thank you all."

Louise handed back the microphone to the announcer. The crowd cheered. The band struck up a boisterous rendition of "Happy Days Are Here Again."

"Congratulations," Delmer said, reaching out to shake her hand. "You raised a beauty."

"Thank you. So did you. I can't believe mine weighs more than yours. Could the scale be wrong?" she said.

"Not a chance," he said.

The crowd began to disperse. Delmer stayed next to her until they were out of earshot of everyone.

"I want to apologize for my bad manners at your inn. I'm glad you won."

Louise stared at him. "You are? You've worked hard to grow the biggest pumpkin. Mine is a fluke."

"No. I got carried away. Winning became so important to me, I became jealous when I heard about your pumpkin. I went to the inn to check it out." He paused, looking very uncomfortable. "I snuck into your garden before dawn."

"I know."

"You do?"

"Yes. My sister saw you. She'd been out jogging. She also saw your friend go into the garden and interrupt you."

Delmer hung his head and nodded. "I owe him an apology too. And a thank-you, for stopping me from doing something nasty."

"Would you really have harmed my pumpkin?" Louise asked.

"I don't know. I guess I'll never know. But your kindness to Genevieve and me, even when I was so rude, made me realize there are more important things than winning."

"Well, let's give you the benefit of the doubt. At any rate, I don't intend to do this again," Louise said. "One giant pumpkin is enough for me. It's turned my life upside down."

Delmer gave her a hint of a smile. "You don't like the limelight, do you?"

"Not really," she said. "If I'd known, I never would have planted those seeds."

"Congratulations," Genevieve said, coming up next to her husband. "I heard your comment, Louise. Why did you plant them, if you don't mind my asking?"

"To prove to my sister that I could grow something. Jane is the gardener in our family. I'd seen a patch of giant pumpkins years ago and I was so impressed, I bought a few seeds as souvenirs. Then I forgot about them. This year I found the seeds and decided to give them a try. I thought if I managed to grow anything, maybe it would be respectable."

Delmer laughed. "Much more than respectable," he said. "I don't suppose I could talk you out of some seeds."

"My friend Craig will have the seeds. I'm sure he'd be happy to sell you some. He has a flower shop and nursery in Acorn Hill."

"Did he advise you on fertilizer?" Delmer asked.

"No. I tried something I had read about in a novel, but truly, I have to thank the Lord and my sister for my success. You're a gardener, perhaps you've heard the verse about sowing and reaping."

"Oh yes," Genevieve said. "One person plants and another harvests, but the Lord makes the crop grow. Is that the one you mean?"

"That's it. I looked it up, because I was puzzling over this great pumpkin. I did feed it something unusual, but I had no control over its success. Not really. The Bible says, 'So neither he who plants nor he who waters is anything, but only God, who makes things grow' (1 Corinthians 3:7). My sister has been working the garden and building up the soil for a long time. I came along and planted these little seeds that someone else provided. And that's what came of it," she said, pointing to her pumpkin.

"If you're not going to raise them again, would you tell me what you fed it?" Genevieve asked.

"Why not?" Louise leaned forward and whispered in Genevieve's ear.

The lady gave her a stunned look. "You're kidding."

"That's the honest truth. Six ounces every day."

Genevieve looked at her husband, then at Louise, and began laughing.

"What did she say?" Delmer asked.

Still laughing, his wife said, "I'll tell you later, after I've sworn you to secrecy."

"This is serious business," he said. "If it'll help me grow a champion, you can be sure I'll never tell."

"Come visit us again sometime," Louise said. "I promise we won't serve pumpkin for breakfast."

"We'd be delighted," Genevieve said. "Now go enjoy the carnival. They have pie-eating contests and they'll be cutting up the entries in the largest pumpkin pie contest over there," she said, pointing to a large striped tent.

"Thanks. We will, but we want to be back in Acorn Hill before dark, so we won't be able to stay long." Louise said good-bye and went to join Craig, who was waiting patiently.

Craig frowned in the Wesleys' direction. "I couldn't help overhearing part of your conversation. That's the guy who wanted to sabotage your pumpkin?"

Louise nodded. "He apologized. He's had a change of heart."

"That's good. Gardening is such a peaceable, happy occupation, I can't imagine anyone getting so caught up in winning a competition that he becomes bitter."

"Neither can I. But I've learned something."

"What's that?"

"It takes a lot of work to produce a successful garden. You and Jane have my total admiration and respect."

Craig smiled and touched the brim of his cap, giving her a slight bow. "Thank you, ma'am. And your wonderful seeds are going to help my business. Will you share your fertilizer secret with me?"

"Yes, but not until I tell Jane and Alice. Speaking of whom, I'd better call them with the good news."

"Here. Use my cell phone. I'll go see about getting our prize beauty loaded for the trip home."

Louise smiled as she punched the numbers into the little phone. Jane and Alice were going to flip over her news.

Chapter Twenty-Seven

"*M*y goodness. Look at all the cars. It seems we have a welcoming committee," Louise said as Craig parked the truck up the road from Grace Chapel Inn. "Good thing we left the trailer at your nursery."

"You're a celebrity," Craig said.

"Not I. The pumpkin."

When Craig opened the inn's front door for Louise, a crowd met them, standing and applauding as she entered. She'd received applause for her piano playing from auditoriums filled with people, but this outpouring from her friends touched her heart. She spotted her sisters in the back of the room. They were both smiling proudly.

"Oh my. I don't know what to say. Thank you." She held up the trophy. "This is for Jane and Alice, who put as much work into watching out for that pumpkin as I put into making it grow."

As they all laughed, Jane said, "We'll treasure it always. You did get pictures, didn't you?"

"I took lots of pictures," Craig said.

"I want a photo of the winner for the paper," Carlene said, making her way to the front of the room. "Is it parked outside?"

"No. We left it at Craig's nursery," Louise said. "Besides, I've had enough pictures taken."

"You can look through my pictures and use what you want," Craig told her. "They're all digital."

"Good. You're famous, you know," Carlene said.

"Only because this wasn't a record-breaking year. At least not at Baskenburg. I'm sure there were larger pumpkins at other weigh-offs. The largest on record is six hundred pounds heavier than mine."

Lloyd stepped forward. "It doesn't matter. There's always someone to break a record. On behalf of Acorn Hill, we're proud of you. As mayor, I proclaim that's official."

"Are you going to grow another one next year?" Fred asked.

"Not on your life. Jane can if she wants or you can, Fred. Craig will be glad to supply the seeds. For myself, I don't care if I never see or taste another pumpkin again."

"That's too bad," Jane said, coming forward. "Dinner is ready. In your honor, we have stuffed pork loin with all the trimmings and for dessert, pumpkin cheesecake."

"Pumpkin cheesecake?" Louise said. "Well . . . maybe just tonight. I love your pumpkin cheesecake."

That earned a laugh as everyone filed into the dining room.

Rev. Thompson asked the blessing, thanking God for Jane and Craig's safe trip and for the bountiful meal. Jane started the food around.

Louise stood.

"What do you need?" Jane asked. "I'll get it."

"I thought I'd have a glass of buttermilk."

"Oh dear. We're all out. I put what was left in the biscuits. I'll get some more tomorrow."

"No buttermilk? Oh dear." Louise put her hands to her heart dramatically and sighed. "I suppose it's all right. I won't be needing it anymore now that the pumpkin is gone."

"Why?" Jane gave her a suspicious look.

"That was my secret weapon. I've been fertilizing the pumpkin patch with buttermilk. It's an old folk secret that I read about." She beamed with satisfaction.

"Buttermilk?" Jane repeated. "You fed your plants buttermilk? I've never heard of such a thing. I thought you were drinking an awful lot of it."

"Buttermilk?" Craig said. "Amazing. I can't imagine why it would work, but something did the trick. I'll have to research that. Who would have thought?" he muttered.

Louise entered the kitchen the following Friday afternoon. Jane was sitting at the kitchen table, putting a self-stick label on the back of a bag of cookies. Each small package held two cookies that the ANGELs had baked and bagged.

"Ah, the cookies for after the race. Let me help." Louise sat at the table and picked up a sheet of printed labels. "Are these all oatmeal chocolate chip cookies?"

"Yes. The oatmeal raisin cookies are in the other box. We need to label them also." Jane peeled off a label and stuck it to the back of a bag.

"Your friend Carrie Gleason just checked in," Louise said.

Jane nodded. "I registered two women on her committee earlier. I told them you have piano lessons in the parlor this afternoon, but they're welcome to meet in the library or the dining room. It sounds like they're well organized."

"Organizing is what they do, isn't it?"

"I believe so. They put on charity races for different groups. I gather it's a business, but it sounds like a passion too. The women are very excited about tomorrow."

"Are they racing?" Louise put a finished bag in the box with the ones Jane had completed and picked up another bag.

"No. They're handling registration and taking pledges. I think Carrie is the only one of the organizers who is running." Jane smirked. "Figures." She looked up at Louise.

"Uh-oh. My attitude is showing. I'm afraid I haven't done a very good job of letting go."

"This weekend is going to be hard on you, isn't it? Alice and I can serve breakfast, but you're still going to run into her sooner or later. Would you like to pray about it?"

Jane looked at her sister. "I would. I've tried to think good thoughts about Carrie, but it isn't working very well."

"All right." Louise put down her bag and reached out for Jane's hands. Jane took her sister's hands and bowed her head.

"Dear heavenly Father, this has been quite a time of learning humility in our household. Thank You for my sister who supported me and never teased me about my clumsy gardening. I know I didn't grow that pumpkin on my own. It wouldn't have grown so large if Jane hadn't prepared the soil so well. It wouldn't have grown so large without Your sunshine and rain. Now Lord, please pour Your sunshine on Jane's heart and help her to let go of these feelings of inadequacy she has around Carrie. Help Jane see the special gifts You've given to her. Help us to be thankful for what we have. Lord, watch over Carrie and touch her with Your sunshine too. Bless her for helping people less fortunate, who are suffering from diabetes. We ask these things in Jesus' name. Amen."

Jane opened her eyes. "Amen. Thanks, Sis," she whispered. "I'll try to remember to pray for Carrie tonight before I go to bed and tomorrow, before we run."

Louise smiled. "You're welcome. I'll keep praying for both of you." She picked up another label and another bag. "So how's the pledge drive going?"

"I'm not sure. Aunt Ethel is handling it and she's gotten off to a good start. I've gotten some nice donations from my friends in San Francisco. Otherwise, I've left it up to her. She seems happy to do it."

"I imagine so. Alice and I will stay on the sidelines with Aunt Ethel and cheer you on."

"I couldn't ask for better cheerleaders." Jane got up and brought another cardboard box filled with bags of cookies to the table. "These are the oatmeal raisin cookies."

"That's a lot of cookies. How many bags did the girls make?"

"Two hundred. That's how many Carrie said to plan for. I think a lot of people are staying in Potterston."

"We have two more reservations to check in. Will you watch for them while I give piano lessons?"

"Sure will. I think I'll put out popcorn and pumpkin bread for snacks tonight. I still have plenty of pumpkin and squash to use up."

"Maybe next year we should cut back on the pumpkins."

Jane grinned. "Do you think buttermilk would work on those long gourds? With your success, we could grow a ten-footer."

"Oh no, you don't. From now on, the only buttermilk we use around here is for cooking. Of course, I might have a little nip now and then."

Jane shook her head. "I don't know how you acquired a taste for that stuff, but you're welcome to it."

Carrie came down the stairs as Jane was checking a mother and daughter into the Garden Room.

"Hi, Jane. Nice room and the inn is lovely."

"Thanks. I hope you enjoy your stay."

"I'm sure that I will. Well, see you later. I'm heading into town. I'm looking forward to racing you tomorrow." Carrie went out the front door, her short, dark hair bouncing with her lively steps.

I bet you are, Jane thought. She turned and smiled at the new guests. Both were below average height. The mother was heavyset. The teenager was of average build and had lovely smooth skin and bright hazel eyes. "If you'll follow me, I'll show you to your room. Are you here for the race or to enjoy the fall colors?" she asked as she started up the stairs.

"I'm running," the teenager said. "Mom likes to shop."

"I'll watch the race from the sidelines, but I'm looking forward to browsing through your shops. We passed a bookstore and an antique shop. That's my kind of sports," the mother said. "I'm glad Tory is interested in exercise, though. What a lovely home you have. Maybe I'll buy a book and sit in your living room and read."

"You're welcome to do that." Jane told them about the different places they could get dinner. "I'll set out a snack this evening. We'll have an early breakfast for runners in the morning. Breakfast will also be served from seven to nine. Let me know if you need anything."

She left them and went to the kitchen to make early preparations for Saturday's breakfast. She planned to have it ready for Alice and Louise to serve while she readied herself for the race.

Jane got out her list. Three of their guests were entered in the Harvest 10K Run plus the two helpers. That left only two guests for regular breakfast. With the race in town, she'd planned conservative, health-conscious meals. She prepared batter for stone-ground corn waffles that Louise and Alice could toast in the morning. As the waffles cooked, she made piecrusts for broccoli-and-cheese quiches. She made an extra quiche for dinner and had just put everything in the oven when the bell rang at the reception desk. She started to remove her apron, then heard Louise's voice in the hallway. She couldn't help hearing Carrie's voice also.

"I won't be eating breakfast here," she told Louise. "I need to be out early to help with setting up."

"Jane is serving an early breakfast for runners and helpers," Louise told her.

"That's all right. I carry special food with me."

Jane heard footsteps running up the stairs. The kitchen door opened and Louise came in.

"One less for breakfast," she said.

"I know. I heard. She carries *special* food. Well, she doesn't know what she'll be missing. I have a great breakfast planned for the runners. Her loss." Jane hated the negativity she heard in her own voice. She hated the knot that she felt in the vicinity of her heart. She gave Louise a pained look, trying to communicate her regret.

"It's all right," Louise said. "Treat her with kindness and respect, and let it go."

Jane nodded. *Let it go*, she thought. *How can I? I'm behaving like the self-centered person I accuse her of being. Lord help me get over this judgmental attitude I have toward Carrie. She probably has a good reason for carrying her own food. It's not a reflection on me. She doesn't even know me. Amen.*

༄

Jane was up and dressed for the race before she put out breakfast for the early birds. She set a platter of fresh cut fruit and a basket of whole-grain bran muffins on the table when she heard footsteps on the stairs. She looked out into the hall and saw Carrie.

"Good morning," she called out. Carrie turned.

"Good morning. Are you in the mood to race?"

"I am. I just put out some fresh fruit and bran muffins, if you'd like some. I have homemade granola as well."

Carrie looked inside the dining room. She was dressed in a royal blue outfit with racing stripes down the sides of her shorts and a matching top and jacket. She gave Jane a friendly smile. "Looks good, but I have a power bar. That's my usual breakfast. Gives me just the right mix of carbs and fiber, and it's low fat, you know. Maybe I'll take some fruit." She put several slices of apple and some dried cranberries in a napkin. "Gotta run." She laughed at her own pun. "See you in a while." She took off, walking quickly down the hall and out the front door.

The sun was up and there wasn't a cloud or wisp of mist in the air. It promised to be warmer than usual. Jane preferred it cool for running, but she couldn't complain. After a week of cold nights, the glorious autumn colors were popping out in force. The race was to start at nine o'clock, so she had plenty of time.

The two organizers who worked with Carrie came in. They greeted Jane, then sat down and ate quickly.

"This is wonderful," one of them said as Jane poured coffee for them. "We don't usually get such a great breakfast. May we take a muffin with us?"

"Of course. I'll wrap them in plastic for you. Would you like to take coffee with you?

"Oh yes. That would be wonderful," one of them said.

Jane went to the kitchen, wrapped the muffins, filled to-go cups with coffee and put lids on them. Then she gathered up the items and took them to the women. They thanked her and hurried off with their food to set up for the race.

A man who looked about forty came downstairs, dressed in black spandex running shorts and a long mesh T-shirt. His running shoes looked expensive. Jane had seen the man and his wife come in. The woman looked athletic, but obviously pregnant.

"Good morning. Joy is sleeping in. She's tired a lot lately." He glanced at Jane. "I see you're dressed to run. Do you compete often?" He sat down and started filling his plate with small portions of everything.

"No. This is my first road race. I ran in high school, but that was a long time ago," Jane said. In her mismatched modest outfit with inexpensive running shoes, she hardly looked like a habitual runner.

"Well, good luck. My wife and I run marathons, but we

may have to curtail that for a while, although we're looking for racing strollers now."

"Fresh air is good for everyone," Jane said, not sure what else to say.

"Yes. Joy can't wait to get back to running."

"Would you like some coffee?"

"No thanks. Not before I run. Joy is off caffeine too."

"I have decaf or tea," Jane said.

"Water is fine." He took a long drink to prove it.

"I'll let you eat then. Holler if you need anything. I'll be in the kitchen."

He'd left by the time Tory and her mother came downstairs. Jane glanced at her watch. There wasn't much time before they needed to check in for the race.

"I'll just have a small bite now with Tory. I'll come back for breakfast after she checks in."

They both filled their plates with fruit. Tory spread peanut butter on an apple slice and ate a handful of granola.

"Now watch what you eat," her mother admonished.

"I know, Mom," Tory said. "I have to have enough energy to make it through the race."

"All right, dear." She turned to Jane. "I'd love coffee, thank you. Do you have hazelnut creamer?"

"Yes." Jane handed her a small cream pitcher. "This one is hazelnut."

Tory reached for a muffin. Jane had chosen them especially for the runners' breakfast. They were Clarissa's heart-healthy muffins with oat bran, wheat bran, pineapple and raisins. They provided plenty of carbohydrates and protein.

"Is there anything else I can get for you?" Jane asked.

"No, thank you. We need to go," the mother said, looking at her watch. "Come on, Tory."

"Okay, Mom." Tory stood, leaving the muffin untouched.

"Let me get a paper plate for you," Jane said.

"No, thanks. I've had enough," Tory said. She grabbed half a banana and followed her mother out of the room.

Jane carried their plates to the kitchen. Alice had taken the quiches out of the refrigerator. Louise was stirring a pan of long-cooking oatmeal.

"Isn't it time for you to leave?" Alice asked.

"Yes. I'm just about ready." Jane removed her apron.

"We'll be praying for you," Louise said. "Just remember, reach for the prize."

Alice gave them a quizzical look. "Yes, we'll be praying," she said. "If we can get the guests fed in time, we'll meet you at the finish line."

"Thanks." Jane gave them a smile, then went out the back door and jogged toward downtown.

Chapter Twenty-Eight

*T*he parking lot behind Town Hall was packed with people. Most looked like runners. Jane signed in. They gave her a bright yellow bib with the number 153 on it. Judging by the line behind her, she thought the entries might hit two hundred.

The sun was already getting hot. Jane was glad she'd left her warm-up jacket at home. Several of the runners were shedding theirs and leaving them in a pile at the registration table.

She put on her number bib, then looked around for Eleanor. She didn't see her anywhere. The coach was still fighting her way back from bronchitis.

Vera waved to Jane. Sylvia Songer came over and wished her luck.

"Are you running?" Jane asked her.

"Not in the race. I'm running a sale today. Some storeowners got together and we decided we'd put out some sidewalk sales. Look at all these people," she said, smiling. "I'm expecting a record number of shoppers today."

"I hope you have a great sale."

"Thanks. See you tomorrow at church," Sylvia said.

Jane saw Tory with her mother. They were talking to Patsy Ley, who had come to watch. Over by the registration table, Lloyd was talking with the registration ladies from the inn. He was dressed in his official mayoral outfit, with sports coat and bow tie. He looked a little out of place among the shorts-and-spandex-clad crowd. Ethel was standing behind him, holding on to his arm. Jane thought she looked chic in a lavender knit warm-up suit that appeared quite stylish with her carefully curled and sprayed red hair.

Runners began stretching out in earnest. Jane looked at her watch. They had twenty minutes before the race would start. She walked around in a little circle, shaking her legs out, loosening up. She went through her normal routine of stretches, and felt as ready as she could be. Glancing up, she looked right into Carrie's eyes, ten yards in front of her.

"Watching you, I feel like I'm seventeen again," Carrie said.

At that moment, Jane felt sixteen and squaring off against her toughest competitor. This was it. Today she was going to beat Carrie Gleason. She nodded at Carrie, silently challenging her. Carrie smiled. Challenge accepted.

"Will all runners get ready to report to the starting line," Lloyd called over a loud speaker. "Five minutes to the start."

Shaking out her arms and legs, Jane moved toward the starting line. The street had been cordoned off, blocking all vehicular traffic. She found a place near the front. There were perhaps twenty people ahead of her. Looking over to her right, she saw Carrie take a place just even with hers.

Tory was right in front of the crowd next to several teenagers from the high school track team. They were calling to someone. Jane looked over. Eleanor Renda stood on the sidewalk in front of the antique shop. She was waving at the teens. She saw Jane and raised both hands, pointing her thumbs high. Jane returned the gesture. On the other side of the street, Lloyd and Ethel stood on a platform with three race officials. Ethel waved to her.

Jane took a deep breath. This was her race, but she wasn't alone. She wondered who was there for Carrie. She'd stayed alone at the inn. Jane hadn't seen her with anyone. Somehow, that seemed a little sad.

"Ready runners?" Lloyd said over the speaker.

A resounding "yes" rose from the crowd.

"Go at the sound of the shot. Ten . . . nine . . ." Lloyd counted down the seconds. The starting gun went off. Jane surged forward with the crowd, elbow to elbow, getting jostled, taking care not to trip over nearby feet. They ran down Hill Street to Village Road, then turned right to make a big circuit through town.

This was the easy part, level and paved. The mass of

runners stretched out. Jane saw teenagers and a few younger men and women ahead of her, but she seemed to be in the lead of those her age. Tory was near the front. The girl was fast. Jane didn't see Carrie. She didn't dare look back. She set her pace, knowing she had six miles to go, and the hills were still to come.

All along the way, friends cheered her on. The course rounded Chapel Road and then headed north past the Fire Department and the Cat Rescue Shelter. Hearing her name shouted from the crowd of spectators gave Jane a spurt of energy. Her legs stretched out with each stride. She passed the pharmacy and Fred's Hardware. Fred and Vera were shouting her name. "Go Jane! Go Jane!" Her feet pounded in time with her name. She felt energized, euphoric.

Passing the inn, she saw Alice and Louise standing on the front porch waving and calling out encouragement. The Leys and the pregnant guest were with them. On the hill, she poured on the power as if Eleanor were next to her, racing her. The wind blew wisps of hair back off her forehead. The faster her feet went, the quicker her ponytail flipped back and forth.

The course left the road and headed toward Fairy Pond. Here the mass of runners funneled into a path too narrow for a crowd. Jane got by several runners, then fell into line, settling in with the general pace. The midmorning sun shone through the trees, casting the runners' shadows onto the pond. Jane caught her reflection, along with the others, a line of carousel horses, up and down, up and down in alternating order. Then they were past, sprinting down the path through the trees, then breaking out into the sunshine, running along the road past fields of cut hay. The bright sunshine caused Jane to raise her arm and wipe the moisture off her forehead.

Eventually, Bellwood Farm came into view. Carol and Sissy Matthews were handing out cups of water along with Rose Bellwood. Several of the teenaged runners grabbed two cups, gulped one down and poured the other one over their heads. Jane thought about it for a second, grabbed one cup, yelled "thanks" and gulped down most of it, then patted a dab on her neck and face. It felt cool and refreshing.

In the few seconds she slowed for the water, several people passed her. Carrie was not among them. Tory was still ahead, running hard. Another hill was in sight. Jane steeled herself for the climb and mentally paced herself. She didn't have on a watch, but she felt sure she was ahead of the time for her fastest run so far. They'd passed the halfway point.

A hill slowed her a little. Those in the lead pulled ahead by a few yards. Jane heard steps right behind her. They got closer and closer. She glanced over, then let out a breath of relief. It wasn't Carrie. The runner pulled ahead slowly. Jane willed herself to increase her pace, using this new runner to challenge her.

Jane's heartbeat thudded against her chest. Her lungs burned. Her legs ached. She grabbed a drink at the eight-kilometer checkpoint. Tory still ran ahead of her. The girl was good. They started downhill toward town. The road wound around several wide turns. After the first of them, Jane heard feet pounding hard behind her, closing fast. Just as the runner overtook her, she glanced over. Carrie.

Carrie passed her as if on wheels. Jane stared at her rival's back in disbelief. Carrie raised a hand and waved, but she didn't look back.

Jane couldn't help admiring Carrie's long, even strides. They looked effortless. The woman was a powerhouse. She knew how to run. Eleanor would be impressed. Carrie rounded the bend in front of them, passing several other runners. Jane's heart sank. *Here we go again*, she thought. *By the time she reaches the finish line, she'll be doing her hippity-hop victory dance.*

Jane refused to give up. She poured on the steam, forcing her legs to move faster, her breathing to grab deeper, her mind to grow more determined. Around the next curve—no Carrie in sight. One curve to go, then the last stretch into town to the finish line.

She could see downtown as she rounded the curve. Then she saw something that stunned her. Carrie had stopped. She was leaning over someone. Someone was down.

Carrie had it well in hand. This was Jane's chance. Keep

on running. She was about to beat Carrie Gleason. Smiling, she drew up alongside, then began to pass her.

Rats, Jane thought. She stopped, turned and jogged back.

It was Tory sprawled on the ground, her head down, looking pale as death. Carrie looked up.

"Diabetic," she said.

Jane reached into her pocket and pulled out a pencil-thin, plastic-wrapped tube. She pulled the plastic off and reached out with it toward Tory. "It's fruit leather. It should give you enough carbs to make it."

Tory looked at her with a blank stare.

"She's had a sugar crash. Here." Carrie took it and held it to Tory's mouth. "Suck on it like it's a candy cane," she instructed.

Tory let Carrie push it into her mouth. She blinked and began sucking on the dried fruit.

"I usually have a snack. I can't believe it," Carrie said. She looked at Jane and smiled. "Thanks. Go on ahead. I'll wait with her and help her in."

"I could send someone out to pick her up."

Tory pushed to her feet and staggered. She looked ready to cry. "I've got to make it. Please. I can go on."

"You're in no shape to run," Carrie said.

"I'll walk. I've got to. I promised my grandma I'd make it. She just lost her toe. They amputated it because of her diabetes. I can make it."

Jane looked at Carrie. "How about the three of us. We're almost there. You and I can walk her across."

Carrie looked at Tory, a worried expression on her face. "You sure you want to try to walk in. It's still quite a distance when your sugar is so low."

"Please. I'm sorry that I made you stop."

"Sometimes losing is winning," Carrie said. "Come on. Put one arm across my shoulder and one across Jane's. What's your name, by the way?"

"Tory Winters."

"Hi, Tory. I'm Carrie. Glad to meet you."

The three of them limped into town. Just before they got to the finish line, Carrie looked down at Tory and said, "Get ready now. Any time you cross the finish line, you're a winner. Then you get to whoop it up, just for making it. Okay?" She looked at Jane and winked.

Jane nearly dropped Tory. *Any time you cross the finish line, you're a winner. Then you get to whoop it up, just for making it.*

"Okay, ready to sashay," Jane said, getting into the spirit of it. They reached the line together.

"You put your left foot across, you put your right foot across, you put your whole self across and you shake it all about," Carrie sang out as they carried out her commands.

"You do the hokey-pokey and you turn yourself around," Jane added, as the three of them whirled around in a circle, shaking their arms and legs and laughing like giddy teenagers.

"That's what it's all about," Tory said, huffing to catch her breath, finishing the ditty. She hung on to Jane and Carrie, and laughed as her mother came over, bewildered.

Tory sobered. "I'm sorry, Mom, I didn't do so well. Jane and Carrie had to help me. I feel better now."

The mother gave them a grateful smile. "Tory was just diagnosed three weeks ago. We don't have this figured out yet, but she insisted on running this race for her grandmother who has diabetes too."

"You just tell your grandmother you finished the race a winner," Carrie said.

Jane wanted to hug Carrie, but she wasn't sure if she had the right, after the unkind, unfair thoughts she'd had.

"Carrie, how about coming back to the inn for lunch after this is over? I owe you a meal."

"You don't have to do that, Jane."

"Oh yes, I do. And I'd be delighted. Please?"

Carrie tilted her head and looked at Jane. "All right. I'd like that. Right now I'd better see how our volunteers are doing."

"Okay. See you later." Jane turned and saw Louise and Alice standing on the sidelines. They were smiling, but Louise had tears in her eyes.

"Congratulations, little sister," Louise said. "You finished ahead of Carrie by a toe."

"I . . . I did?"

Alice burst out laughing. "I've never seen anyone finish a race quite like that."

Jane grinned. "Pretty classy, huh?" Thinking how they must have looked, Jane laughed. "I don't know about you, but I need a cold drink and a warm shower. Then I might be ready to face the world again."

The three sisters made their way through the crowd and on to Grace Chapel Inn. Jane left Louise and Alice relaxing on the porch, while she went upstairs to shower.

"I have an apology for you," Jane told Carrie as they sat with Louise and Alice on the front porch, eating chicken-and-pesto paninis and Waldorf salad. "I wanted nothing more than to come in ahead of you today. I've always been jealous of you, since high school, when I never could beat you in a race."

Carrie looked startled. "Seriously? But you had so much going for you. You were pretty and talented and lived in this beautiful house. I wished I could paint like you. I knew someday your art would hang in a museum. Me? All I could do was run and that didn't come naturally. That's why I did a victory dance, just for crossing the finish line."

"But you were always first. I thought you were conceited."

Carrie laughed. "Me? Of what? I barely made it through school with a C average. I never dated. No one ever asked me to the prom or even to a football game." She reached over and put her hand on Jane's arm. "I'm sorry, but it's nice to know someone thought I could do something well."

"That, you could. And I learned something today about winning. You said it. Sometimes losing is winning. It's like the Bible says. 'Many who are first will be last.'"

"'And many who are last will be first.' Matthew 19:30. That verse always gives me hope," Carrie said.

"Winning doesn't always mean coming in first," Louise said.

"Although in your case, you did," Alice said. "Louise won first prize for the largest pumpkin at the Baskenburg Giant Pumpkin Weigh-off last weekend," she explained to Carrie.

"Really? How big was it?"

"Just over one thousand forty pounds."

"Wow. I can't even imagine how big that is."

"But it's a fluke," Louise admitted. "That's a case of the first shall be last, because I don't have a green thumb. I can't grow weeds. Jane is the gardener."

"No matter. You won and we have the trophy to prove it," Jane said. She stood. "I have something for you. I realized it's for you when I came around the corner and saw you leaning over Tory. I'll be right back."

Jane ran up to her room, grabbed a large, flat paper sack

from her closet and hurried back to the porch. "Phew! I think I'm done running for today," she said, sitting down across from Carrie. She slipped a canvas out of the sack and handed it to Carrie.

"Oh Jane, I can't accept this. It's beautiful."

"I painted it for you. I just didn't know it at the time. I was sitting at Fairy Pond, enjoying the solitude and beauty and peace, when a runner came by. It was as if the Lord said, 'Here, paint this for someone special.' I didn't know what He had in mind until today. It's for you."

Carrie's eyes grew luminous. "I can't tell you how much this means to me. My last year here was difficult for a lot of reasons. My mother was sick. She died a week before graduation. My dad took it hard. Then we moved and I never came back. I needed to come back to make peace. If it weren't for you and Tory, I still might not have found that peace. Thank you. I will cherish this."

"I hope this was the first *annual* Acorn Hill Harvest 10 K Run. Next year, I'll give you a real race."

Carrie smiled. "Okay, you're on."

"Yoo-hoo. Where are you?" a voice called from the hall.

"Out here, Aunt Ethel," Alice called back.

Lloyd and Ethel came out to the porch.

"We used the back door. I couldn't wait to tell you," Ethel said, holding up a piece of paper. "Jane, you raised more pledges than anyone else. Nine hundred and fifty dollars." She handed Jane the certificate.

"But Aunt Ethel, this should have your name on it. You raised most of the money for me."

"Some of it," Ethel said. "I was happy to help."

Jane looked at Carrie and grinned. "See, I can't lose with a team like this."

"And that fact is a blessing for our organization," Carrie said.

"Acorn Hill is the big winner, with all the visitors in town," Lloyd said, ever the concerned mayor with an eye to the town's welfare. "Yes indeed, a win-win situation, all the way around."

About the Author

*S*unni Jeffers lives in northeast Washington. She and her husband live on a farm with an aging Scottish Highlander cow and an elderly Arabian racehorse. Sunni has won the Romance Writers of America Golden Heart, American Christian Writers Book of the Year and the Colorado Romance Writer's Award of Excellence.

A Note from the Editors

Tales from Grace Chapel Inn was created by the Books and Inspirational Media Division of Guideposts, a non-profit organization that touches millions of lives every day through products and services that inspire, encourage and uplift. Our magazines, books, prayer network (OurPrayer.org) and outreach programs help people connect their faith-filled values to daily life.

Your purchase of Tales from Grace Chapel Inn makes a difference. When you buy Guideposts products, you're helping fund our many outreach programs to military personnel, prisons, hospitals, nursing homes and educational institutions.

To learn more about our outreach ministry, visit GuidepostsFoundation.org. To find out about our other publications, such as *Daily Guideposts* and *Guideposts Daily Planner*, visit Guideposts.org or write Guideposts, PO Box 5815, Harlan, Iowa 51593.